Project: Wonders

EDIN

Autumn Equinox

Trigger warning: This body of work contains language and scenes that may be considered offensive. It depicts gun violence, physical violence, racism, sexism, homophobia, etc.

Self-published by the Author.

ID: yrw22k | ISBN: 978-1-7367748-5-4 (Paperback)
Subject: Fiction – Fantasy. Science Fiction. Action/Adventure. Superhero Fiction. Young adult. Political Thriller.

ATTN: To all the queerdoes who need a hero.

You are less alone than you know.
You are worthy of love.
You are worthy.

And to Addison. The queer hero this world needs but doesn't deserve.

ΛE

WILLIAM MATTHEW HOWARD

BIRTH-DATE: 19 JUN 01

SEX: Male

CURRENT HEIGHT: 5'11"

EYE COLOR: Violet.

HAIR COLOR: Red.

INSTALLATION: Seattle, WA, USA.

NATIONALITY: American.

ETHNICITY: Mixed Race (White,
Filipino).

FAMILY:

Daniel Howard (Adoptive Father)

Cassandra Howard (Adoptive Mother)

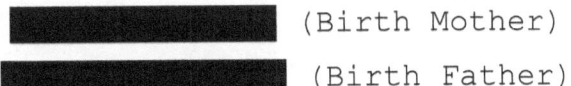 (Birth Mother)

(Birth Father)

19 JUN 18.

12:30.

FERGUSON GYM, SEATTLE COLLEGE, Seattle, WA.

Nia made him nervous. She was energetic, vivacious, and bombastic, the complete opposite of Billy. She made him feel dull and lifeless. What made matters worse was that he very much wanted her to like him, a sensation he was not used to. He usually never cared about what people thought about him, but that all changed when he met Cai, his first serious boyfriend.

Billy looked down at the mats below where the final round of the tournament would soon begin. He saw Cai getting prepped by his father and coach, Alfonso. Nia and her daughters, Alex, Chica, and Eva were cheering like crazy, and the match hadn't even started yet.

Cai stepped out onto the mat and looked up into the stands. Billy swooned. He thought Cai was incredibly handsome. His smooth, milk chocolate brown hair, his light brown skin, his soft face, his petite but muscular frame. In addition to his physical features, he was also kind, sensitive, and fun to be around. He made him feel like the luckiest boy in the world.

"YEAH! GO CAI!" Billy screamed, squealing slightly as he did.

The announcer's voice boomed through the loudspeakers. "AND NOW, COMPETING FOR REGIONAL TOURNAMENT CHAMPION - RICHARD BROWN AND CAIO MEDEIROS!"

Billy and the others all screamed as Cai crossed the floor with the swagger of a rockstar. He bowed to his sparring partner before the referee called for the match to start.

Billy was sandwiched between Cai's mother and sisters, who were all screaming at Cai in Portuguese. Down below, Cai was bouncing around like a jungle cat. He kept low to the ground, keeping his swings swift and light, hitting his competitor in all the right places.

Billy noticed that Richard was significantly taller than Cai. It seemed ridiculous that the two would have to fight against each other, but the people in charge didn't seem to care. He asked Nia about this and she said, "It's a weight class thing. Cai is tiny but stocky and that giant's as skinny as a tree branch."

"Oh," Billy said before returning his attention to the match. "GO CAI!!!!"

Cai smiled into the audience, causing a distraction that Richard monopolized to get in one good swing straight to his gut. He went down. Belly to the mat. An immediate and universal gasp from the audience was followed by a deafening hush.

Billy, and Cai's family, stood up with worry, shock, and fear. He looked seriously injured, but he tried pulling himself back up off the floor. Billy could very clearly hear Cai's dad yelling at him to stay down. He would rather see his son lose than get mauled.

Cai, however, refused to stay down. He quickly regained his composure, and his confidence, and performed a swift leg sweep. Richard went toppling to the ground like a puppet that just had its strings cut. By the time he regained his footing, Cai had already re-assessed the situation and decided on a new strategy.

He kept his head up and started baiting Richard, teasing the skinny goliath, swishing and dodging around. Richard spun around and around before finally...

BAM!

A single, blunt, kick to his face, which was an astounding feat considering said face was at least a foot above Cai's.

Richard stayed on the ground as the referee counted him out. A once silent stadium erupted into thunderous applause. Billy was screaming, filled with pride and joy. Cai had won.

The referee lifted Cai's hand as he announced his victory. He ripped off his headgear and looked up into the audience, making direct eye contact with Billy. He smiled and nodded, as if to say, *'This was for you. Happy birthday.'*

A few hours later.

Cai, and his entire family, came over to Billy's house to celebrate both Cai's win and Billy's birthday. The two families also wanted to take advantage of the momentous occasion to get to know one another.

"Congratulations, again, Cai!" Billy's father, Daniel, said as he gave the boy a high five. He was a simple, middle-aged white man with a slight gut and no hair on the top of his head. He was always seen in a short-sleeved button up, dockers, and an ugly tie found on sale.

"Thank you, Mister Howard. And, by the way, these are my parents, Alfonso and Nia."

Alfonso was a taller, burlier version of Cai, his muscles stuffed into a tight workout shirt and sweatpants. His long, curly brown was pulled back into a ponytail that went halfway down his back. While his height and muscular stature made him sometimes seem intimidating, his welcoming and jovial demeanor gave off a relaxing aura.

Meanwhile, Nia was a hair shorter than her son, and her skin a few tones lighter, reflecting a sweet caramel. She stayed fit like the rest of her family but didn't have the same athletic energy. Like Alfonso, she consistently wore workout clothes, and kept her smooth, honey blonde-dyed hair in a ponytail.

Hellos were exchanged between the two parties while Billy's mother set up the food on the table. Nia joined her to place her own contributions to the feast.

"Mom?" Billy called out from the garage. "Can I come out now?"

"Not yet!" Cassandra was a picture of maternal energy. She always wore loose-fitting sweaters over simple, flowing, often dark colored clothes. She had a love of turquoise jewelry rivaled only by her love of Billy. Her hair was curly and frizzy, and she rarely wore makeup, her work-from-home job as a computer technician kept her from caring too much about her appearance.

Cassandra pulled out the ice cream cake from the fridge. Nia assisted by lighting the candles.

"Oh, thank you, Nia!"

"Oh, it's no problem at all."

They ran it over to the table together.

"Okay, now!"

Billy opened the door into the kitchen and was welcomed by everyone singing "Happy Birthday." He was embarrassed, but the kind of embarrassment you felt when you didn't want people to see how incredibly happy you were. He was embarrassingly happy.

Billy's life had changed dramatically since he had met Cai. He was going out more. He had made so many new friends. He was going out to restaurants and eating food he'd never thought to try before, like Brazilian, Andean and Ethiopian. He was seeing new things, like martial arts competitions and black and white movies at the Paramount Theater. He had even started working out more, and, as a result, quit smoking. His habitual cigarette use had made jogging more than half a mile every day incredibly uncomfortable.

His parents had also noticed the change and were very happy to know that their son was in such kind and encouraging hands. Ever since Billy was a child, he never really, truly fit in. He was never harshly bullied or teased any more than other children, but he never actively participated in anything. They would encourage him to do more than just sulk around the house, surfing through Tumblr or playing vintage video games, but because they were his parents, the more they told him to explore and try new things the more reclusive he became. Cai changed all of that.

Cai walked over to him and put a birthday hat on his head with a kiss on the cheek. Their parents let out a collective "aww" at the sight, making Billy blush even harder. Cai was, of course, blush-less. He was very proud to be Billy's boyfriend and very happy to be with him.

Before Cai, Billy didn't have many close friends, and his extended family was limited to an aunt and uncle who lived in Florida with their three kids and never visited. So, his birthdays were always rather stale. He didn't like to admit it, but after years of pretending to be okay spending his birthday with just his parents, now he had a room full of people who cared enough about him to sing happy birthday, and he couldn't be happier.

While Billy and Cai ate cake and watched a movie on the living room couch, their parents amassed in the kitchen, *discreetly* watching the young couple from a distance.

Cassandra smiled. "They really are a cute couple, aren't they?"

Nia sighed. "I know, right?"

That evening.

Billy's parents were playing it cool. They were going to let Cai sleepover, even going so far as to allow the two to share the pull-out sofa in the living room. They didn't mind the lack of privacy.

Just having the chance to be close to one another meant the world to them.

Cai's parents had already left, and Billy's eventually went upstairs. The two snuggled together on the pull-out, watching a romantic comedy. It didn't matter though. It became white noise as they looked into each other's eyes. Billy held Cai in his arms and felt the universe around him slow to a gentle halt. It felt as if a powerful energy was being exchanged between the two. Their hearts became one in a brief, magical instant.

"I love you, Billy Howard."

Billy so desperately wanted to say, "I love you too." But before he could even form the words, he felt every nerve in his body begin to fever and fry. Complete sensory overload. He couldn't breathe. His brain felt like it was on fire. He started seizing and shaking. His eyes rolled up into his head.

The last thing he heard was Cai screaming for help as he fell into darkness.

He looked up. He looked around. A grey room. Grey ceilings. Grey walls. Hard, cold, steel tables, and chairs. It wasn't his home but, in a way, it felt like it was.

'Where am I?'

A white, bald man walked in wearing a long lab coat and horn-rimmed glasses that framed his muddy brown eyes above his crooked nose and a thick mustache. Without a word, he picked him up and took him to another, grey room where a bleeding man laid flat on a metal slab. He placed his hands on the man's head and suddenly his mind was filled with sounds and pictures.

He saw shoddy, lean-to houses and tents in the middle of a barren wasteland under a blazing, unforgiving sun. People were screaming, running away from explosions coming from the far distance, and rapidly getting closer.

He pulled his hands away from the man's head and the visions were taken from his mind's eye.

'Where am I? Who am I? What am I?'

And then a voice. A man's voice with a cold, Bronx accent. A voice that stirred long-forgotten memories and sensations, all of them painful. "It's time to wake up, Billy."

He saw Nia Medeiros' face, but she was different. She was so much younger-looking than she was when he last saw her. A glowing, youthful goddess of love and motherhood, looking down on him with a bright, beaming smile.

She called to a nearby Alfonso, who fell into a sunken Billy's faded view. His eyes felt like they were new. Everything was bright and terrifying, but in Nia and Alfonso's arms, he felt warm, safe, and protected.

He was at the Medeiros Family Gym where Alfonso was teaching a kids' Capoeira class. Billy was struggling to keep up and felt embarrassed surrounded by the other, more competent students. Noticing his struggle, Alfonso pulled him aside after the class and started speaking to him.

"Have I ever told you where Capoeira came from?"

Billy shook his head.

"When the Portuguese came to Brazil, they brought slaves with them, who brought many wonderful and amazing African traditions. One of them was a form of dance fighting called Engolo.

"The slaves who escaped formed Quilombos - villages far away from the white slavers. Of course, they knew that the slavers would try to kidnap them back, so they turned Engolo into Capoeira. They transformed it into a way to fight and protect themselves.

"For a long time, Capoeira was outlawed. Now we celebrate it! We dance and we fight to remember those who came before us, who fought so that we could live here, in the *'Land of the Free,'* and be proud of who we are and where we come from.

"Remember that, Cai. Remember where you come from. And remember that I love you. No matter what happens, no matter what you do, in my eyes, you can never fail as long as you just try."

He was surrounded by strangers on an overwhelmingly crowded dance floor. He needed to find a bathroom. He pushed open a door that led out into the dark of the night. He saw the outline of a boy in the dark and instantly became nervous and embarrassed. A motion detector security light turned on, coating them both in bright, white light.

Billy was looking at himself.

The other Billy tossed out a brisk, "Hey."

A flush of heat ran through his body. He felt an amazing, and almost instantaneous, attraction to him.

He let out a timid, "Hey."

He looked up to see Richard Brown staring down at him with a bloodlust. He was afraid but remembered that his father was there, and his whole family. He looked up into the audience and Billy saw his own worried face looking down at him. He had people in his corner, and he wasn't going to let them down. He spun and struck, putting Richard in his place: the ground.

"I love you, Billy Howard."

2

23 JUL 18.

13:45.

MT. ST. HELENS HOSPITAL, Seattle, WA.

Billy woke up in a white hospital room. Bright fluorescents were blaring down at him from the ceiling. An IV connected his arm to a bag on a pole. A breathing tube was stuck in his nose. He tried to pull it out, but his arms were too weak. His muscles felt limp, almost dead.

"Where am I?"

By his side was an emergency call button. He started pressing it and within seconds, a nurse had frantically entered.

"Oh my god!" He shouted before running right back out into the hallway. "We need a doctor in Suite E706!"

Minutes later, a doctor wearing wire-framed glasses with her hair pulled back into a tight bun entered the room.

"Hello Billy," she started. "I'm Doctor Irene Gupta. How are you feeling?"

"What happened?" He asked as she started performing some routine tests on him. "I feel like I was asleep forever."

"Oh, don't be silly. You weren't out for more than a month." She shined a flashlight in his eyes.

"A month?!"

"Yes, you were very lucky. Some coma patients never wake up. Your pupils are dilated, your reflexes are dull, and your heart rate is a little high, but considering what you've been through, that's to be unexpected."

Just then, his mind raced back to the sound of Cai's terrified voice as he fell into darkness. "Cai! Is he okay?! Oh my god, what the hell happened."

"Billy, I'm going to need you to relax, okay? I know that this is all very stressful for you, but everything is going to be fine. Cai is fine. Your parents are on their way, and then we'll talk about what we're going to do next. Okay?"

Billy took a deep breath. "Okay..."

Billy's parents arrived soon after. A tearful Cassandra wordlessly pulled Billy into a suffocating hug. Daniel kept his distance.

"That gown does nothing for your complexion, Billy," he joked.

"Thanks, Dad... Mom, is Cai okay?"

"Cai is fine. He's been very worried about you."

Daniel chimed in, keeping his distance. "We all have, buddy."

"He's visited almost every single day."

It was then that the doctor decided to pull focus. "Do you remember what happened before you went out, Billy?"

"Oh god... Cai told me he loved me, and then I just... blacked out. And then I had the strangest dreams..."

Irene was very intrigued by this. "Hmmm, really? What kind of dreams?"

"Well... actually... it was about my boyfriend's parents."

"And what were they doing?"

Billy refused to be distracted by her questions when he had so many of his own. "Doctor, please... What happened to me?"

Irene took a deep breath. "From what Cai told us, you suffered some sort of seizure, and that seemed to have caused you to go into shock Thankfully, you got here before any major damage was done to your brain."

"A seizure?"

"Yes, that was the initial prognosis. By the way, Cassandra, Billy is adopted, right?"

"Yes... But, if we're going to talk about this, can we at least speak in private?"

"Mom, please. I'm not a kid anymore. You can talk about it in front of me."

Cassandra sighed. "Okay. Yes, Billy was adopted through a private agency when he was four. It was a closed adoption. So, we don't know anything about his birth mother if that's what you're planning on asking."

"Nothing?"

Cassandra shook her head.

"Not even whether or not he has a history of epilepsy, or cancer, or *anything* in his family?"

Daniel stepped in. "We took him to a pediatrician, gave him all his shots, and got all the tests. The doctor said he was perfectly healthy."

"Well… I don't know what to say then. He doesn't seem to have epilepsy, meningitis, or any kind of infection that could have caused his *'episode.'* This all happened on his birthday, am I correct?"

They all nodded.

"Well, then, I think we should run a few more tests before we make any decisions on how to move forward."

"And how long might that take?" Cassandra asked.

"It won't be too long, just a few more weeks."

"A few more weeks?!" Billy parroted with a whine. "Oh god. Mom?"

"Doctor, please, I don't know-"

"Misses Howard, may I call you Cassandra?"

"Sure…"

"Cassandra. I understand your concerns, and that you want your son home as soon as possible, but we have to find the cause of the seizure in order to prevent it from happening again. And if it happens again, it's highly likely that it'll be worse than last time."

Cassandra looked over at Billy with apologetic eyes.

All Billy could say was, "Fuck."

Noon, the Next Day.

Billy was picking at his lunch with a plastic fork while using the TV as background noise when Cassandra walked into his room with Cai following closely behind.

Billy had to remind himself that he was attached to an IV to keep from jumping at his boyfriend, wrapping him up in his arms and never letting go.

"Aww, baby!" Cai embraced Billy, also being very mindful of all the tubes and machines attached to him. "How are you doing?"

"I love you too."

Cai put on an electric smile. He had been waiting so long to hear Billy say those words. "I love you so much. And I've missed you."

Cassandra quietly ducked out, letting them have their privacy. Cai held Billy's terrifyingly weak hand.

Billy started to cry. "I'm so sorry."

"It's okay. It's so okay."

"I didn't want to scare you."

"It's okay. I love you."

"I love you, too."

Cai wiped Billy's tears away and kissed his forehead, pulled up a chair close to his bedside, and held his hand. "So, how are you doing, cutie?"

"Well, the bed is fine, the food is fine, but this overhead lighting is killing me."

"Oh my god, you're ridiculous. Seriously, talk to me. Is everything okay?"

"Seriously? I'm fucking scared."

Wanting to be as supportive as possible, Cai shoved his fear down his throat so he could better focus on Billy's feelings. "Do they know what's wrong?"

"No! They don't! That's what's so fucking scary."

"Well, shit."

"Right?! I just wanna go home and cuddle with you."

"Aww," Cai gently rubbed Billy's cheek. "Don't worry babe. I'm sure it won't be long till they figure it all out, and then we get to take you home."

"Yeah... in the meantime... Do you think they'll let us do it in here?"

Cai giggled and gave Billy a quick kiss. They both felt a rush of sparks that quickly dissipated as Cai's phone started ringing.

"It's my mom. Hold whatever thought you had in your gross little mind, okay." He started speaking to his mother in Portuguese. "Hey mom, what's up? ... Yes, he is. I'm so happy... No, no Ma I don't think he's contagious. He had a seizure, not measles."

Billy responded. "I'd prefer the measles to this."

Cai stared at Billy with wide eyes before saying "Ma, I'm gonna call you back."

Billy faintly heard Nia's voice screaming, "What's going on?! Is Billy-" as Cai hung up.

"Billy, how did you do that?" He said, in English, with wide eyes.

"How did I do what?"

"That!" He quickly flipped back to Portuguese. "You're speaking Portuguese. Have you been taking classes?"

"What? No, I...."

"Ali! Right there! How are you doing that?"

Billy was beyond confused. "Was I really speaking Portuguese?"

"Not anymore, but you definitely were a minute ago."

"But that's impossible."

"What are you talking about?"

"I've never spoken a word of Portuguese in my life. I mean, I'd been trying to learn it - for you - but..."

Cai stared at him incredulously. "But that's impossible..."

"Right?! I go into a coma and wake up speaking Portuguese? What the fuck is going on?!"

"Okay, okay. Calm down. We don't need - We'll figure this out."

Cai put his hand on Billy's. Suddenly, Billy felt another spark course through his body, like he had just shoved his finger into a light socket. Vivid visions and sensations flooded his mind in the short moment their hands touched.

Cai's mother was holding him as he cried on their living room couch.

"Shhh... shhh... It's going to be okay, baby. I'm sure he's going to be fine."

Nia started softly singing a tune Cai knew by heart. A lullaby she had been singing to him his entire life.

"Mom… stop, that's not helping. I'm really scared, and I don't know what to do."

"There's nothing you can do baby. All we can do is be there for Billy and his family. That's all."

Cai pulled his hand away. "Are you okay? Do you need me to call a doctor?"

"I felt it."

"Felt what?"

Billy started to cry. "I'm so sorry. I know I scared you and… I'm so sorry."

Cai pulled Billy into a hug. "Shh, no it's okay. You didn't scare me, but… Billy, what's going on?"

Billy started singing the same song Nia sang from his vision.

Cai pulled back. "Wait… What? Did my mom teach you that? No… that can't- I'm so confused."

"I heard it! In my head! You were crying *about me*. You were with your mom. You were really scared. And then she started singing that song. I could see it all in my head. I could feel it. All of your pain and your fear. You thought I was going to die and… God, I'm so sorry!"

Cai didn't know what to say. He had always felt like the two of them shared a deep connection, the same way most teenagers feel about their first loves, but this was on a completely different level. Billy was reading his mind, and there was no denying it. He knew that he couldn't deny it. He wanted Billy to believe that he believed him.

He took Billy's hand again. "What do you see now?"

With Cai by his side, Billy's fear was replaced by strength as he tried to concentrate and repeat the process.

More sparks.

Cai had visited this hospital before when he was nine years old. It was a very heavy winter. Seattle hadn't seen one like it in years. His parents were out so his sisters were the ones who were supposed to be watching him, but, unfortunately, they were too preoccupied with fighting to focus on babysitting their little brother.

"You stole my butterfly clip!"

"Girl, please…"

Another boy - Cody - showed up. He was special. Cai really liked him and really wanted Cody to like him back. So, when Cody suggested they try doing "Parkour" around the building ("Like on the TV!"), Cai didn't think twice. Of course, when he slipped on a patch of ice and fell six feet onto the icy ground, breaking his arm in the process, he wished he had.

His parents were furious at everybody: Cai's sisters, Cai, and Cody. Cai's sisters felt so guilty. Cai felt so stupid. Cody never spoke to Cai again out of shame.

Billy let go of Cai's hand and came back to the present. "Seven years ago. You came here after you broke your arm."

"How?"

"You were playing with this kid, Cody. You slipped and fell. You felt so bad."

Cai looked at Billy with an incredible sense of awe. "Oh my god. **I'm dating a psychic.**"

A few days later.

Billy was having trouble handling his newfound "gift." He didn't know what triggered it and he didn't know how to turn it off. He wore gloves and full sweats to physical therapy, avoided touching people, refused to be touched, and insisted on doing his workouts alone.

"If you want, you can practice on me."

Billy gave the visibly excited Cai a shocked stare. "Cai... I really don't want to."

"You might as well. You're stuck here with nothing better to do. Plus, I'm straight-up allowing you to get to know me a hell of a lot better than you already do!"

"Cai... I don't want to get *better* at this. I don't want *this* at all. Whatever this is-"

"Psychometry."

"What?"

"What you do. What you have. Reading the past through touch. There's a name for it. Psychometry. I looked it up."

"*Why* would you look it up?"

"I was trying to be supportive."

"Well, is there a cure for it?"

"I don't know... As far as I know, or as far as the internet knows, you're the only one who has it."

"Well... That's just... wonderful."

"Could be worse."

"How?"

"Could be raining," Cai said with a cute smile.

Billy stared at him, hoping he had also gained the power to make people's heads explode, before realizing he could never blow up a head so beautiful.

"Or you could be like the Incredible Hulk and turn into a rampaging bitch monster whenever you're angry."

"You mean an even **bigger** rampaging bitch monster than I already am?"

Cai laughed. He hoped Billy's show of humor represented progress, but then Billy's eyes filled with tears.

"Cai... What am I gonna do?"

Even without psychic powers, he could sense all of Billy's fear and desperation.

"We need to get you out of here. If something happens, if someone touches you... well... It's going to be okay. We'll deal with it. I'm going to help. No matter what. I promise."

Billy took in Cai's words. "Can you get my mom?"

A few minutes later.

It didn't take much to convince Billy's mom to try and get Doctor Gupta to let him leave.

"My son is ready to go home and I think it's about time he is allowed to do so."

"Cassandra… it's not like Billy took a little nap. He was in a coma. And we still don't understand what caused said coma. So, it is in my professional opinion that he does not leave this hospital until we can run every possible test to ensure that it's not a chronic condition and prepare for any possible relapse. Have I made myself perfectly clear?"

"That's true but you've had many weeks to figure that out. And since my son hasn't had a single seizure since then, and he is, to quote your professional opinion, 'as healthy as a horse,' I think it's about time we call a spade a spade and chalk this up to a one-time, freak accident."

Billy tensed at the word "freak," which Cai noticed. He reached out for his hand, but he pulled away, scared he wouldn't be able to stop himself from seeing another unwanted vision.

Doctor Gupta pulled the hyper tense mother aside. "Cassandra, I cannot stress enough how much of a bad idea this is. Billy needs doctors right now. I've been going over his MRI, and there's some unusual activity in his occipital lobe and his temporal lobe that needs to be looked into."

"Is it serious?"

"*I don't know.* That's why he needs to stay here. I know a specialist I'd like to bring in, a neurobiologist. I think he-"

"That won't be necessary."

"Please, I-"

"I **know** what my son needs."

She resisted the temptation to perform an eye roll. "I highly doubt that."

"Do you?"

"I'm sorry, but it's not like I don't know what I'm talking about. I'm a *doctor*. I'm not trying to scam money out of you by keeping your son here longer than he needs to be. I'm trying to make sure your son doesn't die. Not only that, but so he can live a healthy life free of the burden, or fear, that something like this - or something even worse - could happen again."

"Same, Doctor Gupta. And right now, my son wants to leave. He no longer feels comfortable here and since he doesn't seem to need physical therapy, hasn't shown signs of anymore *'episodes,'* and can feed himself without a tube, I no longer feel like a hospital is the right setting for my son to get better."

Gupta had to stop herself from bringing up her belief that Billy's biological mother might be a key factor in his condition, but she knew it would only make the situation worse. Nothing, in her opinion, was more unstoppable than a mother who thinks she knows better than a doctor about what's best for her child, especially a white, upper-middle-class mother.

"There's no way to change your mind, is there?"

"Doctor Gupta," Cassandra said as she planted her feet by her son. "The only thing that would stop me from walking out of this hospital with my son today would be a bullet."

She sighed in defeat. "Okay, I'll let him go. But I'll be making sure to note that it's against the doctor's orders. I don't need any unnecessary legal flack for this. And I expect him to be back for a follow-up exam in two weeks. If he so much as gets a headache, I want to know about it."

Cassandra agreed to the terms and, within a couple of hours, Billy was on his way back home.

"I think we should celebrate," a chipper Cassandra said as she drove the two boys away from the hospital. "Cai, how would you feel about having dinner with us?"

"I'd-"

Billy cut him off. "He can't. He has stuff to do with his family."

"Oh, really?"

Cai took the hint. "Yeah... yeah my dad needs help at the gym."

"Ok, well, still, feel free to drop by anytime. You're as good as family to us."

"Thanks," he said, a hint of sadness in his voice. He knew Billy needed time, though, so he kept it to himself.

They dropped Cai off along the way. He tried patting Billy on the back, but he was deflected by a sudden shoulder jerk. Cassandra held her tongue as he quietly exited the car.

As soon as they got home, Billy ran upstairs and locked himself up in his room, preparing himself for complete isolation.

3

12 AUG 18.

15:45.

HOWARD HOUSEHOLD, Seattle, WA.

Over the next several days, Cai texted Billy every few minutes and called several times but received no response. He eventually decided to go and try to talk to Billy in person. When he arrived, Cassandra greeted him at the door.

"Hey, sweetie, I haven't seen you in a while." She closed the door behind her as she stepped outside. "How's it going?"

Cai was pushing back tears. "Things are going great, Missus H. Just... great... is Billy home?"

"He's in his room... but I don't think he wants to see anybody."

"Oh... yeah... I-I figured."

"Hey, sweetie... Cai... did anything happen at the hospital? Between you two? Did you... have a fight or something?"

He tried his best to hold back the floodgates behind his eyes. "Could you just... Could you just tell him that I'm sorry? And that it's okay if he's mad at me... I just- I just wanna see him again."

"Oh honey," She pulled him into a tight, motherly hug. "Do you wanna come inside? I'm sure Billy would come out of his room if I told him you were here."

"No, thank you. He needs space. I get it. I'm just gonna… walk back home."

"Walk? Honey, that'll take hours."

"I could use the exercise. See you later Missus H."

Watching as Cai pathetically dragged himself off into the distance, head hanging low, Cassandra's pity for the sullen and defeated boy was replaced with a sudden fury. She marched herself up to Billy's room and banged on the door.

"William Matthew Howard, you open this door *right now*!"

A quick and firm, "No!" blasted from the other side.

"William, if you do not open this door immediately, I am letting myself in!"

"Do not come in here! *I mean it*!"

"I am giving you until the count of three!" She was shocked at herself, treating Billy like he had regressed into the temperamental child he used to be.

"Mom, please…"

"One!"

Silence.

"Two!"

More silence.

"Three?!"

"Mom. Seriously. **No!**"

Cassandra used the key to her son's room to force open the door. Within, she found herself perplexed at the incredibly bizarre sight in front of her. Billy was completely covered from head to toe, with a scarf, gloves on, and a long sleeve, turtleneck sweater. It was the middle of summer, and ninety-plus degrees outside, making him more uncomfortable. To counteract the heat Billy had the room set to a refrigerator-level temperature.

"Billy, what in the world is going on here?"

"Just go away, mom!"

"Do not use that tone with me, young man. I am your mother! And I demand you tell me exactly what is going on."

"Just leave, please. I just want to be alone right now."

Cassandra sighed the sigh that many mothers use from time to time. The sigh that says, *'I have no clue what is going on with my child, but I am not giving up.'* She walked over to his bed and sat down. He inched away from her, turning to the other side.

"Billy, I don't understand what's happening here, but that's okay. You don't have to tell me anything until you're ready. But that does not excuse how you've been treating Cai. That poor boy almost burst into tears on our porch."

Billy just cocooned even further into his bed, out of a combination of fear, shame, and sorrow.

"Just talk to him... Okay? He deserves way better than how you've been treating him lately."

He took a long pause, before saying, "Go away."

With a defeated sigh, Cassandra said, "Fine." She got up to leave, but before she closed the door, she turned back. "By the way: Cai? He misses you. And he said he's sorry."

Cassandra closed the door. Just as she did, she heard Billy's soft cries from within.

Later that day.

Billy tried to sleep, but the vision of a crying Cai kept him from going down. Cai's words at the hospital echoed in his mind: *'It's going to be okay. We'll deal with it. I'm going to help. I promise,'* and forced him out of bed. He went to his laptop and started doing some research. After some digging, he found the information Cai had told him about at the hospital.

"Psychometry: the extrasensory ability to perceive a person's past, present, or future through physical contact. An object in that person's possession can also stimulate the effect."

Billy sighed. All that he could find was information about people who've claimed to have the power and even more about what people *"believe"* having psychometry might be like. But he found absolutely nothing about how to control it or, more importantly to Billy, getting rid of it.

Frustrated, Billy slammed his fist on the desk. He got up, kicked his chair away, and hit his bare forehead on the wall. He started to hear his parents' voices in his head.

"Don't tell me to calm down, Daniel!"

"I'm just trying to-"

He pulled his head away. Their voices left his mind. Curious, he removed one of his gloves and pressed his hand against the wall. He was shocked by the full vision of his parents in their room, having a very heated conversation. About *him*.

"-just wanna know what's going on."

"Cass, he's a teenage boy. He had a massive health scare. He's probably... withdrawing because he's afraid it'll happen again. That's what I'd be doing if it happened to me."

"Is this happening right now?" Billy said to himself as he listened on.

"No. No! It's more than that. *Something happened.* Something between him and Cai. I can just sense it."

She held her head in her hands. Knowing she needed him, Daniel reached out and held her in his arms.

"Cass... you keep talking about what's going on with Billy but... how are *you* feeling?"

Cassandra started to cry. "I'm scared. My baby is obviously in a lot of pain and I don't know what to do."

This completely caught Billy off guard. He had always seen his mother as such a strong woman. She could get emotional but not in the way he was seeing her at that moment. She wasn't just scared for Billy. Billy was scaring her.

Billy let go of the wall. He threw off all his layers before running straight to his parents' room, surprising them both.

"Billy?" Cassandra said.

He wrapped his mother up in the biggest hug and let whatever she was thinking about, whatever she had to show him, race through his mind's eye. He almost drowned in her memories, but he wasn't afraid. He needed perspective. He needed to see through her eyes.

The doctor tried to be as nice as he possibly could, but there was no real way to explain this kind of problem to somebody in a "nice" way. Daniel held her hand as the doctor told them both through the news.

"I'm sorry, but it's likely that you'll never be able to conceive a child. Not naturally at least."

The hopeful Daniel asked what he thought were the right questions. "What about hormone therapy? Or In Vitro? Surrogacy?"

"Mr. Howard… Cassandra is not capable of-"

"Don't." She said through her teeth.

"Pardon?"

"Please, don't talk to my husband like I'm not in the room. Talk to *me*. Tell *me* what *I* need to know. I deserve that much."

"Well Cassandra, your condition has left you with very few viable eggs. We managed to take care of the infection and removed most of the cysts, but this is going to be a long process, and by the end of it, you won't have many options, if any at all."

This man wasn't acting like the same doctor who, only a few months before, told her to keep her chin up. He was not the same doctor who went above and beyond to try and keep her comfortable throughout this whole experience.

Cassandra felt betrayed; betrayed by this doctor, betrayed by her own body, and betrayed by life. She had always tried to tell herself that not having children didn't make someone less of a person. *'We're not animals. We shouldn't be pushed through life by the biological need to pass on our DNA.'* Yet, there she was, feeling ashamed that she no longer had the option and feeling stupid for not trying to have children earlier.

A few months later, after all the medical drama was over, Cassandra found herself in a church. Growing up, she wasn't the most devout catholic girl, but she knew that if there were ever a time to put faith in a higher power, now would be it.

She just sat there in the pew, full of fear, and full of mourning for the children she would never be able to have. Finally, after some time, she said to herself "Why not?" and decided to start talking to the omnipotent being in the sky her parents tried convincing her existed.

"Dear God... I'm just going to start by saying I'm sorry. This is the first time I've ever really looked to you for... anything. I guess I've worked hard all my life to not feel like I need help from anybody... not my family, not my husband... not even you... but now... God, please. If you're up there, I need you. I need help, I need guidance. Daniel says it's going to be fine, and he'll support whatever decision I make. He says we can adopt. We don't even have to have children if I don't want to. We can do whatever I want... but I don't know what I want anymore. I'm so scared... I feel so... screwed over. I'm so angry. I feel like I've lost a dream I didn't even know I wanted to see come true until I was told it'll never happen... God... What am I supposed to do? Please, tell me, what am I supposed to do?"

After a few moments of looking up at the ceiling, she realized she would never get her answer just by sitting there. She started to leave, spotting a small collection box near the door on her way out. She stopped to donate whatever spare cash she had in her purse before a young priest crossed her path, placing something on the bulletin board nearby.

Is Fostering Right For You?

It was a literal sign.

True to his word, Daniel supported Cassandra in her decision and they immediately started the paperwork and training to become foster parents. They went through a private organization called "Garden," heavily recommended to them by one of Daniel's coworkers. The counselor told them that if all went well, they had a six-month window of opportunity to commit to adoption.

Through some miracle, it only took a few days before a child became available. A five-year-old boy named Billy. They went to the foster center to meet him, and Cassandra took one look at him and knew he was her son. They started the adoption process on the spot.

Despite all that they'd been through, despite all the hardships and the scares, Cassandra had never once lost faith in Billy. She never lost faith in the idea that everything that had happened to her was meant to bring him into her life. She was meant to be Billy's mom.

Billy cried as he pulled himself away. He felt all the love his mother had in her heart for him in a single, overwhelming instant.

He let out a soft, "I'm sorry."

"It's okay."

She let Billy leave without trying to stop him. Whatever he had been going through, it didn't matter anymore. Somehow, she knew he was going to be okay.

Billy rushed back to his room, grabbed his phone, and called Cai. At first, it went straight to voicemail, which he understood upon considering all the phone calls from Cai he had ignored.

He called again, and this time, Cai answered.

"Hey."

"Hey... I'm sorry... For everything..."

"It's okay. You needed space. I get it. You're going through something. And it's something I'll never understand, no matter how hard I try..."

"Can you meet me tomorrow? Noon, at the thrift store in the international district?"

"Why?"

"I'll tell you tomorrow, okay? And Cai?"

"Yeah?"

"I love you."

A brief pause. "I love you too, Billy."

4

13 AUG 18.

12:00.

"HOPE-FULL THRIFT STORE", Seattle, WA.

Billy waited at the front of the store, having discarded his many layers and replaced them with. At noon, on the dot, he saw Cai walking towards him through the parking lot. Billy ran straight to him, fully intending to provide him with all the affection he had been withholding the past few weeks but was stopped by Cai's heavy frown and outstretched hands.

"No. Sorry. I can't."

"What? It's fine. No. I promise. I don't care anymore. I love you, and I want you to touch me. It's okay now!"

"No, it's not that. It's just..." Cai took a deep breath. "I don't want you in my mind right now. I've been feeling a lot of bad shit lately and I'm not sure I'm ready to have *you* deal with all of that right now, especially since I know I haven't completely dealt with all of it yet. I'm sorry..."

"Oh... No, I get it. I don't want to make you uncomfortable."

"No, you don't get it, I don't want to make *you* uncomfortable."

"But I've been such a dick to you. I pushed you away and you were the only one who knew what I was going through."

"But I don't, Billy. Not really. And I never will. That's what I had to figure out. Everything you're going through is so unique, and strange, and... I'm trying not to say the wrong thing right now... This is huge. You're allowed your time..."

Billy sighed. "All you wanted to do was help me. I feel like an asshole."

"You're not an asshole, Billy. And I still wanna help you. I am here for you; in whatever way you need me. I'm not going anywhere until you tell me to go. Just tell me what you want me to do."

"I want you to-" Billy stopped himself. "Okay. Come on."

"What are you gonna do?"

"I'm going to try and read every one, and everything, in this building."

"Whoa... Okay, so you're trying to go back to the hospital?"

"Practice is supposed to make perfect."

"Billy, this is the largest thrift store in town. I can't even begin to think about how overwhelming this is going to be for you."

Billy looked deeply into Cai's eyes. "As long as you're here with me, I know I can do anything."

"Billy..."

"I get it. I know you think I don't, but I do. I don't want you to forgive me cuz I know you still need time. I just want you to be here for me. If that's too much to ask for right now, though-"

"It's not. I'm here. And I'm not going anywhere. Let's go."

"I promise to take it-"

"Slow. I got it, Billy."

Together they walked into the store. They made their way to the antique section where they found a box of old silverware, faded to a heavy iron color from years of careless use.

Cai squeezed Billy's shoulder. "I'm right here."

"Don't be afraid to shake me if I'm gone for too long."

Billy touched a spoon and felt a sea of memories wash over him.

Her mother had wanted her to meet somebody. A young man from her church. She tried her best to refuse but, at some point, there was just no way to say "no" to her mother any further.

'And besides,' she thought, *'what would it hurt?'*

"Whoa," Billy said as he emerged from the vision.

"What'd you see?" Cai eagerly asked.

"A young woman living in the twenties. Her mother called her a *spinster*. She was, like, *twenty-two*... It was sad."

"Aww."

"I think it turned out fine though. Towards the end, I could sense excitement and sweetness. I think the guy her mom set her up with turned out to be *'the one.'*"

"Wow. You *saw* all that?"

"It's not just seeing... I don't know if I can explain it. It's almost like when I touch something, I can see the world in four dimensions... up, down, left, right, center, none of that means anything anymore. I become whatever memories I see."

They ventured further into the back and found an old, beaten down couch, with a gross, green fabric with brown triangles popping up here and there. To Billy's horror, upon touching the couch, he realized the brown triangles used to be yellow.

The owner had died recently. Harry Marsh. 87 years old. Born March 31st. Married to June, who died ten years earlier. His kids had to sell it to pay off his funeral bills. It killed them to do it. It was the couch they grew up on, but they had to. Despite that, the person they sold it to didn't realize the emotional worth of the couch and gave it away after a few months.

Billy pulled himself out of the vision without taking his hand off the couch. "I think I'm getting the hang of this. Also, I should've brought hand sanitizer."

"You are," Cai said. "I'm honestly super impressed. Let's keep going."

Cai took Billy back into the literature section and handed him a copy of "Gone With the Wind."

"Try to find specifics."

"You want me to write a psychic essay?"

"No, I mean, like, tell me how it got here."

Billy closed his eyes, performing a brief read. "Garage sale."

Another book: Of Mice and Men.

"College student. Uses aliases when he hooks up with girls. Huge asshole. A girl left it at his place, and he gave it up even though he knew she needed it for school."

Treasure Island.

"Adult virgin, by choice."

"Wow. You're amazing."

"*You're* amazing. Thank you for helping me."

Cai blushed. "Let's try people now. You need to learn how to touch other humans without reading them. But try not to dive too deep. You never know what you're gonna get."

"I promise to avoid catching a psychic STD."

He tried hard not to laugh, wanting to put on as serious a front as possible. "Close your eyes."

Billy complied, and Cai gave him a sweet but restrained peck on the lips.

"Mmm," Billy gave a surprised moan. "You had eggs for breakfast."

"Wow, you saw that?"

"No, I smelled it. Your breath is terrible."

"Oh my god, fuck you," He said through a laugh.

Billy spent the next while working to read as many people as possible without looking suspicious. He "accidentally" bumped into a middle-aged man, touching his bare forearm with his own. He learned that he had met his first wife in high school and his second wife at their high school reunion.

He helped an elderly woman up out of a recliner that she'd sunken into. She had a doctor's appointment last Thursday. Everything was fine except for her blood sugar, so they put her on a very strict diet.

Billy saw a girl he knew from school, Lilah Watkins. He greeted her with a high five. She failed math, so she was going to have to take summer school.

"This is amazing," Billy said. "I feel like I could fly."

"Yeah… wait, can you fly?"

"Not yet. But if you kiss me, I'm sure I could."

"Oh my god, you're ridiculous," Cai said. "I have an idea. Come with me."

A half hour later.

They found a secluded section of a heavily wooded park. Cai looked around to make sure they were as alone as possible.

"What's the plan?" Billy asked.

"First, we stretch."

"We stretch?"

"We stretch," he said with a big smile.

Cai began doing basic muscle stretches which Billy did his best to mirror. For fifteen minutes, they warmed up their bodies without saying a single word.

"Okay, now, step two."

"Step two?" Billy asked.

"Step two, I'm going to kiss you."

"Blush."

Cai tried to be stern but couldn't keep himself from smiling. "Concentrate. This is gonna be pretty intense, but I want you to try to focus on one thing: my martial arts skills. Try to keep that in the center of your mind. Let everything else that's in me, that's between us, just go."

"That might be hard considering how much I love kissing you, cuz that's all I'm gonna be thinking about."

Cai smiled. "I get that, just remember, I'm right here. Always."

"Same."

And they kissed. They kissed in that special way two people kiss when they've been kept away from each other for too long. They had to remember what kissing each other felt like.

Intense, passionate, and beautiful, the world around them faded away as a shock flew through Billy's body. He felt Cai's psyche blend with his but pushed the memories he was mining through a heavy filter.

Cai pulled himself off of Billy, splitting their addictive connection. "Okay, now brace yourself. I'm going to test something out on you. And if I'm right, it won't be as terrible as I know it's going to look."

"What do you-" Before he could finish his sentence, Cai performed an incredibly swift jumping, roundhouse kick. One Billy barely managed to dodge. "How did I do that?"

"You can read memories. I figured, if you focused hard enough, you could absorb skills - like playing the piano, speaking other languages, or, in my case, kicking butt." Cai put up his fists and started lightly bouncing around. "Now show me what I can do."

"You wanna fight me? Cai-"

"Billy, I think it'll do us both some good if you just try and kick my ass."

"But-"

Cai took another swing, but Billy dodged it again. His reflexes had become so much more heightened than they were normally. His focus had become airtight as he managed to obtain Cai's ironclad attention span.

Cai kept on throwing punches, testing Billy, and working very hard to understand his limits, while secretly also getting out some of the frustration that had been building up the past few weeks. Out of reflex, Billy sent a punch straight to Cai's chest, throwing him back a few feet.

"Oh, shit! I'm so sorry! I'm so, so sorry! Are you okay?!"

"It's fine," Cai said with a grunt and an impressed smile. "Keep going!"

The test resumed. Eventually, Billy stopped apologizing whenever he nearly hit Cai and started fighting, looking for openings and opportunities to strike. As the evening went on, their play battle became more like a dance. The two boys swayed and swung around each other in a very elegant form.

Billy was struck with a thought. "Wait a minute: are we doing ballet?"

Cai giggled. "Maybe."

"When did you learn this?"

"I trained for a couple of years back in middle school to help my form. It emphasizes core strength, flexibility, and precision movements."

"How am I doing by the way?"

"You're doing great! Though, maybe next time, I'll have you focus more on my ballet training. You're all over the place."

The two boys laughed as they continued to sweep and sway. Billy grabbed Cai's hand and pulled him close. They started to waltz, no longer dodging or weaving through each other.

"Billy..."

"I know. It's okay. I'm sorry."

Cai nodded. Pressing his head against Billy's, he shared everything he'd been bottling up the past few weeks without him. All of Cai's fear, self-loathing, sadness, pain, and all anger flew through Billy's mind. Tears began streaming down their faces as they pulled away from each other.

"Oh my god," was all Billy could say.

"I feel terrible about everything I felt towards you. I was scared you'd hate me. I hated myself. Billy, I'm so sorry."

"No! No... I don't hate you. I can't hate you. You're amazing. And I can't... I can't tell you how much having you in my life means to me. How much it's changed me. I love you."

"I love you too, Billy."

Their lips touched once again.

Billy's mind was filled with images of every time the two had kissed. He felt their first kiss from Cai's lips. He felt Cai's love, his passion, and his need to be with Billy.

Billy pulled away. "Come with me."

A half hour later.

Billy drove them to a quiet, often overlooked part of town before turning off the car. Cai didn't need to ask why they were there. He just pulled Billy on top of him.

In a heated instant, they tore each other out of their clothes as they shared their first intimate moment in what felt like forever. This time, it wasn't just sex. It was an exploration of intimacy far beyond the limitations of the flesh. It was powerful, emotional, sexual, and psychic.

Billy felt Cai's heart through his chest. He felt his heartbeats through Cai's hand.

"I have an idea," Billy said. "Promise to keep an open mind?"

"Yeah!" Cai said, with a nervous excitement he'd never felt before. "Go for it!"

Billy opened the door between their minds, bridging the psychic gap between the two. Cai could feel and see through Billy's eyes just as easily as Billy could see through his. At first, it almost overwhelmed the two, but their combined mental strength, willpower, and incredible trust in one another kept them from drowning in each other's thoughts and memories. Instead, they swam in that moment, surrounding themselves with the physical and emotional sensations cascading through their bodies. Their minds intertwined as their hearts beat as one.

When the moment had come and passed, Billy broke off their connection. Their time in each other's minds was over and they were back together in the real world. Spent, physically and mentally, they fell asleep in each other's arms.

He was back in the grey room. The same one from the dream he had the night Cai told him he loved him, the night he fell into the coma. The same grey room from a long-buried memory now erupting up to the surface, calling out to him and demanding his attention.

'Oh no. This place again. What is happening?'

'Billy?'

'Cai? What are you doing here?'

'Your powers must've pulled me into your dream while we were sleeping. Or maybe this is a side effect from being connected for so long. Or maybe, we've been dreaming the entire time, and this is reality! Who knows? Are you okay?'

'I don't know. I've had this dream so many times. I think I've been here before.'

'Ok, so we're having a dream about your past?'

'No,' a cold voice said from behind the two-way mirror. The man stepped forward into the light. He was the same bald scientist with the thick horn-rimmed glasses from earlier, but older, with a heavier lid and more lines on his face. His mustache had grown grey, his hair had grown out on the sides. 'This is his present. And I need him here - **NOW**.'

They were both shocked awake.

"What?!" They said at the same time, their minds still linked.

"What was that?" Cai asked.

"I- I don't know." Billy hurriedly put his pants back on and climbed into the driver's seat, starting the car and driving off into some unknown direction.

"Where are we going?"

"I don't know… But I need to be there. *Now*."

"What? Was it about that place in your dream?"

"You remember it? That really happened?"

"Of course, it happened. And who was that weird guy in the lab coat?"

"Gehrig."

"Gehrig?"

"Gehrig. Doctor Franklin Gehrig. Where he is is where I need to be."

"Billy, do you think this has something to do with your powers?"

"I **know** it has something to do with my powers. I don't know how. God, I wish I fucking did. I feel like I'm going insane, but I need to find him. I need to go back to where it all started."

"'*Where it all started?*' Do you even know where you're going? Stop the car!"

Despite being on an intense mission, borne of subtle and intuitive instinct, Billy did as he was told. He gave Cai a look of mixed fear and longing.

"I'm scared, but I know this is what I have to do."

"Okay… first off." Cai pulled up a map of Seattle on his phone. "I need to know where we're going."

Billy maximized the map until it showed the entire world and then pointed to a random spot of blue in the middle of the Pacific Ocean, further confusing his already dumbfounded boyfriend.

"There…"

"There? But there is no there! No islands. No nothing!"

"I need to go there, Cai. I just… I need to go."

"How are we supposed to get there?"

Billy closed his eyes. "Someone is waiting at the airport for me. Someone I'll know as soon as I see them."

"Okay… but I don't give a shit about who's waiting at the airport. I'm going with you, no matter what."

Cai squeezed Billy's hand. Once again, he had managed to keep his mind safe from Cai's memories. He was evolving, getting better by the literal second. He would've been terrified if it weren't for Cai.

"Thank you."

5

13 AUG 18.

20:45.

SEATAC AIRPORT, SeaTac, WA.

As Billy predicted, someone was waiting for him inside the airport. Security had been given advance notice to tag Billy and have him escorted to a restricted area of the building, bypassing all security checks in their way.

Nobody seemed to mind that Cai was tagging along. As they were being guided through the airport, Cai grabbed Billy's hand and opened the psychic door between them sending his thoughts into Billy's mind. *'Stay calm and hold onto me, I'm not going anywhere.'*

They were taken to a private gate, far away from any passersby. Their guide quickly abandoned them and ran back into the main part of the building. Waiting for them was a soldier. Upon seeing Cai, he pulled out his pistol. Billy jumped in between them out of instinct.

"Who the hell are you?" He asked aggressively.

Cai stood his ground. "Who the hell are *you*?"

The soldier ignored Cai, locked eyes with Billy, and said, "His name was Adam and he wanted to stay."

Through their connection, Cai felt a surge go through Billy's body, and then straight through his own. The hairs on their skin stood on end.

Something had been unlocked within Billy's mind. Something terrifying and strong, that started to pull him towards the soldier like a magnet, but Cai held on and remained both his physical and mental anchor.

"What just happened?" Cai asked.

The soldier never dropped his gun. Billy never got out of the way. Cai never thought about running without Billy.

The soldier repeated himself, this time more impatiently. "His name was Adam and he wanted to stay!"

Billy and Cai felt the surge again, and the pull, but Billy resisted once again with Cai's help. As long as he held Cai's hand, he knew he wouldn't be made to do anything he didn't want to do.

The soldier pulled the walkie on his jacket up to his mouth, all the while keeping his gun poised on the two. "Beta, this is Alpha. Psych is compromised. I repeat. Psych is compromised. I need back-up, now! Over! Get down on the ground! Hands up!"

Cai and Billy exchanged a knowing glance before letting each other go and doing as they were instructed. "Alpha" started walking slowly towards Cai, ready to take a kill shot.

Billy capitalized on the man's tunnel vision by sweeping his leg across the floor, causing him to fall to the ground like building blocks. Cai sprang up onto his feet and kicked the soldier's pistol across the floor before cannonballing onto his chest, pinning his arms down with his legs and punching him in the nose with enough force to knock him unconscious.

Thinking fast, Billy grabbed the soldier's face, inserted himself into his mind, and absorbed as much information as he could.

Private Steven Halbard. U.S. Special Forces. Code name: Alpha. He had just called for "Beta," the backup squad composed of three soldiers accompanying him on this "retrieval mission." "Delta," the pilot, is staying behind to ready the jet when they've acquired him.

Letting go of Private Halbard, he pressed his hand to the floor and had a vision of the other soldiers coming down the hall, each of them heavily armed.

"They're coming! Go!"

Cai sprang into action, jumping off the unconscious Halbard and sprinting to the door.

"Take the other side," He directed Billy before crouching down.

The soldiers burst in, armed and ready for a fight, but the two boys were just as prepared. Through his brief connection to Halbard, Billy had divined their formations, tactics, and training well enough to predict their moves before they made them.

He grappled the soldier's gun arm, holding it in place as he kneed him in the side, and threw him into the soldier behind them.

Cai grabbed the second soldier's hand, strategically placing his fingers on pressure points that put him in crippling pain. With the man out of sorts, he flipped him onto the ground and swiftly kicked him in the head.

The third soldier pushed his comrade off of him and jumped back up onto his feet. He pointed his gun at Cai, ready to take a kill shot. But before he could pull the trigger, Billy ran up behind him, wrapped his arms around his neck, and, with all the strength he could muster, twisted it until it snapped.

The man fell to the floor with a heavy, thunderous drum. Dead.

"Oh my god!" Cai couldn't believe his eyes. "Billy, you just-"

"He was going to kill you," He said, in a chilling voice.

"Yeah, but-"

"Cai… I know It's scary. I'm scared too, but I can't afford the luxury of second-guessing myself right now. He was going to kill you. So, I killed him first. End of story."

Billy started searching through the dead man's jacket.

"What are you looking for?"

Billy pulled out a small plastic case that resembled a miniature first aid kit. Opening it, he pulled out three hypodermic needles filled with a clear liquid.

"This."

"What is that?"

"Their 'contingency plan.' Just in case I didn't come quietly."

Acting fast, Billy stabbed the needles into one of the soldier's necks.

"Whoa!" Cai shouted. "What are you doing?"

"The same thing they were going to do to me. There's enough sedative in these things to knock someone out for a full day." He gave each of the still-living soldiers a dose. "I figure a little bit for each will keep them down until it's too late for them to stop us."

Cai had gone quiet. His head was too full of insecurity and doubt to say anything, and Billy didn't need to read his mind to sense that. He put his hand on Cai's shoulder, but he just shrugged it away. Billy sighed with frustration.

"Cai, I get it. Please. We have to keep moving."

Cai took his hand and opened the connection between the two of them. He allowed Billy to feel his fear that whatever was going on was going to turn Billy into a completely different person if it hadn't already. He was afraid that he would lose Billy again, but this time he wouldn't be able to get him back with a text and a phone call.

When they let go, Billy was about to try and reassure his boyfriend that everything was going to be fine. However, he was interrupted by the sudden sound of a voice coming from the soldiers' walkie-talkies.

"Alpha. Beta. This is Delta. What's your status? Over."

Billy, acting on the instincts stolen from the soldiers, grabbed the closest walkie and tried to imitate Halbard as best as he could. "Delta, this is Alpha. Psych is down, repeat, Psych is down. We are headed back your way. Begin making takeoff preparations. Over."

"Copy that, Alpha. Over and out."

"Billy… are we really doing this? I mean, this is a terrible idea, right? We are in way over our heads."

"Cai… I read their minds. *They know where we live.* Not just me. Both of us. 'Over our heads' is an understatement."

Cai was shocked. "Are you sure?"

"Whoever they're working for, they've been watching me my entire life. They're the reason behind all of this… and I want to know- I **need** to know why."

As goosebumps made nests all over his body, Cai took a second to collect his thoughts. '*Am I ready for this? Can someone ever be ready for something like this? I just saw my boyfriend kill somebody… And he just shrugged it off. But what if I had been in his position? … I don't know anymore. I don't know anything anymore. What if we get hurt? What if other people get hurt? Innocent people… What if Billy gets… God, I can't even think about that. But I didn't come all this way just to abandon him. No matter how scared I feel - and I feel fucking scared right now - I refuse to let him go through this alone.*'

Cai forcibly replaced his fear with courage and prepared himself for the worst.

They ran through the gates and down onto the tarmac where an ominous, unmarked black jet waited for them.

"That's not creepy at all," Cai quipped.

They climbed up the stairs into the plane. Billy pressed his hand onto the deck of the cabin to check and see if there were any hidden surprises.

"Nobody's left but the pilot."

"Okay," Cai took a deep breath. "What's the plan?"

They heard a noise coming from the cockpit.

Billy let out a quick "Shh," before grabbing Cai's hand. *'Follow me,'* Billy said through their psychic link.

They slowly walked towards the cockpit and split up, covering both sides of the door. They knocked. "Delta" popped his head out.

"Commander, when will we-"

Cai cut the man's sentence short with a punch to the throat, stunning him. Cai pulled him out of the cockpit, onto the ground, pinning him down. Billy pulled out the last of the sedative and stabbed him in the neck. Delta tried to resist but eventually stopped struggling as he lost consciousness.

Cai was completely out of breath "Okay... Are you sure you can do this?"

"Positive."

"Okay. I believe in you."

Billy braced himself and placed both hands on the pilot's temples. Focusing with all of his might, he felt a surge of psychic force flow between him and the other man. Launch codes, protocols, mechanics, all the ins and outs of operating a military jet filled his mind and, in a split second, he was an expert pilot.

"Alright, let's go," Billy said, ready to finally find out where he came from.

6

12 DEC 17.

20:35.

XAVIER PREPARATORY ACADEMY, Seattle, WA.

Billy was standing outside, behind the gym where they kept the gas tanks that heated the entire school. He was about to light his cigarette when a thought came to his mind. *'Wait… is this safe?'*

He moved a few feet away from the gas tanks, further into the dark of the night. He lit up and took a hefty puff.

'Ugh, what am I doing here? This is so stupid. Why do school dances have to be the actual worst? The only thing that could possibly outweigh them in general terribleness is trying to find a decent place to smoke in freezing weather. It's so fucking cold. Can somebody please just murder me before the hypothermia does?!'

The door to the gym opened, spooking Billy.

'Shit, I think I spoke too soon.'

A boy that Billy didn't recognize stepped out, looking lost and confused. In an effort to be friendly, but also appear tough, he shot out a stoic, "Hey."

"Hey," the boy quickly said back.

He was short, but muscular, with dark skin and very handsome features. He was also wearing a full tuxedo which made Billy, dressed in his school uniform, feel underdressed.

To him, his uniform was, at the very least, semi-formal. It was a pair of khakis and a short-sleeved, white button-up shirt with his school's insignia on it, topped off with a navy jacket and black boots, both of which he wore daily.

Worried that he might rat him out for smoking, Billy nervously tucked his cigarettes back into his pants before coolly saying, "Sup?"

The boy seemed embarrassed. "I, uh- I thought this was the bathroom."

"Oh. No, that would be *inside* the building."

"Yeah, I figured. I don't go here."

"You don't say?"

"I do say."

"Cool... So... what brings you... here?" He cursed himself for how awkwardly that fell out of his mouth.

"I'm friends with Chloe Fellan."

"Chloe? Cool..." Billy had no idea who that was.

"Yeah, I normally don't go to other school's school dances, but she got dumped at the last minute, and I have a heart, so... here we are. *Not* in a bathroom at somebody else's Winter Formal. Woot."

"Oh... Poor Chloe."

"Yeah... Well... I gotta go... find a bathroom. Wish me luck!" The boy gave a nervous chuckle before running back into the building.

"Good luck."

After getting caught by the bathroom kid, a pair of classmates he didn't recognize popped out to engage in some heavy petting. He relocated to the football field only to be nearly caught by a nosy teacher, trolling for troublemakers. He eventually made it all the way through to the farthest end of the parking lot, praying he wouldn't have to relocate again.

Attendance to the formal was mandatory for the Junior class as part of a "participation grade," which annoyed the generally asocial Billy. He wasn't the type of person who had fun at anything that involved large groups of people. His mother tried to convince him that the dance would be a good way to make friends. The only flaw with that plan was that Billy didn't want to make friends outside of the ones he'd already found through online gaming. To Billy, the best friends were friends you didn't have to see in person.

Billy heard the scuffle of feet behind him and rolled his eyes as he replaced his lighter in his jacket pocket and prepared to relocate yet again. He turned to see that the boy from before had managed to stumble upon him once more.

"Oh, it's just you," Billy said.

"Sorry. I'm beginning to think I'm just not destined to pee tonight. This school is like a maze."

"It's actually the eighth circle of hell, but close guess."

"Yeah, I'm assuming the architect was the guy from Saw. Hey, can I ask you a potentially weird favor?"

Billy raised his eyebrow. "What?"

"I know we only just met. We don't even know each other's names, for Christ's sake. By the way, I'm Cai."

"Billy. Charmed."

"Hi, Billy," Cai said with a quick but brilliant smile. "I need to pee, like **right now**. I would pee my pants but that would mean losing a problematically large deposit on this tux."

"Okay?"

"I am going to urinate on one of these trees. All I need you to do is make sure nobody walks in on me. Do you think you can do that?"

"Uh…" He takes a moment to look around before giving his answer. "Sure."

"Thank you!" The tuxedoed boy gleefully runs over to a nearby tree and begins immediately relieving himself.

Billy went back to his smoking.

"You smoke?" Cai asked as he craned his neck.

"Only when I'm stressed…. Which is all the time…"

"Oh? What's got you stressed? Is it me?"

Billy laughed smoke through his nose. "No. I just hate these things. Dances, you know?"

"I get that. Chloe told me attendance was, like, mandatory or whatever. It's why she refused to come without a date."

"Yeah…. That would be horrible…"

"Are you here with anybody?"

"No."

Cai suddenly felt the urge to shove his entire foot into his mouth. "Oh, sorry…"

"Don't be. Unless you were the sadistic matchmaker who ensured nobody would be interested in coming to a mandatory school function with me, I think you're fine. Besides, I've never had a date before, why should tonight be any different?"

A normal person would probably have taken that as a cue to stop the conversation, but Cai felt an overwhelming desire to keep talking to Billy, whom he found oddly fascinating. After finally finishing his business, he turned around to better converse with his newfound pal.

"Well, why do you guys need to come to this thing anyway?"

"Conformity."

"Oh... okay.... I'm sorry. If it makes you feel better, from what Chloe told me, this school is pretty terrible."

"I mean *duh*."

Cai giggled like an idiot before wanting to slap himself. His cheeks were flushed. His eyes were fluttering. He was crushing hard on this strange, backdoor smoker and had no idea why.

Cai pushed words through his puppy love daze. "I mean, who would want to come to a prep school anyway? Uniforms, early starts, late releases. And the classes are, apparently, stupid difficult."

"The only kids who come here are kids whose parents can afford to send them here. They should be called 'privilege schools'. Every year, we get new computers, new sports equipment, new textbooks. If a teacher doesn't do a good enough job making sure all the kids pass, they get fired. It just screams 'we're better than everybody else!' But the privilege of coming here comes with a price: if you don't fit in, your life will be miserable. There are overpaid white dudes in three-pieces all over the place, ready and completely willing to bitch at you for falling out of line. And if you're like me and walking the straight and narrow is hard for you, then falling out of line is what you do best."

"You seem normal enough to me... of course, we just met and I'm not the best judge. I mean, I'm left-handed and I pee in public in front of strangers."

"And I'm a triangular peg being shoved into a round hole." Billy took a drag from his cigarette. "Not that I don't want to fit in. I'd love to. People would bother me less if I flew under the radar."

"People bother you? Like *'bully'* bother you?"

"Not really... not in a long time, at least."

"I get that, I used to get bullied by some idiots at my school until I learned how to give a purple nurple with my toes."

"Good for you. My experience has been... different."

"I mean, every single one of my experiences seem super unique."

"Must be fun."

"Meh... anyway, we just deviated away from the point. How do people bother you?"

Billy sighed. "You ever walk into a room and know exactly what everybody thinks about you? Every single one of my classmates are white, and if they're not white then they're straight, and if they're not straight then they're doing their very best to pretend to be. The bullying isn't obvious, but they are looking down on you. They're more than willing to exclude you. To ignore you. So, it doesn't matter how rich your parents are because you'll never stop being an *'other.'*"

Cai looked at Billy with understanding, and, for the first time, Billy took a very good look at Cai. He saw his big, round, beautiful brown eyes. He saw the softness of his face, his sleek chin, and his wavy black-brown hair.

"I get that."

"You do?"

Cai shivered out a solid, "Yah. I do."

Billy had just noticed Cai wasn't wearing a jacket. "Are you cold?"

"I think so."

"You don't know?"

"For some reason, I've never felt warmer."

"Uh... I don't know if this is inappropriate or not but, my car is a little ways away."

"Why would that be inappropriate?"

Billy bit his tongue. He didn't want to say the wrong thing. He found himself wanting to kiss Cai, but his fear of saying or doing the wrong thing kept him from taking the chance. Sensing Billy's wariness, Cai closed the gap between them and gave Billy the most electrifying kiss he had ever had in his life.

Fifteen minutes later.

The two boys were frantically making out in the back of the ridiculously large SUV that Billy's father had bought him. In the back of his mind, he wondered what parent would ever buy a car with such a massive back seat for their teenager. The answer was the kind of parents who don't think they have to worry about their son having sex.

The extent of Billy's sexual experience was minimal due to his secluded nature. He was a "not completely out but not denying it" gay. He grew up in Seattle, one of the most "gay-friendly" cities in the country and was raised by parents encouraging him to not be afraid of his sexuality. However, that just made him want to be afraid of his sexuality. As the story so often goes, when a parent encourages their teenager to do anything, even having sex, it usually has the opposite effect. He had made out with a few boys and gotten to third base with a select few, but this time it felt different to Billy. This time it was full of heat, strong and deep.

Cai's skin began to fever under Billy's touch. Their body heat melted the world around them. Their hearts raced ever faster together. Billy ran his hands down Cai's side, closing in on his pants, but stopped himself before he went too far.

"Is this okay?" Billy said, through hot and heavy breaths.

"Feel free."

Billy moved his hands up into Cai's shirt, feeling the hot, sweaty skin underneath. He was in heaven. A teenage fever dream.

Billy paused to turn some music on, wanting to set a certain ambiance. It took an awkward minute, but he found a "sexy beats" playlist that was too enticing to pass up.

He returned to his backseat buddy and felt Cai's hands pull him back in before running down his back, grabbing at the bottom of his shirt, desperately trying to untuck it from his pants. Billy helped him out by unbuttoning his shirt before pulling it off, exposing his smooth, defined chest to the young, handsome stranger.

Cai began kissing and nipping at his skin, working his way up until he latched onto Billy's neck, eliciting a few heavy moans before moving back up to his lips where he resumed their passionate kissing. Cai pulled Billy on top of him as they fell into the flattened backseat. Billy had never felt more wanted in his life. Never had he ever felt more **desired**.

Cai was very careful about making sure his tuxedo was gently removed and placed somewhere safe. Despite being in the throes of youthful passion, the young man was very meticulous and centered - a focus that he had developed over time. After successfully disrobing, Cai pushed Billy down back into the seat and went straight to his ear.

"Can I blow you?" He said in a hot, breathy voice.

Billy wanted to say yes but his anxiety had other plans. He was worried Cai might think he was too small, and then, for a second, he thought he might be too big. *'Oh god, is there such a thing as too average???'* Then he worried he might climax too soon. *'Oh shit, what about pre-cum? I pre-cum so much sometimes...'*

Cai could tell there was some sort of internal conflict going on in Billy's head, so he stopped trying to pull Billy's pants off. "Billy, are you okay?"

This question jerked Billy back to reality. Despite being emotionally and physically overwhelmed, his desire to be transparent with his partner shined through to the front of his senses.

"I need to tell you something…"

"What?"

"I've never…"

"Oh my gosh… You've never had sex before?"

Billy drooped his head in guilt. "No."

"Ah, shit," Cai had never even considered this and suddenly felt full of shame. "Oh god, I'm so sorry. Am I being too forward? Am I making you uncomfortable? I didn't wanna make you uncomfortable."

"No, you're not. Please…"

"I can go if you want."

"No! Please, don't! You're perfect. I'm just… I'm just *really*…"

"Billy, I get it. We don't have to do anything that you don't want to do, especially anything you think you're not ready for."

"And I really want this."

"Why? We just met."

"Cuz you're hot…"

"And?"

Billy drew a blank. "You're... hot?"

Cai chuckled. "I know that. But do you really want your first time to be with someone you met while he was peeing in the parking lot? I mean... it's not my job to tell you how to live your life, but still."

Billy drew more blanks. "Honestly? I have no clue... My entire life, I've wanted someone like you to notice me. To... want to do this type of thing with me."

"Just so we're clear, I'm into you. I'm into this. I think you're super sexy and cool, and you're attracted to me so you're obviously intelligent. But I'm not a virgin. And my first time was... not great."

"Why?"

"I didn't know him. He didn't know me. So, he had no reason to care about me or what I liked or what I wanted. It didn't help that I didn't know what I wanted anyway."

"That sounds terrible."

"I wouldn't call it terrible. Unpleasant, but not terrible. I don't think he knew what he was doing either."

"Can I ask an awkward question?"

"Shoot."

"How many guys have you been with?"

"Hmmm... I don't know. I guess I lost track after fifty."

Billy had to keep his jaw from dropping. "That's very impressive."

Cai raised his eyebrow at the clueless Billy. "It's three. I've been with three guys. Oh my god."

"Oh, wow. I'm sorry."

"Don't be sorry. I wish I had that kind of experience under my belt. I could probably make you go like a geyser just by looking at you."

"Probably. Yeah... So, um... Ever been with a girl?"

"Nope. Never had the interest. I kissed a girl once, the prettiest girl in school, all the guys wanted her, and she only wanted the glorious god standing before you. But one peck and I knew I was as gay as a unicorn farting glitter while running down a triple rainbow to get down to a big gay, unicorn orgy. How about you? How long have you known you were gay?"

"Oh god, it feels like forever now. I had swimming lessons when I was eight and my teacher was-"

"Hot as fuck?"

"The hottest. Hotter than all the fucks. A volcano of hot manly fuckness. But not nearly as hot as you."

"Blush," Cai said with a coy smile.

"Anyway, we were practicing the backstroke and I kept sinking so he had to help me stay up in the water and-"

"Oh my gosh, I know exactly what you're going to say."

"Yup, super boner. I was so embarrassed."

"Oh nooo!"

"I nearly ran on water getting out of that pool as fast as I did."

Cai ran his hands through Billy's thick but silky red hair. "You're cute."

Billy giggled like an idiot. "Blush."

"Can I ask you an awkward question?"

"Go ahead."

"What hair dye do you use? This color is gorgeous."

"Thanks, but it's natural."

"Shut up."

"It's true."

"That is fire engine red hair. And you are a fire engine red liar."

"It's barely a dark apple, calm down."

"Hand to god."

"I'm sorry, I was unaware that there were any red-headed Asians. I mean, except the ones in K-Pop bands."

"What can I say? I'm special. The world took one look at me and said 'not weird enough. Let's make him an Asian redhead'."

"Which side of the family did you get it from?"

"I don't know. I'm adopted."

"Oh." Cai didn't know what to say to that, so he just said, "Nice..."

"It's no big deal. I love my parents. And my birth parents... I barely ever think about them. Never had to... Hey, do you wanna change topics?"

"I'm always down for an abrupt conversation restart."

"Where did you get those..." Billy started pointing at Cai's stomach. "Things covering your body?"

Cai looked down at himself and became very confused. "Do you mean muscles?"

"Yes! Muscles. I don't have those. Where can I get them?"

"They're pretty expensive but I heard you could get them at a gym for pretty cheap."

"Yeah, but I heard that requires a lot of work."

"That is very true. I've been working out like four times a week since I was five."

"Holy shit, why?"

"I'm an MMA fighter. It comes with the job."

Billy's mouth was agape. "That is so cool."

"Thanks," Cai said with a proud smile. "I think so too."

Billy looked at Cai with his bright, violet eyes. "You really are beautiful."

Cai started stroking Billy's hair again. "You're beautiful."

"So… I'm beginning to realize that we are not going to be having sex tonight."

"No, we are not."

"Oh."

"But we are getting to know each other. And, in my opinion, that's so much better."

Cai laid down and invited Billy to join him. Billy pulled a blanket out from under the passenger seat and spread it over the two of them.

They kept talking, time passing without them ever realizing it as their eyes never left the others' gaze. Eventually, and without trying, they fell asleep in each other's arms.

Meanwhile, back inside, a young Chloe Fellan couldn't help but wonder, *'Where the hell is Cai?'* As she watched her now ex-boyfriend dance with her ex-best friend.

There were two other kids in the playpen with him. A frizzy haired, silver eyed Hispanic girl and a large, deformed child, with pale skin and pointed ears.

The girl began playing with the metal toys she had been given. After a few moments, they began levitating around her as she giggled. The other child's hand became fluid as it formed and reformed into various shapes - a square, a circle, a triangle, and then a cross.

A man in a lab coat came towards him and picked him up, taking him to another room and laying him down on a strange slab. A series of walls close in around him and he felt a strange sensation as a bright, green light above him started to glow and pulse.

Then, after a minute, all he could feel was pain as his brain felt like it was bursting into flames from the inside out.

Billy shouted as he woke up in a cold sweat, startling Cai who was sleeping next to him. They were both still in their underwear from their earlier encounter. After Cai calmed himself down, he looked to Billy with concern.

"Are you okay?"

Billy took a moment to remember how to breathe. "Yeah... sorry... bad dream. I think."

Cai grabbed his phone, panicking at the sight of the current time. "Holy shit, it's midnight! I was supposed to be home hours ago! My dad is going to murder me."

"Oh my god, I'm so sorry! I'll drive you home!"

The two started getting dressed as fast as they could. After giving Billy his address, the red-haired speedster sped off, leaving skid marks in his wake.

Not wanting there to be any silence between them, Billy tried making more small talk. "So... how do you know Chloe?"

"She goes to my dad's gym. We've known each other for a few years."

"Your dad's gym?"

"Yeah, my dad runs a gym. It's small so we make most of our money teaching Capoeira."

"Oh... wow... That's cool."

"Yeah, I think so too."

An awkward silence began crushing the connection between the two. To break through it, Billy offered Cai his aux cable. He was simultaneously too nervous to play the music that he liked and desperate to find out what kind of music Cai loved.

"Play whatever you like."

"Really?" Cai joked. "You sure we're not going too fast?"

Billy smiled. "Yeah. I wanna know what kind of music a handsome stranger like you listens to."

"Alright but be warned: my taste is corny as hell."

The first thing he played was "Teenage Dream" by Katy Perry. Billy looked at Cai with wide eyes.

"What? What's wrong? Oh god, do you hate this? It's okay if you do. I can change it."

"No. You don't understand. I. Love. This. Song."

The two bopped along to the boppiest of bops from the mid-eighties to the mid-2010s before finally arriving at the apartment building where Cai lived with his family.

"So," Billy started. "This is where you live."

"Yes. This is my place. This is the place that I live in. This building. Right here."

"It's nice."

"It's an apartment building."

"I see that. Looks very pretty."

"It's alright. It's a lot easier to live in since my sisters all left."

"You have sisters?"

"Three of them. Triplets."

"Jesus…"

"Yeah, they suck. But they can occasionally be tolerable."

"Hey-"

"Yes?" Cai jumped.

"Can I get your-"

"Yes! Yes! Yes!" Cai was shamelessly eager. He had met a very nice somebody and very much wanted to meet him again.

After exchanging information, the two parted ways with a prolonged kiss. The sound of Billy's phone ringing - his mother - eventually separated them. He ignored the call.

"Text me," Cai said.

"Of course."

With that, Billy began driving back home. Along the way, he received a text:

Cai: Hey! I know I probably seem like a huge dork for texting immediately after seeing you, like, 10 secs ago but I was worried Id forget too text you in the morning so hi! I just wanted to say that I really hope you get home without dying so we can see each other again soon!

Billy was in awe. He couldn't believe that he'd met such an adorable someone who was showing incredibly obvious indications that he was as dorkishly attracted to Billy as he was to him.

Pulling into the driveway, Billy knew he had to play it cool in front of his parents. He didn't want them figuring out what had just happened. He was still feeling the hormone high and was worried that talking to his parents about a boy he'd just met would cause a crash that he could never recover from.

Walking through the door, his mom and dad were still up waiting for him, just as Billy expected.

"Hey, honey!" His mother said in a ridiculously chipper tone, a sign that she'd had a lot of coffee to get herself through the night. "*You're* getting in *late*! I take it that means you had a good time?"

"It was okay," he said with the swiftness of a master pickpocket. "Goodnight."

His mother flew between him and the stairs in a caffeinated blur. "Hey-hey-hey, you don't get off that easy." She looked her son up and down. "Oh my god, you met a boy!"

Billy was embarrassed she saw through him so quickly, but he was hardly surprised. His mother might have been psychic for how much she could figure out about her son just by looking at him. He could feel the crash set in and needed to find his bed before the ultimate explosion.

"Oh my god. I'm going to bed."

"No wait tell us how it went! What's his name?"

"Mom, please, I do not want to have this conversation... I'm very tired."

"I bet you are!"

"Oh my god, MOM!"

"Oh, come on! This is just as exciting for me as it is for you!"

"I can't see how that's at all possible."

"Please! Gab with me! Why can't we be that mother and son who talk about everything?"

"C'mon Cass," His merciful father intervened. "Billy obviously doesn't want to talk to you about this."

"Thank you, dad."

"Let the boy go to bed… I'm sure he needs it. Goodness knows how many calories he burned dancing the night away with his new boy toy." He gave an evil smile as his son's face turned beet red.

"Oh my god!" Was all he could say as he jumped around his mother to escape the madness that was his parents' unconditional love and support.

He flopped onto his bed, emotionally exhausted. Then he remembered he had to do something before he could allow himself to go to sleep.

He opened his phone, pulled up Cai in his messages, and sent him a text:

> BILLY: Hey Cai! Good news: I didn't die. And I had an amazing time. Free this weekend? Maybe we could see a movie or something? Or we could get dinner or whatever. IDC as long as I get to see you (Newsflash: I'm a dork too.) Goodnight!

7

14 AUG 18.

00:27.

SOMEWHERE OVER THE PACIFIC OCEAN.

Cai had been a nervous wreck throughout the entire flight. As soon as they had taken off, he lost all his cool. Billy was in the cockpit, piloting a jet into the middle of nowhere with nothing but a brief, psychic crash course to prepare himself, which scared Cai almost as much as whatever unknown terror may be waiting for them at their destination.

He started to ask himself an overwhelming amount of questions. What was waiting for them? Would they be able to escape? Would he ever see his family again? Who will they be by the time this is all over? Cai had no idea what his life had suddenly turned into, and he was praying for a quick resolution. Deep down, though, he knew that something terrible was going to happen.

They started to descend. Cai jumped out of his seat and ran into the cockpit.

"Is this it?"

"Yes," a robotic Billy responded. "Buckle up. The fasten seatbelt sign is on."

Cai sat down in the copilot's seat and strapped himself in. Looking out the windshield, he saw what appeared to be a man-made island rise from beneath the ocean. At first, he thought the dark of the night was playing tricks on his eyes but, looking closer, he saw the outline of a dark, metallic castle fortress.

"Holy shit. What is that?"

"EDIN."

"Eden?"

"Experimental Developments and Intelligence. E-D-I-N."

"And that's where you're from?"

Billy nodded.

"Whoa... I can't even begin to - are you sure you're ready for this?"

"Yes." Billy's gaze was as strong as steel, his body just as tense.

Cai had no choice but to believe him. They did a loop above the structure. Billy pressed a button on the control panel. Down below, a large door opened, and a long runway stretched out from within the massive structure. He gently guided the jet through the narrow passage, stopping at the far end where Cai noticed five other teenagers standing as straight and as stiff as statues in the docking bay, waiting for them.

It was at this point that Cai's fight or flight instinct truly began ringing all the bells in his mind.

"Billy, I don't like this."

"You have nothing to worry about."

"How do you-" He was stopped mid-sentence by the sudden piercing of a needle into his neck, the last of the sedative violently being inserted into his veins. "Billy?"

"It's going to be okay," was the last thing he heard before he descended into the darkness.

(Epilogue)

When the doorbell rang, Cassandra struggled to find the energy to go answer it. She'd spent all of the past two days crying, an activity she had been using to replace sleeping and eating. Daniel, slightly drunk, walked in from the kitchen and tried to pull her up from her seat.

"Come on, sweetie."

"No."

"You need to."

"I don't need to do *anything*, Daniel."

"Okay then, *we* need to answer the door."

The doorbell rang again.

"Ugh... I can't deal with this right now.''

"None of us can, Cassie... but we have to."

With a heavy sigh and the swiftness of a sloth on depressants, she lifted herself from the nest she'd made out of the couch and walked to the door. Opening it, she found Nia Medeiros crying in her husband's arms.

"Cassandra," Alfonso greeted her, his face lined with exhaustion.

"Alfonso." Cassandra welcomed the crying Nia into her arms. "Oh, Nia..."

"I'm sorry. I just can't - How do you do it? You're so... so strong... Billy just got out of the hospital. And now... and now..." Nia's sobs became heavier.

"Come on in, sit wherever."

Daniel appeared out of the kitchen, carrying beers. "Hey everybody. Sorry, I started early."

"Don't worry," Nia said, falling onto the nearby sofa, as she pulled out a flask from her purse. "I couldn't drive and cry my eyes out at the same time anyway. Thank god for tequila."

"Amen," Daniel said.

He offered Alfonso a beer, but he refused.

"Someone has to drive. Have you heard anything from the police?"

"If we did, I promise we would have already told you."

"Oh, I can't take this," Nia said, taking a swig. "This is absolutely absurd. I know my baby and he wouldn't do anything like this. He would never just run away without saying something. Someone took them, I know it."

"Completely unlike him. No note, no voicemail. No warning..."

"Cai wasn't acting at all strange before they... you know?"

"Aside from brooding over Billy, no."

"Billy was just as broody. He locked himself up in his bedroom and didn't come out for days."

"Did you find anything strange that might help us figure out what happened?"

"Nothing… We searched his room, his computer, not a single clue, right Cassie?"

Cassandra was drifting off into space. In her mind, she was searching for her son in the cosmos, searching for clues in the chasms of her memory.

"Cass!"

She snapped back to reality. "What?!"

"Did you find anything on Billy's computer?"

"No… nothing important."

She couldn't stop her mind from racing back to that moment in her bedroom. She was talking to Daniel about Billy's behavior, completely shutting off and shutting out the rest of the world after he had come back from the hospital. Then, out of nowhere, he walked in and hugged her. In that brief embrace, she felt a connection form between the two of them, forged from a strange and powerful force that pierced her heart and mind. That moment kept telling her that Billy was okay. He may have been missing, and she needed to find him, but she knew he was okay.

"Where could they have gone?!" Nia drunkenly wailed.

Daniel had to ask, "Does Cai have any… I don't know… friends out of town? People he'd go to if he needed a place to crash?"

"The only times Cai has ever left Seattle was for competitions, and believe me, he wasn't making any friends. What about Billy?"

Cassandra and Daniel simultaneously both scoffed and laughed.

"Billy didn't really have 'friends.' Billy had player twos. To be honest, we didn't think Cai really existed until we met him."

"To be honest, we thought Cai was joking when he introduced Billy to us as his 'boyfriend.'"

Daniel took a drunken offense to this. "What's that supposed to mean?"

"Well, it's just like you said, Billy wasn't exactly a social butterfly. And Cai was… is a very outgoing fella."

Daniel paused to put drunken thought into what Alfonso had said. "You're right. This is all just so fuckin' weird, you know? Just a few weeks ago, Billy was in the hospital. Before that, we were celebrating his birthday."

Daniel, surprisingly, started to cry and slumped onto the couch next to Nia.

"Oh, Daniel," Nia moved over to offer her crying companion a shoulder.

"Oh great… Now I have a headache."

Alfonso went into the kitchen to grab a glass of water, quickly returning and handing it to Daniel.

"Hydrate."

"Thank you," Daniel said, before gulping it all down in one swig.

Cassandra just kept on looking into space, searching for her son. Alfonso noticed this and went over to her.

"We should go out," He recommended.

"What? Alfonso…" Nia quietly protested.

"I'm serious. There's no phone to wait by. There's no news to be heard. Things aren't going to get any better with us just sitting here. I know our boys wouldn't want to see us like this and frankly neither do I. I care about all of you. Please don't make me watch you kill yourselves waiting for our sons to come home."

It was hard for Alfonso's words to break through the grief of the group. Nia and Daniel did their best to look at themselves objectively and mutually thought, in their own respective ways, *'What are we doing to ourselves?'* Cassandra, meanwhile, just kept staring off into space, drawing everyone's attention.

Daniel clumsily picked himself up off the sofa and walked over to his wife, nudging her back into the conversation.

"What?" She said, slightly startled.

"Cass, we need to go."

"Go where?"

"Anywhere. We gotta leave the house."

"But what if-"

"It'll only be for a couple of hours. I'm sure if they came home between now and then, they'd wait for us. Let's just go."

Cassandra took a second to ponder and softly nodded before getting up and following the others out the door.

"Have you guys ever been to Little Ipanema?" Alfonso asked.

"The Brazilian place on the waterfront?" Daniel asked.

"We've always wanted to go, and I figured-"

Daniel interrupted him. "Let's go eat a fuckton of meat."

They left the house and started walking down the street.

"Wait," Nia stopped. "Are we walking downtown?"

"It's a beautiful day, and we need to work off all that booze."

Cassandra stayed behind a little. She looked back at her house, worrying in her mind about when Billy would come home, but worrying even more about where this innate sense of calm and knowingness was coming from. It felt otherworldly, almost prescient. With her friends doing their best to keep up their spirits, she decided to focus on joining in and keep these premonitions at the back of her mind.

Nobody noticed the dapperly dressed man standing across the street. He smiled to himself as he closely watched the two families begin striding towards downtown. His phone began ringing and he quickly picked up, not wanting to keep the person on the other side waiting.

"Status?" They demanded.

"The families are oblivious. I doubt they'll be trouble for us anytime soon. I'll do a sweep of their houses before heading back."

"And the doctor?"

"Already taken care of."

"No trail?"

"C'mon, red, who do you think you're talkin' to?"

An annoyed silence.

"Have I ever given you any reason to doubt me?" A long, almost telling pause. "Hello?"

"We need you back at base right now."

"Why?"

"It doesn't matter. Your jet leaves at 1700 hours sharp. I want hourly status updates as soon as you touch ground. Base out."

The call disconnected. "Nice chatting with you too… bitch."

"PAVEL MAXIMOVICH VOLKOV"

BIRTH-DATE: 05 NOV 01

SEX: ████████████

CURRENT HEIGHT: ████████████

EYE COLOR: ████████████

HAIR COLOR: ████████████

INSTALLATION: Moscow, Russia.

NATIONALITY: ████████ ("Russian").

ETHNICITY: ████████████████

████████████

FAMILY:

Maxim Volkov ("father", deceased)

Lilya Volkov ("mother")

Anton Volkov ("younger brother")

Mila Volkov ("younger sister")

Dmitri Volkov ("younger brother")

1

20 JUN 18.

16:00.

GOLD'S GYM, Moscow, RU.

As soon as school let out, Pavel would immediately run to the gym. For two hours, he would work every muscle in his body to its limits and beyond before heading to his job as a clerk at a vegetable shop at four. There he would stay until the stroke of midnight when he finally went home to sleep, waking up only five hours later to get ready for school. This was his daily routine.

He was training himself, his dream at the forefront of his mind with every bench press, and every treadmill kilometer. What he wanted most in the world was to become the most renowned and decorated soldier in the Russian military. He wanted to be the hero to Russia his father never had the chance to be, and one that Putin himself would bequeath a medal of excellence.

Conversely, many of Pavel's peers wished to avoid the draft in whatever way they could, usually by running away or using up their savings to bribe the conscription officer. The more privileged young men would use their influence to weasel out of their patriotic responsibility. The working-class Pavel couldn't afford to run, and even if he could, he wouldn't. He also couldn't afford a gym membership, so his friend Mikhail bankrolled a permanent guest pass for Pavel on his account. Like Pavel, Mikhail also wanted to join the army, but not for the prospect of heroic grandeur. Mikhail wanted an escape.

Mikhail was tall, muscular, with a crooked, flat nose, bushy eyebrows, smooth black hair he kept long at the top and short on the sides.

He came from old money - his rigid and fastidious father was the CEO of a weapons manufacturer that made billions of dollars a year in gun sales - which brought with it responsibility and pressure that Mikhail was not interested in. His father's militaristic approach to parenting and their constant fighting only fueled the young man's desire to run away.

On the off occasion, Pavel would say, "Do you know what I would give to *have* a father I could fight with?"

And Mikhail would respond, "Hopefully that annoying mouth of yours."

They would train together every day and afterward, Mikhail would walk Pavel to work, following the same path every time. On this particular day, a car accident blocked the entire road.

"It's okay," Mikhail said. "We'll just slide through this alleyway. It's faster anyway."

Looking down the alley, and knowing what would be waiting for them, a nervous Pavel pleaded with his best friend. "Actually, can we go the other way around?"

"That'll take ages, dummy, and I have schoolwork to torture myself with. We're going this way."

"Ugh."

"What?"

"It's just…"

"Yes?"

"There's this creepy old man down there."

"*My father's in the alley?*" Mikhail joked.

"No, you big idiot. It's this nasty, old tramp. He is always there, and he always says the creepiest things whenever I pass by. Every time, without fail, he pops his head out of the same pile of garbage just to freak me out."

"Pavel, he's a creepy little homeless man. You're a billion feet tall and ninety-eight percent muscle. And I'd like to think I'm just as huge and intimidating. I'm sure we can take him if he tries to put up a fight."

"Yeah, but…"

"But what, Pavel?"

"There's just something about him… Something very… weird… I don't know. I just don't like him."

Mikhail sighed, before adopting a playful smile. "You know, you really shouldn't have told me."

"Why not?"

"Because now I need to know if that creepy old man really is my father, lying in a ditch. I'm going to want pictures."

"Gosh darn it, Mikhail, let's just go the other way!"

Mikhail ignored Pavel and ran down the alley. Halfway down they found the man in question, drunkenly splayed out over the pavement. His shirt was unbuttoned, all exposed skin was covered in mud, and his pants were shredded well enough that the two young men could see his privates. Pavel was disgusted but Mikhail just started laughing.

"Jesus Christ, Pasha, you're scared of this? I've seen more terrifying moles on your backside, which, by the way, I think you should have a doctor look at."

"The minute I can *afford* a doctor, you'll be the first to know. Now please, let's just go."

Mikhail ignored him again, instead deciding to open a conversation with the inebriated man. "We can very clearly see your dick, you know. You might want to start thinking about covering it up, leave something to the imagination."

The man grumbled and mumbled, tossing around in the garbage he had made into his bed before sitting himself as upright as he could with a very pronounced hunchback.

"What are you looking at, you fucking fairy?" He said with a heavy slur.

Mikhail's mischievous smile was quickly replaced with a look of pure fury. "What the fuck did you call me?"

"Fucking fairy. You're a fucking fairy," he slurred out before wheezing out a phlegm filled laugh.

Mikhail took a deep breath before spitting at the man's feet. "Let's go... I'm done with this trash."

The man screamed "FAIRYYYY!" at them as they walked away.

The two didn't speak until they reached Pavel's store when he broke the fevered quiet. "Are you okay?"

"I'm fine. I am so sorry for putting you through that. I promise we'll go the long way next time."

Pavel couldn't help but say, "I told you so."

"You know, it's shit like that that makes me want to get the fuck out of this stupid, fucking city. Everything here is just so... gross. I could have my arm blown off, bleeding on some Chechnyan farmland, and still be happier than I am living here. Just a few more weeks and I can escape."

"You could do that on your own, you know? You have the money."

"*I* don't have money. My father does. And he's the one who decides how it gets spent. Sometimes, I just..." Mikhail wanted to form words for the wishes, emotions, and insecurities bashing around inside his mind, but couldn't find the way. "You could escape too, Pavel. Whenever you want to. No offense, but you're not exactly important or outstanding. Nobody would come after you."

"Mikhail..."

"I get it. Your family."

"They need me."

"That may be all cute and true in your heart, but I know what my dad would say if he were here: *'Don't fall to weakness.'*" He said with a laugh.

The clock tower bell struck the hour, reminding Pavel that it was time for him to clock in.

"I have to go. I'll see you tomorrow."

As Pavel rushed into the store, Mikhail quoted his father one more time. "*'Love is weakness...'*"

Half past midnight.

After another long day of working his body and mind to their respective limits, Pavel finally made it home. He opened the door to see his mother, Lilya Volkov, sitting in her rocking chair, waiting for him to come home as she did every night.

"Hello, mother. Goodnight mother."

A slight, pixie of a woman, Lilya had the worn hands of someone who had been working all her life. Despite being barely through her late 30's, her once honey blonde hair had turned grey and thin from stress. The bags under her dead, blue eyes were almost as heavy as the weight of her children's futures on her shoulders.

Pavel attempted to run out of her line of sight as fast as he could, but Lilya cleared her throat ever so softly, yet with the magnitude of a tornado siren. And it was all that she had to do to stop Pavel dead in his tracks.

"Good *morning*, Pasha. How was work?"

"Fine," He swiftly said as he placed his day's pay in the small, wooden box his family called their "hope chest", just as he did every day. The plan was to use the funds to eventually buy a larger, or less dilapidated, house.

"School?"

"Fine."

"And how about Misha? How is he?"

"Mikhail is also fine, mother."

"Oh good. You know I worry about him sometimes. Living with his father must be so difficult, the way he treats the poor boy. Of course, he also deserves better than he treats himself too. But what do I know? I'm not *his* mother." Lilya's motherhood magic revolved around her mastery of aggressive passive-aggression. She pressed buttons but she wasn't pressing buttons to annoy, but to motivate.

"And I'm certain *he's* very grateful for your worry. Goodnight, mother." He made his way to the stairs.

"Pasha?"

He contained a sigh as he halted and turned. "Yes, mother?"

"Are you okay?"

He resisted the urge to sigh in frustration as he sensed the inevitable, exhaustive conversation on the horizon. "Yes, mother."

"Don't lie. I can tell when you're lying."

Pavel cursed at himself. He wouldn't be going to bed anytime soon. "I'm fine, Mother… are you okay?"

"You know, I worry about you, Pasha."

"*All* you do is worry, mother. You worry so much that *I'm* beginning to worry that you might not have any other settings."

"You work too hard. And too much. It's all much too much. You're too young to have so much weight on your shoulders."

"It's a weight I can bear, mother. It's a weight I choose to bear."

"It's a choice you shouldn't have had to make, Pasha. Children should be allowed to be children."

One of Pavel's buttons was pressed. "I'm not a child, mother! I'm just as much of a man father was when he-"

"When he what, Pavel?"

Pavel felt his face turning red and took a moment to collect himself. "Why do we have to have this conversation every night? Why can't you just let me go to bed and have what little sleep I get before I have to start all over again?"

Meanwhile, Lilya maintained an annoying calmness, having already mentally prepared herself for the task of emotionally combating her teenage son. "You don't have to go to school if you're too tired, Pasha. You don't have to go to the gym or go to work. You can just stay at home and rest."

"Mother, please, you're being ridiculous."

Her calm demeanor crumbled to pieces as Pavel pushed one of *her* buttons for a change. "Ridiculous? *I'm* being ridiculous? You've been working yourself to death to provide for this family. All you can think about is making money and becoming the perfect soldier, the perfect man. You've set your mind on becoming an ideal that will be impossible to achieve. You've set yourself up for failure and I refuse to watch you crumble under the pressure."

He decided to keep pressing. "You mean like father? You don't want me to turn into him?"

"Pasha..." She was caught off guard, "don't change the subject. This isn't about your father; this is about you."

"Everything is about father. What he did to us, to you."

She started to turn a pale pink. She would've turned red, but the years pulled the color out of her. "Pasha, stop."

"I'm not father. I will never be father. Unlike him, I would do anything for this family."

"And we'd do anything for you," She took a breath in preparation. "Which is why I want you to use the money to pay off the conscription officer."

Pavel un-collected himself as his veins nearly burst. "What?! Mother, don't even joke about that!"

Somewhere in the house, his three younger siblings were sleeping soundly. They were so used to their mother and big brother fighting that it had become a lullaby. They snored gently in their beds as Pavel and Lilya's voices escalated.

"I would not joke about this, Pavel," She half-shouted. "Take the money. I'm begging you. Just take the money. Go somewhere. Be somebody else. Do something better than killing yourself."

"I'm not killing myself!"

"You are, Pavel! You're killing yourself for your family and when you enlist, you'll just be killing yourself for your country."

"What would you rather me do? What do you think I'm really worth?"

"Pasha, you are worth so much more than you give yourself credit for. You could go to America. You could be a doctor, or a lawyer, or a dentist, or... flipping burgers in a diner and it would still be better than anything the army can offer you."

Pavel spat on the ground. "I'd rather be shot out of a cannon into a pile of used needles than live in America."

"Ok, don't go to America. Go to Germany, Japan, England, Antarctica, anywhere else that isn't here. Live a life that's worth living, Pasha."

"But what about you, mother? What would you do? What would happen to you without me? Or Anton, Mila, and Dmitry? Don't you want to live a better life?"

She scoffed. "A better life? What better life could be available to an aging widow who cleans floors all day and needs her son's help to pay the bills?"

"I could buy you a bigger house."

"A bigger house? Pavel, I don't need a bigger house. I don't want a bigger house. I only want my children to be happy, and safe."

"Anton, Mila, Dmitri... Don't you want more for them?"

"Of course, I do. And I'll find some way to get more for them. But right now, the only one in this family who cares about moving up in the world is you."

Pavel could feel himself unravel. He so desperately wanted to be a soldier. He so desperately wanted to fit in. He wanted so many things for himself and his family, and to be told by his mother that he shouldn't want these things, as if he were an infant who couldn't make decisions for himself, made him so angry.

"How dare you?"

"Pavel?"

"How dare you try and take my dream away from me."

"I'm not trying to-"

"This is all I've ever wanted my entire life. It's all I've worked for. And I won't allow anybody to take it away from me. Especially not you!"

"Darling, I-"

"No! Don't talk to me. I hate you!"

And with that, he ran out the door into the dark streets of Moscow as it started to rain.

2

21 JUN 18.

00:55.

MARKOV ESTATE, Moscow, RU.

Pavel ran to Mikhail's extravagantly large manor home and knocked on the door, knowing his best friend would still be awake to answer it.

True to his reputation, Mikhail cracked the door open, still wearing his gym sweats. His eyes were slightly sunken in from having been watching television for several hours straight. Yet another thing Pavel was jealous of was his friend's access to entertainment. The thought of a television in the Volkov household, to him, felt like a fantasy.

"Pavel?" He softly said, his quiet voice filled with concern. "What's wrong?"

"Can I come in?"

Mikhail hesitated to answer, knowing his father would not respond kindly to a midnight visitor. "No, sorry, but... um... Come this way." He grabbed an umbrella and escorted Pavel to the pool house that doubled as a guest apartment so they could talk in confidence. "What's going on?"

"It's my mother... she's just so..." Pavel couldn't form the words, he was so upset. "Ugh."

"What happened this time? Another one of her '*talks*,' I'm assuming."

"When is she ever *not talking* to me?"

"Fair point. But still, she's never made you this upset. What happened?"

"She wants me to… god, I can't even say it. It's so… disgusting."

"She asked you to run away?"

"How…? How did you know?"

Mikhail had to swallow an amused chuckle. "Pavel, the only thing I honestly think that would ever really get you this pissed off would be if someone told you that you couldn't be a soldier. I try to avoid thinking about what would happen if- I mean, sometimes I wonder what if you're wanting to do it for your family or if you just really want to be a soldier."

Pavel started to cry. "I just… I don't know what else I can be…"

The sight of his best friend crying threw Mikhail off. He didn't know what to do. He escorted Pavel to the bedroom, laid him down to rest, and let him cry himself to sleep as he slept on the floor nearby.

They were an infant, no older than four. They had three fingers on each pale, white-skinned hand, and were dressed in a strange, black uniform that looked like a wrestler's singlet.

They sighed with a heavy gust of boredom. The grey of the room reflected onto their skin and they became grey to match to entertain themself. They changed their fingers from three to six to ten to seven before changing it back to the original three. They produced a nose and made it grow longer and wider until it covered their whole face.

They laughed at themself. In their opinion, noses were very weird and unnecessary.

Several people in lab coats entered, picking them up and taking them to a grey room where they sat them at a large, metal table with a variety of strange dishes placed in front of them. They were forced to eat nails, wood chips, and bones. It all became like cereal in their mouth. Acid felt like sparkling spring water.

They were given a picture of a little boy with blond hair, fair skin, and blue eyes. Looking into a hand mirror, they forced themselves to change their face to match the boy, succeeding in becoming a perfect duplicate.

A man with horn-rimmed glasses, a shiny head, and a mustache squeezed his shoulder with a smile.

"It's time to wake up, Changeling."

He awoke with a great pain overtaking his body. His skin felt as if it was on fire. The flames spread to his muscles, bones, and brain. He felt like he was being slowly submerged in lava, melting down like ice cream.

He screamed at the top of his lungs, which Mikhail echoed from the floor as he was scared awake.

"What's wrong?"

Mikhail's worried voice sounded like a distant echo. Pavel mustered what strength he could through the pain and ran outside, hoping the cold air might freeze his body until the burning would subside, but the pain wouldn't stop.

Pavel ran out into the street, his bones vibrating with every step. He could hear Mikhail running after him.

"Pavel, wait!"

Pavel wouldn't stop running, though. There was something wrong with him. It wasn't just his body, but his mind as well. Something that he couldn't understand, or control was pulling him into the night and away from his friend.

There was a park close to Mikhail's house that Pavel ran into, despite his better instincts. He ran past sex workers, drug dealers, addicts, and undercover police officers. He needed to be away from people. Mikhail followed, but no matter how fast he ran, Pavel outran him by a mile.

Not seeing the tree root poking out of the ground, Pavel fell and rolled, finding himself near a pond. Attempting to regain his composure, he gathered his thoughts and considered drinking some of the pond water to ease the burning. But upon looking into the black, polluted, trash-filled pool, he decided not to.

Looking deeper into the water, he saw a strange figure staring back at him. A creature with snow-white skin, slight, black slits where the eye sockets should be, a ridged and pointed nose with a heavy bump in the middle that almost looked like a horn, a completely hairless head, no eyebrows or locks, and pointed, elf-like ears.

It took him what felt like an eternal moment to realize that the reflection in the water was his own. He couldn't believe his eyes until he touched his now bald head. As he did, he noticed that his hands had also changed, instead of five digits he now possessed three: two fingers and a thumb on each hand. He had become a monster.

He screamed in shock.

From a distance came a response from a worried Mikhail. "Pavel?!"

Pavel heard his friend's footsteps come running in his direction and, out of fear of how Mikhail might respond to his new appearance, dove headfirst into the pitch-black water. Mikhail passed by and, not being able to find Pavel, ran in the opposite direction from where he came.

Relieved but still confused and terrified, Pavel swam to the other side and pulled himself out, running out of the park and into the city streets. The burning had stopped, but now he looked like a freak and wished for nothing more than to be hidden from any and all eyes.

He found his way to the alley from before, knowing that only drunks and the homeless would be there, already asleep. He hoped it would be quiet enough for him to try and get a grip on whatever was going on. He sat on the ground and tried to catch his breath.

The trash nearby started moving, startling the already emotionally dismembered Pavel. Looking towards it, he found the drunkard from before, tousled in a bed made from trash.

"Oh no."

The man took one look at the disfigured Pavel and, with a huge smile on his face, said, *"He looked for an answer. He'd hope. He'd pray."*

And without any warning, Pavel instantly blacked out.

3

22 JUN 18.

08:00.

#818 REGAL ESTATE APARTMENTS, Moscow, RU.

"Wake up!"

A man's voice shook Pavel awake. He had a massive headache and couldn't move or speak, as if he had been bound and gagged with an invisible rope. He wanted to scream for help, but his mouth stayed sealed.

"Sit up," the same voice called from the nearby kitchen.

Pavel felt like his mind and body were being hijacked as he did exactly as he was told. Sitting upright, he found that he was in an incredibly expensive and luxurious apartment, complete with furniture that altogether would cost what Pavel's parents paid for their house a hundred times over.

The man continued. "I'm sure you have many questions, so feel free to speak."

"HELP!" Pavel screamed.

"No screaming."

Pavel's voice turned into a quiet whimper. "Help…"

"Calm down. You're in no danger. Trust me. There's no need to worry. You're still in Moscow if that's what you're concerned about. In my apartment, to be precise."

"Who are you?"

"A friend."

"Why did you bring me here?"

"I live here, so it seemed to make the most sense."

"Why didn't you take me to a hospital?"

"Because there's nothing wrong with you."

Remembering the events of the previous night, Pavel refused to believe that. "Have you not seen me?"

"Of course, I have, and there's *nothing* wrong with you. Go ahead. There should be a mirror on the wall to your left. See for yourself."

A sense of hope washed over Pavel as he felt the invisible restraints lift from his body. He jubilantly ran to the mirror, as if fireworks were popping out from beneath his feet. He began to think that what he had seen in the water wasn't his reflection, but a nightmare brought on by whatever wretched fever had overtaken him. However, that hope was replaced by terror as he was greeted by the same monster as before.

He wanted to scream, but whatever spell his captor held over him kept him from doing so. "What is happening?"

The man appeared from out of the kitchen. very tall and tan wearing expensive, designer clothing, balancing several bowls in his arms like a waiter. He placed them on the coffee table in front of the couch.

"You may talk, but no screaming. God knows what the neighbors would think."

Pavel let out a deep breath. "How can you say there's nothing wrong with me? I'm hideous."

"Beauty is in the eye of the beholder, Pavel."

"But... wait, what? How do you know my name?"

"Sit down and I'll tell you everything I think you need to know.

"I don't want to sit down," Pavel said as he sat down.

The man pushed the bowls across the table toward Pavel. Looking down, he saw that they were filled with dirt, twigs, screws, nuts, bolts, and nails.

"Sorry I didn't have more to offer. This is all I could put together on such short notice."

"What am I supposed to do with this?"

"Eat it." The man said with a goofy smile.

Pavel, still with no control over his body, started shoveling handfuls of the random scraps put in front of him. Despite all his assumptions about how a human's body is supposed to respond to eating inedible materials, he found his teeth rose to the occasion as he chomped through the loose bits of metal, wood, and soil.

"I would've given you a proper salad but we're trying to fatten you up. I'm sure you've noticed by now that your body doesn't operate like a normal human's. That's because you're a metamorph - a shapeshifter. You can change shape at will, presumably to be able to perfectly impersonate other people. Super handy, right? On top of that, you can absorb any and all kinds of mass - assimilate it, if you want to get technical - to increase your own. My friends and I call you 'Changeling'. Any questions?"

Pavel nodded his head as he swallowed the last of his "meal."

"Ask away then."

"What is going on?"

"I just told you. You have superpowers. And someone must train you how to use those powers so they can be put to good use. That's why I'm here. Any other questions?"

"Who are you?"

"Oh, come on, kid. You know who I am."

Pavel shook his head. The man responded by hunching over, messing up his hair, and adopting a drunken look on his face.

Pavel would have gasped if there were any shock left in his body. "The man in the alley? You've been harassing me for over a year!"

"I like to think bullying builds character."

"Why are you doing this?"

"I'm in charge of taking care of you."

"By terrorizing me and taking me hostage?"

"If you look at it objectively, what's the difference between what I'm doing and how school works?"

"Can't I just go home?"

"Do you think they'll want you, the way you look right now? That's not your home anyway, kid. Not really."

"What do you mean?"

The man sighed. "You're going to hear all this eventually, so I might as well tell you now. Your family, your *real* family, abandoned you when you were a baby."

"What?! That's impossible! My mother-"

"Don't interrupt."

Pavel shut his mouth.

The man continued. "This - how you look now - is how you're supposed to look. We, my friends and I, took you in and performed a few invasive genetic reshaping treatments. I'm not a scientist, so I can't even begin to imagine what they did to you. All that matters is that you're a changeling now! Of course, then, what to do with a changeling? *I* was the one who suggested that we drop you out here in Moscow. So, around the time all the experiments and tests on you were finished - I'd say you were about four? Maybe? We looked for a Russian family visiting America with a child-"

Pavel's face became contorted in discomfort at the notion of being an American.

"Yes, you're American. It's a shock, I know, but you'll get over it. Anyway, we found the family, had them detained at the airport before they could board their plane, and then had you copy their kid's appearance. Then, the guy in charge of everything - I want to say his name was Garry? Or Gear? Whatever, he used this weird little machine that convinced you that you were the real Pavel, giving you all his memories, hopes, dreams, blah-blah-blah. Then we turned on this little machine in your brain called an ANT which turned off your powers so you could grow up normally without going all goopy and weird. Do you have any questions so far?"

Pavel nodded.

"Without screaming, you may ask your questions one at a time."

Pavel began, speaking softly as commanded. "If I'm not the real Pavel, then, where is he?"

"As far as I know, he's living somewhere, perfectly alive and happy. Or he's dead. I don't care. Keeping track of him is not my job. Next?"

"What's my real name?"

"I don't think you ever had one. So... 'Abandoned Baby'? 'Changeling'? Yeah, Changeling's probably your real name. That's what I'm going to call you from now on, anyway. Next."

"What is the point of all this?"

"Oh, that is privileged information, but I promise you, you'll find out on your own soon enough. Next."

"How come you chose me?"

"You were an abandoned, unnamed baby left as a ward of the state who had exactly what we needed for this operation. Why wouldn't we choose you? Any more questions?"

"Yes."

"Then speak up. We don't have a lot of time for this."

"Why now?"

"I will admit, this is all kind of ahead of schedule. We planned on reactivating you at a very specific time and place. However, I can't help but marvel at the coincidence..." The man started to mutter off into his own world.

"What coincidence?"

"Hm? What? Oh, nothing. Privileged information. None of your business. Don't ask about it again. Or about my plans.

You'll find out when you need to find out. This next one's your last question, so don't waste it."

"You said I can shapeshift into anyone, so couldn't I shapeshift back into me?"

"What do you mean? You already are you."

"I meant can I shapeshift back into *'Pavel'*?"

"Of course, you can, I just don't know why you'd want to."

Pavel wanted to cry. He wanted to say, *'Because I liked being Pavel.'* The man could easily tell what was weighing on his mind.

"You're not Pavel. You never were Pavel. You're Changeling. And I'm in charge of taking care of you, but I only have a few days to get you ready for your **big debut**. We need to get you into shape-shifting shape, so be quiet and do everything I tell you to… Oh wait, you don't have any choice." The man chortled.

It was at this moment that Pavel realized that he'd never see his family again. He thought of his mother, and how much he missed her. He prayed for her, knowing how much she would be missing him.

Over the next few days…

The "training" the man put Pavel through was both grueling and perplexing. He was forced to eat whatever materials the man would put in front of him. This included furniture of varying sizes, like a coffee table and an easy chair. To accommodate this, his teeth became pointed and razor-sharp while his saliva became like acid, breaking down everything he ate until it went down like oatmeal, and if the "food" was too large his mouth would grow in size until it could encompass the entire object.

They practiced Pavel's ability to mimic faces. The man would show Pavel pictures of other people and had him imitate them repetitively until he had made an exact replication.

After he'd mastered face changing, they visited a morgue.

"This is where the real fun begins," the man said, with the giddiness of a child. "Full body morphs! I'm going to have you shapeshift into every corpse in this room."

'*Jesus Christ...*' a disgusted Pavel thought, his innermost thoughts now his only refuge.

"Take your clothes off."

Pavel had no choice but to expose himself to the monstrous man who had taken him hostage. He felt disgusted, embarrassed, and violated, but steeled himself for what atrocities the man, who once exposed himself in front of the juvenile Pavel, was going to make him perform.

He had him force his body into the shapes of the morgue's deceased residents, mimicking their appearances. At first, no matter what he did, he would always do something wrong. He'd be missing a mole here and there, or the hair would be an inch or so off, or his skin would have just the slightest touch of lively pink where there should be dead grey. His mysterious instructor was a stickler for detail.

He was forced to take on female shapes, morphing his genitalia to match. This brought upon its own level of discomfort. He felt as if he were violating these now dead women by perfectly mimicking their naked forms, only to be meticulously inspected by the deranged man. However, taking the shape of a woman didn't bother him as much as he assumed it would. As time went on, he began to enjoy the freedom that came with no longer being himself. He could escape, mentally, into whatever face or body he was forced to present.

Pavel didn't have many resources available to properly investigate the many terms for the many options and identities known to the modern world. Russia was not a welcoming place for those who didn't conform to the cis-heterocentric patriarchy that permeated their society.

Mikhail would occasionally let Pavel use his laptop, and, though it annoyed Pavel, they would watch this television show from America that wasn't allowed to be broadcast in Russia. A character from the show, who was assigned "female" at birth openly identified as "gender-neutral" and went by "they/them" pronouns. It was this memory that resonated deep within Pavel's soul as he poured over his current circumstances in the quiet solitude of his mind. "They" and "them" were limitless words. "They" could be used to describe an entire group of people or just one person. "They" was meaningful and made Pavel feel meaningful.

The eager, militant, conservative Russian-raised part of Pavel's mind decided to throw itself into Pavel's inner monologue. '*That's absurd though! Who cares about a weird and delusional woman on an American tv show? She's nothing more than a servant of queerocentric, American neoliberalism. It's all complete nonsense.*'

In his identity confusion, Pavel began to argue with himself. '*But, then again, I thought the concept of superhumans was just a comic book fantasy until just a few days ago. Now I'm shapeshifting into corpses. Mikhail has been trying to open my mind to other ideas besides the ones I grew up with. Maybe...*'

'*God what is going on with my life? Just the other night, I was an ordinary teenager fighting with my mother about my future. Now, I'm fighting with myself over how I should identify. What does it matter? My life is over.*'

Pavel's heart sank. '*I don't think I'm ever going to escape this. I don't know what this man is going to do to me, and I don't know where I'll wind up at the end of it all... all I know is that I want my mom... I want my brothers and my sister... not that they'd be able to help me escape, but at least they'd be able to help me figure out who I'm supposed to be. I don't know who, or what, I am anymore. I want clarity. Would* neutrality *bring me clarity? Or, at the very least, a brief pause for the endless confusion I'm feeling?*'

'*This show that Mikhail made me watch, the* 'gender-neutral person' *said that gender was just a construct. That it was a* 'societally assigned idea forced upon us at birth based entirely on our genitals.' *And I am nothing more than a constantly shifting mass of biology and anatomy. I can be whatever I want... I can be whatever sex I want. So, what does the* 'concept' *of gender mean to me now?'*

Within Pavel's mind, a conclusion appeared, like a beacon of light and understanding. *'Gender is meaningless. But I don't have to be.'*

They. Them.

Pavel began to wonder how none of the doctors or medical examiners that worked in the morgue ever managed to wander in. They also wondered how the man obtained the clearance to come into this place in the middle of the day with a random teenager. Everything about this situation was beyond belief to them. They were almost happy they couldn't ask questions.

The man lifted one of the bodies as best as he could across from Pavel, holding it upright a short distance away.

"Okay," he said with glee. "Now we're going to do something really fun. I want you to extend your finger outward, like a tentacle, and then make it as hard and as sharp as a knife. Then pierce it straight through this thing's heart. It should be here, on the left side of her chest."

Pavel lifted his hand Focusing with all their might, they felt their body insert mass into their finger, stretching it outward like a great blade until it managed to reach the corpse.

"You're on the right track," the man said, encouragingly. "Now, pierce it through the chest like a bullet. Reverse and full throttle forward."

Pavel's new tentacle pulled back and sliced clean through the body's chest, piercing it with little effort.

"Wonderful!" The man shouted, joyfully. "Just wonderful! Okay, now onto something even harder. I want you to change your flesh into metal."

'*How could I possibly do that*?' Is what Pavel would have asked.

"I know what you're thinking: 'how could I possibly do that?'"

Pavel wanted to roll his eyes.

"But what you may not realize is that while you've been on a diet of nothing but metal, wood flakes, and a bunch of other crap the past few days, you've also been metabolizing all of it. Assimilating it. Trust me when I say that this will be far too easy for you. Just focus on what you want yourself to be, and then you will be it. Be metal!"

Pavel focused. and as they did, they felt their skin begin to burn. They winced at the pain but continued, nonetheless. The flesh of their finger had turned into steel, taking on a silvery chrome color in the process.

"Woot-woot! Now, extend your finger again, but this time, pierce her right through the skull."

Their now metallic finger became liquid metal. It struck forward at the body's head, making a quick, clean hole.

"Excellent! Beyond excellent! Marvelous! You're progressing right on schedule. You may pull out now."

Pavel retrieved their tentacle from the corpse's head and pulled it back into their body and felt a slight surging sensation as it changed back into a flesh and bone finger.

The next day.

The man had Pavel take on more unconventional shapes, having them turn their fists into shovels, and then their feet into flippers. They learned to grow wings out of their back, extend their neck like a giraffe, and grow a variety of different tails. First a bushy, horse's tail, then a long, furry, cat's tail, then a scaly, dry, lizard's tail.

At first, changing shape was painful, as if their whole body was turning inside out repeatedly, but the more they did it the easier it became, and the greater their powers would become. Despite their progression, though, none of it made Pavel's feelings on their imprisonment any better.

'*Perhaps this is hell,*' they thought. '*I sinned in some way and have gotten myself trapped in this demon man's lair. Doomed to spend the rest of eternity here. Going insane in the prison that is my mind…*'

4

29 AUG 06.

23:00.

ANCHORAGE INT'L. AIRPORT, Anchorage, AK.

Maxim and Lilya planned a short vacation for themselves and their children, Pavel and Anton. They had been offered free plane tickets through a lottery at Maxim's work. Lilya was concerned about flying while pregnant, but her husband convinced her that they needed to jump on the "once-in-a-lifetime opportunity."

They decided to go to Alaska, the cheapest place they could travel to without bankrupting themselves. Once there, the family rented a car, stayed in a small room in a small bed and breakfast, and saw as many sights as possible. The time away from home was so overwhelmingly relaxing that it nearly broke all of their hearts to go back to Moscow.

When they arrived at the airport for their trip home, the family was pulled aside by security after they had found a "suspicious item" in their luggage. This turned out to be an ordinary can of locally sourced Alaskan salmon that Lilya had hoped to take home with them. As a result, they were forced to spend several hours detained in a small room with uncomfortable chairs after being told there was "an issue with their passports." They were eventually released and given a complimentary flight rebooking for their troubles, only to realize that Pavel was nowhere to be found.

"Where is our son?!" Maxim, the only member of the family who spoke English, shouted at the TSA agent.

"Isn't he with you?" She responded with a smile, pointing at Anton while forcefully escorting them to their gate.

Max looked at her incredulously. "I have **another son**! Where is my **other son**, *Pavel*?"

"What? Oh no. I'm so sorry. Trust me. This almost never happens. I wonder where he could be?"

"We have not seen him since before you pulled us into your interrogation room for *seven hours*!"

"Sir, please lower your voice. I would hate to have to take you into custody again."

This pressed the incredibly small button that made his anger dissipate. He repeated himself in a calmer voice. "Can you please help us find our son?"

"Yes, I can, sir," She stopped at a nearby computer panel. "Now, what is your son's name?"

"Pavel Volkov."

"How old is he?"

"He will turn five in November."

"Awww, how exciting!"

No matter how hard he tried, he could not understand this woman's behavior.

Lilya, in a frenzied confusion, pulled her husband aside. "What is going on? Where is Pavel?"

"She didn't even know we had another son! This woman is impossible!"

"Oh my God, Max. I cannot believe this. What if they never find him?"

"Lilya, please, remain calm. For your sake, for Anton's and the baby's, just go and sit down while I deal with this. We will find our son."

Lilya tried to contain her panic but it continued to creep out. She could sense that something was wrong and knew that there was nothing she could do.

Meanwhile...

Doctor Gehrig felt he had to personally supervise the transition for Changeling, as the necessary procedure was incredibly delicate. He wasn't able to test the "Neural Transceiver" that was supposed to perfectly map and copy the five-year-old Pavel's brain waves before transposing them over the shapeshifter's mind. In addition to his wariness, he was also invested in understanding Changeling's mentality.

Unlike most children their age, Changeling was a blank slate. They did as they were told and felt what they were told to feel. Now the doctor had to take this shallow shapeshifter and completely mold them into an entirely different person using a pre-existing blueprint.

After taking several hours to map out Pavel's mind, they were finally ready to finish the job. Gehrig, suddenly feeling rather sentimental, attempted a farewell.

"Hey," He said, in an embarrassing attempt to be informal.

"Hello, Doctor," Changeling responded in a hollow monotone.

The complete lack of childishness in Changeling's voice always made Gehrig uncomfortable. It didn't make him feel like he was talking to an adult. It made him feel like he was talking to an alien impersonating a human child.

"Well... This is it. We're saying goodbye today."

"I know, doctor. Goodbye."

"Listen, Changeling..."

The child stood at attention. "Yes sir!"

"At ease."

Changeling relaxed.

"The world is not an easy place to live in. If our time together can teach you anything-" He paused as he came to a sudden realization and laughed at his own foolishness. "You won't even remember this... You won't remember anything. Fuck."

"Doctor?"

Gehrig looked at Changeling and saw a child's innocent eyes staring up at him. In a rush of sadness, and shame, the doctor embraced Changeling, but the child assumed he was attacking him and started to cower in fear. The sight of this only made him feel worse.

"I'm not going to hurt you! I promise!" He said this knowing the child had no reason to think this was anything but an empty promise. "My God... I am the single most terrible person on the planet. I've done terrible things. I'm **doing** terrible things.

Things I know I shouldn't be doing, but I have to… because if I don't then somebody else will… and they'd probably be worse… Or maybe that's just something terrible people tell themselves so they can sleep at night."

He looked into Changeling's deep, pitch-black eyes, puzzled and fearful.

He continued his empty confession "At least, for now, I can take some small comfort knowing that all of the pain I've caused you and the others… that at least you won't remember it. If only I could be that lucky…"

He pulled the strap on the device tighter around Changeling's head and flipped the switch. They began to shiver and shake, a side effect that grew more violently as the machine warmed up. The shapeshifter's mind was completely demolished and reorganized. Their semi-liquid form was made completely solid and trapped in the shape of the young Pavel Volkov. After a few moments of torture, Changeling had become Pavel, inside and out.

Afterward.

One of the security agents claimed to have found Pavel eating a candy bar he had taken from a small gift shop near gate twenty-two. His parents nearly fainted from a combination of exhaustion and relief upon seeing their son.

"Pasha!" Maxim embraced his boy. "How could you scare us like that?"

He looked up at his parents with big, apologetic eyes. "I'm very sorry, father. I got lost."

Lilya's feelings of fear and confusion, however, would not subside. She couldn't fight the feeling that something was off. She took a moment to take a good look at Pavel. His eyes were as blue as they had always been, with the tiny flecks of navy and indigo in the same places as they were before. His hair was just as blond and floppy in the bowl cut she gave him. His clothes were the same tattered hand-me-downs from older cousins. As far as she could see, this was her son, but she couldn't shake the nagging feeling that something was wrong. It plagued her until they had reached peak altitude when Pavel fell asleep on her lap.

He whispered, "I love you, mommy."

Suddenly, all the doubt she felt disappeared. This was her child, and she felt terrible for thinking otherwise.

5

28 JUN 18.

22:00.

NEAR THE MARKOV ESTATE, Moscow, RU.

The man had driven the two of them just down the road from Mikhail's house, perplexing and worrying Pavel who became terrified of what this man had planned for his best friend.

"Transform back into Pavel," He commanded.

They immediately did as they were told, returning to the form they thought was their own for twelve years, but now it felt like a costume. To them, "Pavel" was now just as alien as any other form they'd been forced to take the past few days.

He handed them an earpiece. "Put this in your ear. I'll guide you through everything. All you have to do is follow my directions." He paused to laugh at himself. "Wait! I completely forgot. You have no choice. Okay, get out of the car and walk to Mikhail's house."

A confused but obedient Pavel exited the car and stiffly walked to Mikhail's family estate. As they made their approach, they heard the man's voice through the earpiece.

"Walk up to the door and knock."

Pavel knocked and Mikhail answered the door. "Hey, Pavel. Haven't seen you in a bit. How are you?"

Mikhail's incredible calm at seeing Pavel for the first time in what should have been days disturbed them greatly. He should be shocked and asking where Pavel had been since they'd gone missing.

'*What is going on here?*' They asked themself.

The man's voice. "Tell him you missed him and want to talk."

"You missed him and want to talk."

"Son of a bitch... Tell him 'I missed you and want to talk.'"

Mikhail's face was a combination of sentimental and confused. "Really? Uh... okay, what do you want to talk about?"

"Don't say anything. Just hug him. *Tightly.*"

Pavel grabbed Mikhail and pulled him into a squeezing embrace. Without saying anything, Mikhail hugged Pavel back even tighter.

"Go inside and repeat after me."

Pavel entered the house and began: "I've been thinking about you a lot... that's why I left so suddenly that night... feelings had been... stirred."

"Feelings? Pavel, what are you talking about?"

"I..." Pavel began to resist their programming to try and keep themself from saying what the man was telling them to say. They tried to push out a warning or a cry for help until he snapped them back into control.

"Say it! Now!"

"I know how you feel about me, Misha. But I wanted to hear you say it."

"Pavel, I..."

"It's okay… you're safe with me. Misha. I… I love you."

Mikhail's eyes started to water. He looked so full of joy and confusion. A complicated mess of contradicting emotions.

"Pavel…" he started, with a warm resistance. "You… are my best friend. I remember everything we've been through together and said to each other. And all this time I've been so scared. So scared of… everything. I have lived my entire life in fear of my feelings for you."

Pavel couldn't hold back the tears. They didn't want to deceive Mikhail or make him reveal something that would put him in danger, but they had no choice and they tried to keep that at the forefront of their mind.

"And what feelings are those, Misha? Please. I need to know."

"I love you," he said with a great exhale, finally unleashing and owning the truth he'd been concealing for so long. "I'm in love with you, Pasha."

"Now kiss him," the man instructed him.

'No…'

With no other choice, they closed the gap between them and Mikhail and pulled him into a kiss. The man, however, gave no instructions on making it convincing. Mikhail pulled back.

"Pavel?" His face was contorted with sudden regret. "What's happening?"

"Wait for a second…" there was a brief pause. "Don't let him go."

Pavel kept Mikhail in a tight embrace. Their friend started to look concerned.

"Pavel, what's happening?"

"Now! Pull him back in for another kiss, now!"

They kissed again. As they did, the door slammed open. The great, imposing figure of Piotr Markov, Mikhail's father, stood in the doorway. His fury made him look even more intimidating than usual. His dark eyes were filled with a fire borne from age-old hatred and a father's disappointment.

"What the fuck is going on?"

"Quick, turn to metal and pierce him straight through the heart, like a bullet. Make it convincing."

As quickly as possible, they molded their hand into a metallic tentacle and flung it at Piotr's chest, piercing it straight through to the wall behind him, making a wound just clean enough to look like he had been shot. Through the din of their shock, Pavel could hear Mikhail's screams.

"Now do the same to Mikhail but through his skull, from the side, as if he shot himself."

"Oh my god-"

Pavel reared his metallic tentacle back and whipped it clean through Mikhail's temple. Faster than the blink of an eye, they had killed their best friend, and the last shred of the person Pavel once thought they had died as well.

"Are they dead?" The man asked.

"Yes..." They said through gritted teeth.

"Okay. Wait there."

The man arrived at the house a few moments later, wearing a pair of rubber gloves and a hair net. He pulled out a revolver and examined the crime scene meticulously.

"Okay, so, if Mikhail was standing here when Piotr walked in... then-"

He took a shot at the wall behind Piotr's body.

"And then... if Mikhail was here when you murdered him - great job, by the way, very realistic - then..."

He shot at the wall across where Mikhail's body was lying before placing the gun in the dead boy's hand. He had successfully staged the scene of a murder-suicide.

"Okay, we're done here, let's go."

They returned to the car where the man noticed them crying.

"Oh, buddy," he said, in a hollow voice trying to sound empathetic and kind. "I hope you're not too broken up about this. Trust me, it was for the best. I mean, could you imagine? Being gay in a country like this? *Please*. Plus, his dad was a massive dick. Trust me. Neither of them is going to be missed. Now, I know you probably have some questions but, honestly, the sound of your voice exhausts me, all you need to know is that things are going to change for the better." His phone rang. "Orlov," He answered. "Yeah. Of course. No, the kid did wonderfully. It's all we ever wanted and more... Yeah, we're on our way... I promise, ma'am..." He chuckled. "Of course... of course... see you soon. Buh-bye."

They couldn't believe any of this. They had just killed their best friend and his father, and this man was giggling like a schoolgirl. They were filled with so much fury, so much anger. They fantasized about murdering him. They could turn into a tiger and rip him to shreds or morph their fingers into knives and stab him a million times until there was no blood left in his useless, soulless body. The impossible possibilities were endless, but they were trapped, unable to do anything but watch as this man used their fluid, ever-changing body to destroy helpless lives.

They wanted to die.

Orlov drove the two of them to a private airport on the outskirts of the city. Changeling hoped that this was where the man would put them out of their misery, but they knew he would never be that merciful.

"I know you hate me. I don't care but I just thought I'd say this: beauty, like goodness, is in the eye of the beholder. One day, all of this will make sense. And you won't care as much because you'll be too focused on everything else we have planned for you. Now... *'He looked for an answer. He'd hope. He'd pray.'*"

As before, Changeling blacked out.

'Who am I now?'

(Epilogue)

Lilya sat in her living room, consumed with guilt over her fight with Pavel. She had stayed up all night, waiting for him to come home.

"Oh Lilya, you are such a genius. How have you not won an award for 'Perfect Parenting' yet? Stupid woman…"

A knock from the front door, combined with the anxiety induced from a night of no sleep, caused her to jump up out of her chair. She ran to the door with a leap and opened it to find a slightly disheveled Pavel.

"Oh, my baby!" She pulled him into a tight embrace. "Oh, my lord, Pavel, where have you been? I was so worried!"

"I'm sorry, mother," he said in a voice as cool as the winter snow. "I guess I just needed some time to myself."

Lilya looked at the boy in front of her and couldn't stop herself from feeling unsettled. The way he carried himself, the confidence and the poise were so different from the caged, burdened child she had fought with just a few sleepless hours ago.

"Mother," he continued. "I know what we talked about. I know things were heated. I just wanted you to know, my position has not changed. I **will** be a soldier. I have no intention of doing otherwise."

He held his mother's hands in his own. They felt like Pavel's hands, rough to the touch from years of hard work, but still, Lilya could feel something was wrong.

"And mother, my only wish is for you to be happy. I want you to be happy knowing that I am happy. I want you to be happy in a home that you can be proud of, in a country you can be proud of. Please…"

She looked into her son's bright blue eyes. Being without him, even just for a night, not knowing if he was safe or that he was being taken care of, drove her to the brink of madness. If he joined the army, she would surely lose herself completely. If he moved away, if he started a new life, she could rest easy knowing he was far from a battlefield, but one look into his eyes, and she knew she couldn't argue any longer.

"Fine." She said with a proud smile. "You win. Congratulations. And I love you."

"I love you too mother. Trust me, this is what's best for everyone."

His eyes sparkled, something they hadn't done in years. Lilya suddenly felt a lack of ease she hadn't in years. Not since Anchorage.

16 AUG 18.

07:00.

RESIDENCE OF DR. IRENE GUPTA, Mountlake
Terrace, WA.

Irene always stayed on top of her schedule. She never refrained from the rigid and steady beat that she marched to on a daily basis. Timeliness and keeping promises were her strong suits. Even after a three-day, mini-break vacation, she managed to get up on time for work with little resistance. Though she doubted normal people would call working non-stop from home a "vacation."

Before her break, she had been going over some lab work for one of her patients - Billy Howard - who had just recently survived a neurological event that left him in a coma, only to wake up and walk out of the hospital a couple of weeks later. She had been toiling over his MRI scans, trying to understand how the spike in activity in his occipital and temporal lobes could have potentially caused his seizure, but without much progress. She was just at the end of her rope when her fiancé, Bo, reminded her that she could always deal with work **at work**.

On the day of Billy's follow up appointment, she was up at seven on the dot. in the shower by 7:05, out by 7:15, and was completely primped and polished in time for breakfast with Bo at 7:45. At 8 a.m. sharp, she kissed her fiancé goodbye, got into her car, and was on her way to work.

Much to her ire, though, she wound up driving straight into the world of Seattle's southbound morning traffic. After waiting for a half-hour and unleashing a frustrated "Ugh" into the roof of her car, she decided to call her assistant, Jacob, but it went straight to a forwarding message: "We're sorry. The voicemail box of the person you are trying to reach has not been set up yet."

'*Odd…*' she thought. '*And even more frustrating.*'

She decided to call the front desk, but instead of the usual receptionist, she heard the voice of someone new.

"Mount Saint Helens Hospital - Neurological Health Clinic. My name is Linda, how may I direct your call?"

"Um, I'm sorry, who is this?"

"This is Linda at the reception desk for the neurological health clinic at Mount Saint Helens Hospital. If this is an emergency, please hang up and dial nine-one-one. Otherwise, how may I direct your call?"

"Where's Samantha?"

"Who's Samantha?"

"The regular receptionist."

"Samantha no longer works here, ma'am."

"You're joking. What happened to her? Did she quit, or was she fired?"

"Unfortunately, I cannot divulge that information, ma'am, now how may I direct your call?"

"I'm sorry, but this is Doctor Irene Gupta. I *work* in the neurological clinic."

"Oh!" Linda said in a very confused and unprepared tone. "I'm sorry. Please hold."

Irene didn't have time to protest before hearing the terrible muzak they forced their patients to endure. After what felt like an eternity, the receptionist finally picked her back up.

In a hurried tone, she said, "We're sorry ma'am, but we don't have any record of a Doctor Irene Gupta at this ward. Perhaps you have the wrong number," before immediately hanging up.

Irene was in such a state of shock that she didn't realize that traffic had started moving again until the car behind her started honking. She tried calling the clinic again, only to immediately be sent to voicemail.

Shock soon turned to fury as she drove like a bat out of hell towards the hospital. She wasn't worried about getting a speeding ticket; there were far more important things to be concerned with at the moment.

She arrived at the parking garage, where she was met with worse news, this time from Ernie, the security guard

"I'm so sorry, Renie, but... your parking pass has been rejected."

She let out a shaky and heavy exhale. "Are you kidding me?"

"I wish I was."

"Ernie, you know me, right? I work here. Can't you just let me in, please? Just long enough for me to figure out what the hell is going on here?"

"Well, of course, Renie. Park in the first spot you find and head to HR. They can get you a temporary pass until they figure this shit out for ya."

She sighed with absolute relief. "Thank you so much, Ernie. You are a gift from God."

"Nah you don't have to tell me. I know."

After parking, she had to keep herself from bursting into a full run as she rushed into the hospital. Much to her dismay, when she arrived at Human Resources, she received the same level of resistance she had been experiencing all day.

"I don't know what to tell you, hun," the HR officer said, a woman she had never met or spoken to before in all the time she had spent at the hospital. "But there is no record of you working here. Absolutely none."

Irene's hands swallowed her head in an attempt to dull the skull-crushing migraine she'd been nursing the past few hours. "I *cannot* believe this. I feel like I'm going insane. My name is Doctor Irene Gupta. I've worked at this hospital for seven years. I did my residency here. I used to be a candy striper! I work here! Please, let me just talk to somebody - *anybody* - who knows me! My office is in the Neurology Clinic. Room 4103. My assistant's name is Jacob Doby. I know the name of every single nurse in the wing. I have hundreds of patients that require my care. Now please just let me do my job!"

After a brief pause, the annoyed and put-upon woman typed something into her computer. "Ma'am, my information tells me that room 4103 has been vacant for quite some time."

"What?!"

She typed something else. "Furthermore, we have no record of a Jacob Doby working here either."

"So…you're telling me that the office I've had for almost two years is empty? All my diploma, my journals, everything I've ever accumulated in my entire time as a medical professional just vanished into thin air?"

The HR rep's voice became, somehow, even more, cold and condescending. "Honey, from what I'm being led to understand, none of that stuff ever existed in the first place."

Irene was on the verge of a nervous breakdown, and this woman could very clearly see that. And Irene could very clearly see that she didn't care.

"Listen, hun, I can tell this has been a very stressful day for you. Maybe you should just go home and try to relax. Clear your mind. And then maybe this little… *episode* will pass. Hmm?"

Irene looked at the woman like she had just murdered a puppy right before her very eyes. She wanted to scream. She wanted to strangle her, but she took a deep breath and held it all inside as she quietly stood up.

"Thank you for your time," Irene calmly pushed out before walking out into the hallway.

She banged her head against the wall of the elevator as it descended into the parking garage. The doors opened just in time for her to watch as a tow truck sped out of sight with her car latched onto its back.

"What?! NO!"

She tried running after the truck, but her heels dug into her feet, adding foot pain on top of a headache. It disappeared from her view in the blink of an eye. She began to search her purse for her phone, but it, as well as her keys and wallet, had completely disappeared.

"FUUUUUCK!" She screamed out into the empty abyss that had become her life.

She took off her shoes and jogged back to the security gate, but instead of seeing Ernie's friendly face, she was met with yet another hospital employee she had never met before, a new security guard with a face like an angry bulldog.

"Where's Ernie?" She asked, on the verge of tears.

"Taking his smoke break," The man stiffly spat out. "Who are you?"

"I'm," she sighed, "I'm Irene, and I need help please."

"What's wrong?" He said as he voraciously bit into an apple.

"My car just got towed, and I can't find my phone. May I please use yours?"

"No can do." He took another bite.

"Oh my god, why not?"

"Our phone is for official use and emergencies only."

"But this is an emergency! I am stranded here with no way to get home or call for help. Please, just let me use your phone!"

"Hey!" He yelled. "It is not my fault that you parked in the wrong spot without proper clearance. And it's not *my fault* that you were too stupid to keep track of your shit. Now get out of my sight before I call the cops."

Irene was completely over the edge now. She forgot how to breathe. She could feel herself starting to hyperventilate. She ran out of the garage onto the sidewalk. The world was spinning, and the sun was becoming far too bright for her to handle.

She needed to call Bo.

Finding the closest coffee shop, she stumbled up to the front of the line, passing all the irate, under-caffeinated customers.

"Hello," she said to the young barista at the register. "I'm so sorry, my car just got towed, I can't find my phone, and I desperately need to use yours."

"Of course," They said with a smile. "Come on. Come this way."

Irene nearly fainted when she experienced the first bit of goodwill she had all day. "Oh my god, thank you. Thank you so much! You have no idea what this means to me."

The clerk took her back into the office where she tried to call Bo. Every time, though, she was sent to the same forwarding message she received when she attempted to call Jacob earlier.

"We're sorry. The voicemail box of the person you are trying to reach has not been set up yet."

She started to cry. She put her head in her hands, completely forfeiting to the monstrously terrible day she was being forced to endure.

The barista started rubbing her back to help her calm down. "Are you doing okay?"

"No... No, I am not... I am so sorry, but I need to make another call. Do you know the number for Yellow Cab?"

"Oh, no, please, let me call you an Uber."

"I can't let you do that. I live up in Mountlake Terrace."

"Please. It's okay. Consider it a present to make up for the bad day you've had."

She started to cry even harder. "You're a saint."

"Oh, honey... You really have had a shitty day, huh?"

"There are no words for how shitty my day has been."

"Here," They handed Irene a hot cup of tea. "Try to relax while I order the Uber. What's your address?"

The driver took her straight home. As soon as he stopped, she ran right for her ever-friendly front door to find it unlocked.

"Thank god," she said aloud as she entered her home sweet home. "Bo? Are you home?"

No response. She assumed he was out for a jog and forgot to lock the door. So, she went to the kitchen to get herself a glass of water. While she was there, she pulled out an ice pack from the freezer and slapped it onto her forehead before heading to the stairs.

Halfway up, she heard the shower running.

"Bo?" She called out.

No response again.

She ran upstairs and into the bathroom. "Bo? What's going on?"

She looked and saw Bo sitting down in the shower through the glass of the door.

"What are you doing? Bo? Bo???"

She opened the door to find her fiancé, bleeding out from cuts on his wrists, a razor resting on the tile nearby, covered in a red river of blood.

"Oh my god. Oh no. Oh my god. Oh no."

She nearly fainted. The world around her was going dark. She couldn't breathe.

"Oh my god. Oh no. Oh please god no."

She regained her composure enough to start running to the bedroom door, hoping to call an ambulance but she was stopped by a forceful grab to her arm, an unseen assailant who wrapped their arms around her. They placed a pistol into her hand and guided it to her temple, forcing her fingers around the trigger.

"No... please..."

NAHID AZAR NASSIRI

BIRTH-DATE: 10 APR 02.

SEX: Female.

CURRENT HEIGHT: 6'2".

EYE COLOR: Copper Brown.

HAIR COLOR: Light brown.

INSTALLATION: El Paso, Texas, USA.

NATIONALITY: American.

ETHNICITY: Iranian.

FAMILY:

Ebrahim Nassiri (father)

Fairuza Nassiri (mother)

Vida Nassiri (younger sister)

1

Nahid did not fit in. She was a tall, gangly, Shia Muslim living in the most Roman Catholic city on the Mexican border at the height of America's darkest political age. Between the dirty looks from crucifix wearing neighbors and even dirtier looks from red hat wearing neighbors, she was always on a minimum orange alert.

Her family was considerably unorthodox by traditional Muslim standards. Her father, Ebrahim, was born in New Jersey and her mother, Fairuza, was born in Iran. As a result, her dad had a more liberal point of view, while her mother was significantly more traditional.

Neither parent came close to Nahid in height. They each stood around 5 foot 8. Ebrahim kept a thick beard which, along with the peppered bits of grey here and there, aged him beyond his 40 years. Fairuza, when in public, could be seen wearing long, flowing dresses that covered her from neck to knee, while alternating between ten different hijabs, all different shades of floral.

Nahid decided to stop wearing the Hijab when she was thirteen, in a quiet effort to fit in better at school. Ebrahim respected and accepted her decision while Fairuza reacted precisely the way Nahid expected.

"You are breaking my heart!" She said as she clenched her chest, a look of dramatic anguish rapidly consuming her face. "Oh, my goodness, I think I'm having palpitations! The heavens are calling to me! Somebody, call the doctor!"

Thankfully, Ebrahim was a nurse and was able to diagnose her "palpitations" as a simple case of acid reflux, no doubt brought upon by severe melodrama. Nahid and Vida giggled at their mother's histrionics and received a dark glare in response.

Unlike Nahid, Vida chose to wear a Hijab, though hers were always a shade of blue or green. She would pair this with baggy pants and loose-fitting shirts. Their mother would often comment that she looked like a bald boy.

"Oh, how wonderful. Your mother almost died and the two of you are giggling. What next, Nahid? A tattoo? Are you going to get a tattoo, Nahid? A great big tattoo on your face that says 'I don't care if my mother dies! I do what I want?!' Why are you trying to kill me?!"

Nahid could barely contain her laughter. "Mom, please, calm down."

Fairuza having quite had enough gave a great huff before dashing to her room.

All Ebrahim could say was, "You gotta love her," in a typical, flummoxed dad tone.

Fairuza waited an entire day before deciding to leave her room and headed straight for the kitchen. There, she saw Nahid eating a cheese sandwich and the two locked eyes. After a brief, intense silence, Nahid decided to try and reason with her mother.

"I still believe in God, Mom. I still think God loves me. Nothing about me has changed or is going to change, except that when people look at me, they'll see me, not a Muslim girl in a Hijab. And that's all I want."

"Oh, my darling Nahid… There is no shame in wanting to be seen for who you are. But the whole point of the Hijab *is* to be seen for who you are. You are a beautiful, Muslim woman. There's no shame in that either."

"I know that, Mom. But I believe that there are other ways to be a proud Muslim woman without having to conform to tradition."

Her mother heaved a gusty sigh. "Okay… I understand. And I love you, no matter what. And I guess I need to accept that you're becoming your own woman and making your own decisions. So, I guess, this is just a decision that I'll have to accept… But can you promise me one thing?"

"Of course."

"Can you at least wear a headscarf when your grandparents visit? If my mother saw you like this, I'd never hear the end of it. She's soooo traditional."

Nahid rolled her eyes so hard, she was afraid they'd fall out of her head.

When Nahid was fifteen, she decided that it was time for her to start dating. Again, her father was very respectful and kind, and her mother was also very supportive, in her own special way.

"This is wonderful!" She said with enough enthusiasm to light all El Paso. "It's always good to start early! I know some lovely boys at the Mosque who I *know* have looked your way a few times. Of course, it's probably because you're not wearing a Hijab, but that's neither here nor there at this point. Maybe they find immodesty attractive. I don't know, I don't like to make assumptions. Anyway, there's no harm in trying."

"Actually," Nahid said, mustering up the courage deep inside. "I've already found someone."

Fairuza could barely contain her elation. "What?! Really?! What's his name? What are his parents' names? Do they live nearby? Do we know them? Is it Omar and Parisa's son? He's so handsome! I hear he's going to go to med school to become a pediatrician like his father. Or is it Cyrus and Ester's son? Or Navid and Shadi?! O-M-G this is so exciting! When can we invite them all over for dinner? I know exactly what to make! I can-"

Nahid cut off her mother's avalanche of mom-speak. "No, mom! It's nobody from the Mosque. I can confidently say you've never met his parents."

Fairuza managed to become even more intrigued than she was before. "Oooh! A *mysterious* boy from a *mysterious* family. Do they go to a mosque in another town? Or is there a mosque in El Paso I've never heard of? Ebrahim, have they built a new mosque? How could they do that without us finding out? Ooh! Or is it a *secret mosque*? That's a thing, right? Ugh, the current political climate in this country is so exhausting. Does he go to the secret mosque?"

Nahid became more irritated as her mother became more verbose. "No, mom, he doesn't go to a *'secret mosque.'* Or a mosque in another town. He doesn't go to any mosque. My boyfriend's name is Raymond Miller and he's... Not Muslim. In fact, he's very much a very, very, *very* white boy."

Fairuza gave her daughter a bewildered look. She was as still as a statue for almost two minutes, and then, her eye twitched. She clenched her heart and yelled out for her husband.

"Ebrahim! Ebrahim! It's my heart! Oh, my dear graces, it's my heart!! Quick! Quick! Bring me my medicine!"

He handed her a bottle of tums. It had been many years and still Fairuza refused to acknowledge the difference between a stress-induced heart attack and a daughter-induced upset stomach. Additionally, she hadn't figured out that her children knew the difference between when their mother was dying, and when she was overreacting.

"Mom, please calm down."

"Don't tell me what to do," she said through a mouth full of chewable antacids.

Nahid swallowed a chuckle, barely able to contain how entertained she was by her ridiculous mother. "Mom, please."

"Oh, wonderful. Now you are laughing at me. I am a joke! I am a clown! Where is my big red nose?!"

She and Ebrahim were both laughing at this point. "Mom, stop. You're breaking my heart!"

"Ugh!" And with that, she retreated to her room.

The next morning held an awkwardly quiet breakfast for the entire family. Their father, completely inept at cooking, served burnt waffles as a still annoyed Fairuza bumbled into the kitchen.

Nahid meekly smiled. "Morning, mom."

She sat down with a quiet "Humph," and started reading the newspaper.

"I know you're having a tough time with this."

An eye roll accompanied by a "tsk".

"But I want you to know that Raymond is a really nice guy. He's very sweet, and very handsome."

Yet another eyeroll with the most passive-aggressive page turn ever performed.

"And… he wants to be a doctor." This was an incredible lie.

"Really?"

But it was a lie that paid off. "Yup. Super into that medical life."

Fairuza took a deep, conceding breath. "Okay… I can accept this. This is fine. I'm totally fine. But can you please do me one favor?"

"What mama?"

"Don't tell your grandmother, please? If she found out, I would never hear the end of it. She can be very melodramatic, you know?"

Nahid rolled her eyes so hard, she got a headache.

2

17 JUN 18.

17:00.

NASSIRI HOUSEHOLD, El Paso, TX.

Nahid and Raymond broke up just a few weeks before the end of the following school year. It was an amicable split, so the two were working very hard to maintain their friendship, but Nahid could tell that things would never be the same.

As soon as Fairuza heard the news, she went on the warpath. She started calling every Muslim parent she knew in the tri-city area.

"You know what they say! You just need to get back up on the horse... or something, I don't know. I don't like horses much. But we should still try to get you back on the boyfriend train. I like trains much better."

"I'm honestly just looking to spend some time by myself, mom. Figure out who I am before I open myself up to someone new."

"Oh please. You need to keep the love train going and try again! Yes, the train metaphor is definitely working for me."

She sighed. "Mom, I'm barely sixteen. I'm not trying to get married."

"Of course, you're not," Fairuza said with a wink as if she thought they were playing some kind of strange game. "Either way, I found you a date."

"That's nice, mom," Nahid said, with wide eyes. "Now go call him, or his parents, or whoever you found to set this up for you-"

"His parents, dear."

"Chill, now go call them and tell them that I said '*no, thank you.*' I do not - even louder for the back of the room - **do not** want to go on a date with anybody right now."

Nahid marched off to her bedroom and played her music as loudly as possible while pretending her mother didn't exist until, of course, it was time for dinner.

The next day.

Fairuza drove her daughters to school, staying silent throughout the entire ride. However, once they arrived at Nahid's school before she could get her hands on the door handle, her mother quickly locked it, trapping her.

"Mom!"

"Just hear me out, Nahid. I love you and I want what's best for you."

"Oh my gosh, Mom, dating some new guy is not '*what's best for me.*' Now, please, let me out. I'm going to be late!"

"His name is Hassan. His parents tell me that he's very respectful, shy, sweet, and is looking for just the right girl. And I'm sure that girl could be you."

Nahid looked at her mother's big, sad, beggar's eyes, and realized this was a fight she could never win, and the only thing that would get her to stop would be the last thing she wanted to do.

"Ugh… fine."

Fairuza cheered, jubilantly, as if she had just watched Nahid win American Ninja Warrior.

The following night.

Nahid and her mother argued about what she would wear for hours. Fairuza tried, desperately, to convince her to wear a headscarf and only relented after Nahid agreed to wear a floor-length dress. While Fairuza was in charge of who her daughter went out with and partially in charge of what she wore, Nahid was in charge of the location.

She decided on King Pepe's Tex-Mex Restaurant, which was, in her mind, the least romantic restaurant on the planet. She awkwardly shifted around in her dress, one sequin short of a ball gown, on the most uncomfortable plastic chair, and waited for her blind date to arrive. She had the plan all mapped out in her head: tell him the truth, let him down easy, then order the chicken enchilada.

'Or perhaps I should wait until after I eat… he might not want to pay with a broken heart, and I did not bring any cash. Where would I put it? This thing doesn't have any pockets. Ugh, I hate skirts. Ugh, I need a purse. Ugh… I hate purses.'

A handsome young man with flowing dark hair cut short on the sides and long on the top, styled perfectly to make him look like a social media influencer/model, appeared before her, dressed in a full tuxedo. With a velvet soft voice, he said, "Nahid?"

She was almost caught off guard by how gorgeous he was. "Hassan?"

She reached her hand out to meet his. He very nearly was about to kiss it until he opted to shake it awkwardly.

"Hello. Yes. Hi. May I sit?"

"Oh, wow, a *gentleman*," She said, half sarcastically, half legitimately impressed. "Feel free."

Once he sat down, he had to awkwardly shift around to properly seat his coattails. "Have you ordered already?"

"No. I was waiting for you. I didn't want to be rude.

"Aww, that's sweet."

"Yeah…" She had no idea how to make conversation with this random boy she had just met. After a long pause, she asked him the first question that popped into her head. "Do you drive?"

"Oh… um, yeah. I do. Car and everything. You?"

"I- no, never… never learned. Never took the class or anything."

"Ah…"

"Yeah…"

A pregnant pause lingered in the air as neither could think of anything to say.

It was Hassan who decided to cut the terrible silence. "This is awkward, right?"

"Yeah," She said with a hearty chuckle. "This is so frickin' awkward. I'm so sorry."

"No, don't be." He laughed with her. "Let me guess: you do not want to be here."

"Not really, sorry."

"That's okay. Neither do I!"

"Wow! Really?"

"Yup! In fact, my mom forced me to be here."

"Mine too! Wow!"

"Wow is correct."

"Moms, am I right?"

"*So right.* Oh my god, let me tell you about the time I told my mom I didn't want to be a doctor." He started to mimic his mother, but Nahid was convinced he was impersonating her own. "'You're breaking my heart! Bring me an aspirin! Blech!'"

"Oh my gosh, do we have the same mother? You should've seen *my* mom's tantrum when I told her I was dating a white boy."

Hassan giggled. "You and I do have a lot in common, Nahid."

"Really? I mean, besides a ridiculous mother, being Muslim, and being gorgeous-"

"Why thank you."

"You're welcome - I don't see a lot of similarities between the two of us."

"Well, we both like dating white boys, so..."

Nahid was briefly filled with shock before bursting with joy. She laughed so hard it almost hurt. "Ha! Well, color me rainbow surprised."

"Same…" Hassan's moment of truth was followed by the quick and sudden sense of dread that you feel after telling a deeply held secret. "By the way, could you please promise me that you won't tell your mom? I don't need her telling my mom... That would be way too much for me to deal with."

Nahid reached her hand out to touch his. "Of course not, Hassan. I would never, ever do something like that. And if you feel like you need some leverage, I promise not to tell anybody about your boyfriend if you stay quiet about my *girlfriend*."

The biggest, happiest smile grew on Hassan's face as he suddenly realized he was not as alone as he felt.

"*Whaaaat?*" He had to work hard to keep his voice down. "You're gay too?"

"No, I'm bi."

"You're leaving?"

"No, I'm *bi*. As in *bisexual*."

"I was kidding, Nahid."

"Oh, yeah, I knew that." She did not.

"Oh my god, that's so awesome! I can't believe there's another queer Muslim in Texas."

"I mean, with the way things are, I think it's a miracle there are *any* Muslims in Texas."

She awkwardly shifted around in her dress, trying to find a comfortable position and failing miserably. Hassan couldn't help but notice.

"Are you okay?"

"No. I'm incredibly uncomfortable. I really… *really* hate wearing skirts."

"Then why are you wearing one?"

"Why do you think?"

"Laundry day? That's the only time I wear skirts."

Nahid chuckled. "Girl, please."

"You should see me. My legs are everything."

She gave a smarmy smile. "I admire your confidence."

He gave a knowing smile. "Okay, in all seriousness, why is your mom forcing you to wear a prom dress to a tex-mex?"

"Because she's my mom. She's always finding new ways to punish me for not being born the first Iranian Disney princess."

"That's a mood. I've been in this penguin suit so long I've forgotten what jeans feel like. Have you told your parents, by the way?"

"I've told my mom a million times that I hate skirts, but she just keeps buying them. It's ridiculous."

Hassan laughed. "No, I meant about you being bisexual. And your girlfriend and everything."

"Oh, yeah, no I was just kidding." She was not. "It's just not a conversation I think I'm ready to have just yet."

"Same. I'm the only boy in a family full of girls. I'd like to avoid the whole 'I'll never have grandchildren! Bring me an aspirin!' drama…" Hassan's face grew dark. "Or maybe even something worse."

He didn't need to say much else for Nahid to understand. "Do you think you'll ever tell them?"

"I've thought about it. I've pondered on when would be the perfect moment to drop the big gay bomb."

"And when would that be?"

"I'm thinking about an hour before I get married to the man of my dreams. That is if Chris Hemsworth is available at the time. My mom will walk in and be all like 'I have a beautiful girl I think you should meet' and I'll be like 'aww too late, how sad!'"

Nahid laughed through her nose. "I know my dad would be cool, if not incredibly awkward about it. My sister probably wouldn't care... or she'll think it's hilarious. I don't know. For me, the only real problem is my mom, which is something that I hate feeling. I'm dreading talking to my mom about my life. I'm dreading talking to her about this amazing girl I'm head over heels in love with. I'm dreading the idea of having to explain to her what bisexuality is. I'm dreading everything."

"What do you think she'll say?"

"Hold on, let me get my list."

"Funny."

She pulled out her phone and went straight to the file marked "Mom - Bi Reaction." "One: she'll say it doesn't matter if I date girls as long as I marry a nice, Muslim boy, preferably a doctor, and give her a thousand beautiful Muslim grandchildren."

"Oh wow, you were not kidding."

"Two: she'll say it doesn't matter if I marry a girl, as long as *she's* a nice Muslim doctor, and give her a thousand beautiful Muslim grandchildren. Three, she'll-"

"I get it, you have put a lot of thought into this."

"Hassan, every decision I've ever made in my entire life that doesn't fit into my mom's hyper-traditional tunnel vision has driven her closer to insanity. And that's an actual quote from the first time I wore a two-piece to the beach. 'You're going to drive me to insanity! Rent a party bus full of people in slinky little bathing suits, my daughter is driving me to the mental hospital.'"

"But she lets it go eventually right?"

Nahid paused to put thought into what he had just asked. "Yeah... she does. Eventually, I guess. She puts in the effort; I'll give her that much."

"You see, despite all the dark stuff we *think* might happen, at the end of the day we don't know what's going to happen. But we do know our parents will love us no matter what. And yeah, the gay - or bi - thing will throw them, but they'll get over that when they see us living happy, fulfilling lives with whoever we decide to spend our lives with, and realize that us being happy is way more important than them forcing their ideas of what happy looks like on us."

Nahid sighed. "You're right. You're so right that I hate how right you are."

"So, are you gonna do it?"

"Are you?"

Hassan's face became more serious and thoughtful. "Yeah. I will. Tonight, I'll go home, I'll tell my parents I went on an amazing date with an amazing girl. I'll tell them I ate *'amazing'* food in the most uncomfortable chair I've ever had the displeasure of sitting in - seriously, I think my butt is completely flat now, which is terrible because it's my best feature - and then I'll politely explain that you are not available and that neither am I."

"That sounds like a very solid plan, Hassan."

"Yeah, it is, but what about you, Nahid?"

"I don't know. I just don't know. I wish I did, but I don't. I should probably call my girlfriend before I make any rash decisions."

Later.

Nahid told her parents that she and Hassan were going to get ice cream. In reality, he went home, presumably to come out to his parents, while she went over to her girlfriend Lisa's apartment.

Lisa was a college freshman at the University of Texas who lived with her mentally ill uncle, Leon, who rarely left his bedroom. She told Nahid that he was functional enough to make his own meals and take care of himself, but that their family still wanted someone around to keep an eye on him.

The two girls met a few months ago at the Purple Prom, a community dance for queer teenagers in South Texas that was open to anybody under the age of twenty-one who wanted to attend. The school psychologist, and the second person Nahid ever came out to after Raymond, recommended the event to her. Raymond even agreed to accompany Nahid out of solidarity and friendship, even though they had only just broken up a few weeks prior.

About a few minutes into the dance, Nahid spotted Lisa standing alone in the corner and was immediately taken aback by her beauty. She wanted to go over and talk to her but found herself glued to the floor in fear. To her surprise and joy, Lisa was the one who ended up making the first move. She invited her to take a walk through the nearby park, and an enchanted Nahid blurted out a resounding yes.

When she went to go tell Raymond where she was going, he looked at her like she was out of her mind, leaving with someone she had just met, but she didn't care.

The two walked and talked for hours, taking brief breaks to make out on whatever was big enough for them both to lie down on.

They had only been dating a short time, but Lisa already entrusted Nahid with a key to her apartment. She let herself in, spotting Lisa sitting on the floor wearing a white tank top and a pair of boxer shorts with a book in her lap while the TV was on.

"Hey, babe. How was your *date*?" She asked, teasingly.

"Amazing. We had so much in common, and I very nearly fell in love with him. Until he told me that he's gay."

Lisa's mouth dropped. "Whaaaaat?"

Nahid chuckled. "You sound just like him when I told him I was bi. The more I think about it, the more hilarious this night looks in my head. My mom tried to set me up with a boy and he turns out to be just as fabulously leg-butt as I am."

"Leg-butt?"

"L-G-B-T. Legbutt. Duh."

"Oh, okay. You could just say queer, you know?"

"I know, but leg-butt's more fun."

Nahid joined Lisa on the floor just as their favorite show came on. "The Bomb," a tv drama-comedy about a lesbian couple - Fred and Lena - who worked on the bomb squad together. Despite their differing personalities and inability to separate work from romance, it would all come together in the end and bring them closer as partners in and out of the office.

Nahid could never shake the thought that Lisa was so similar in appearance to the actress who played Lena that they could be twins. They both had short platinum blonde hair, dressed in a tomboyish fashion, were precisely the same height, and both were Filipino. Whenever this happened, Lisa would always deflect and point out all of their differences, which were also the things that she thought were ugly about herself: her dark arm hair, the gap in her teeth, and her bacne. None of these things, however, stopped Nahid from thinking she was the most beautiful person on the planet.

She snuggled up under Lisa's arm and, smiling, thought about how lucky she was to have such an amazing girl in her life. The two watched while Fred tried to defuse a bomb in the very same restaurant where she was meeting Lena's parents for the very first time.

Lisa used the commercial break to ask Nahid a very tough question. "When are you gonna tell your mom about us, Nahid?"

She thought about it, and then she thought about Hassan, and then she said, "Tomorrow. I'll tell them tomorrow. I promise."

3

18 JUN 18.

17:30.

NASSIRI HOUSEHOLD, El Paso, TX.

True to her word, Nahid called her entire family into the living room as soon as everybody was home to make a very important announcement. Her mother interpreted the meeting as a guessing game.

"You and Hassan are dating now?! Oh, honey, I'm so proud of you! I hope it's not too late for you two to go to prom together. There's a form for that right? To bring a guest from another school? Do you need my signature for that? Oh gosh, we should invite him over for dinner sometime! And his parents! And, oh! I saw this beautiful dress at the mall, it matches your eyes!"

"Mom! This is a very big deal to me, and I would very much appreciate it if you would let me talk and didn't say anything until I was done. Okay?"

"Yes, darling. Ooh, this is so exciting."

"I just want you guys to know that you are the best parents in the world. Like, the best. You're loving, kind, fair, and you both work so hard to give me and Vida all that we need and more. And no matter what, you guys have always supported me. Even if my decisions confused you," Fairuza adjusted in her seat, aware Nahid was talking about her. "You still learned to accept me for who I am. And you never stopped loving me…"

Fairuza became impatient. "Honey, please, I have food in the oven-"

"Ruzie," Her husband shushed her before encouraging Nahid to continue. "Go on, sweetie."

She took a deep breath. She was so terrified, but then the image of Lisa's smile rushed into her mind and washed any remaining nerves. "I'm bisexual. And I'm dating a girl. Her name is Lisa Lopez, she's a freshman at the University of Texas. She's going to school for sports medicine and lives downtown with her uncle."

The silence in the room was so thick, only a chainsaw would be able to slice through it. /the more intense the quiet became, the faster Nahid's heart started beating.

Vida, mouth agape, blurted out a bewildered, "Whaaaat?"

Her father followed. "Well, that's - just - *wonderful* honey." He got up and hugged his now out and proud daughter. "And *thank you* for telling us! I'm very - proud of you. But uh… if you're dating a woman, doesn't that - mean you're a lesbian?"

"Bisexuals can date anybody, dad," Vida corrected him. "That's the whole point. Duh."

"Thank you, Vida." Nahid felt relieved that at least one person in her family understood what was going on.

"My friend Gina's older sister's friend's cousin Brian is bisexual."

"Good to know," was all she could say to that.

Nahid looked to her mother, waiting for the inevitable, melodramatic "heart attack." Instead, however, the only response she received was an unnerving silence and a petrified glare staring off into space. After a minute or so, she lifted herself off the chair and, without saying anything to anyone, without looking at Nahid, she walked to her room and softly closed the door.

Vida was even more surprised at her mother's behavior than she was at Nahid's announcement. "That was the exact opposite of what I was expecting her to do."

Nahid turned to her father, eyes swelling with tears. "Dad?"

"I think she just needs time sweetie," he said as he wrapped his arms around her.

"But-"

"Just give her time, Nahid. It's going to be ok."

Later that night.

Nahid had been crying into her pillow for hours. She was feeling all the feelings anyone would feel when they were afraid their mother might never talk to them again. Just as she was at the end of her emotional rope, a text came in from the only person she knew could make her feel better, filling her with relief.

Lisa: Hey, you okay? I got worried when you didn't text...

Nahid: No... I'm not. Can I call you? I really need to hear your voice right now.

Lisa: Sorry babe, study time. What's wrong?

Nahid: Everything...

Nahid: Everything is terrible. I've screwed it all up.

Nahid: My mom won't even TALK to me. She's been in her room all night.

Nahid: Oh god, help me.

Lisa: It's gonna be okay. Your mom will come around. I'm sure of it.

Nahid: But what if she doesn't? Please, can't I just come over tonight?

Lisa: If you could you'd already be here. I'm sorry babe.

Lisa: Just give her time. Okay? She'll come around. <3

Nahid tossed her phone across the room in frustration and buried her head in her pillow once again.

(4)

19 JUN 18.

12:00.

RONALD REAGAN HIGH SCHOOL, El Paso, TX.

After spending the entire night crying her eyes out, Nahid fell asleep as soon as she hit her third-period class. It wasn't until he got to the end of the one-hundred-year war that her teacher, Mister Blankenship, noticed her drooling onto her desk.

"Am I boring you, Miss Nazzana?" He said, never once bothering to get her name right. When she didn't respond, he semi-repeated himself. "Miss Nizura!"

The sound of her name being mis-pronounced jerked her awake. "What?!"

"Miss Nizzaria, if you're so tired, why don't you go take a trip to the nurse's office."

Nahid let out a whine. "Oh God, can't I just have an early lunch?"

"Go to the nurse's office, immediately, Miss Nuh-zora."

"Ugh…" Nahid said as she trudged out of the classroom.

'It's almost summer…' She thought as she roamed the halls. *"I took all of my tests… and it's not like you have anything left to teach me anyway… ya jerkwad."*

Just as she was about to head towards the nurse's office, she decided to instead make a beeline straight for the school psychologist's office. The office of Miss Cooper.

In Nahid's opinion, seeing Miss Cooper was the best possible thing for her at this moment, second only to seeing the inside of her eyelids. She was the advisor to the Queer/Gender Alliance, of which Nahid became a recent member. She also had a gay son, so she had an idea of what Nahid was going through and coached her through everything.

When Nahid found out Miss Cooper had a teenaged son, she was completely shocked. She couldn't have been older than thirty. Her hair was a deep, crimson red. Her skin was a youthful alabaster. Her presence in the room was both calming and authoritative like one would expect from a school counselor. Nahid thought she was the most beautiful woman on the planet, second only to Lisa.

Being ever the cool teacher, Miss Cooper let Nahid take a nap on the couch in her office. It wasn't until Nahid was fully rested and ready to go that she started asking questions. "So, tell me, sweetie, what's going on? Not that I mind you napping in my office, but it does raise some concern."

Her voice was like honey, warm and smooth, full of sweetness. Talking to Miss Cooper was like talking to the perfect mom, which Nahid desperately needed.

"I came out to my family last night."

"Oh." Miss Cooper leaned back in her seat. "I probably shouldn't have to ask, but how did it go?"

Nahid struggled to find the words through the torrential wave of emotions she was feeling, mixed with the grogginess associated with waking up from a two-hour nap.

"It was... a lot, to say the least. I mean, my dad's fine. I never thought he wouldn't be. But my mom... My mom..." Nahid started crying again. "She wouldn't even talk to me. She just... She just went to her room. Left dinner burning in the oven. It was so... just not like her. She didn't even come out for breakfast. She's *always there* for breakfast!"

"Calm down, Nahid. Nothing good comes from letting yourself get too upset. You just need to give her some time and some space. She'll come around. I'm sure of it."

Nahid smiled. "My girlfriend said the same thing."

"Well, your girlfriend sounds like a very smart young lady. Nahid, we can't make people do what we want them to do. It's a tough life lesson to learn, and it looks like both you and your mother are going to need to learn it. You're dating a girl, you're bisexual, and that can be a lot for a mom to take in, especially one like yours. She's allowed to take her time. And you're allowed to be angry about her needing to take her time. You want your mom right now and she wants to be alone to adjust to this new information. To adjust to the fact that everything she thought your future would look like is going to change. Neither one of you is wrong for feeling the way you feel. But Nahid, your mom loves you. *Never* forget that."

Later that day.
Nahid arrived home from school and Fairuza still hadn't come out of her room, forcing Ebrahim to prepare microwaved dinners. Seeing the empty chair where her mother usually sat at the table

hurt at first, but then she remembered that there were two other people there with her, talking with her, smiling with her, and asking her how her day was. And two was enough. She would rather be living out loud and proud with two people than live in the closet with three.

Many men were surrounding her, dressed in soldier's uniforms. They beat her with sticks and bats and metal rods. They punched her. They kicked her, and when they were finished, an entire palette of bricks was dropped on her from a hundred feet above her head.

She rose from underneath the wreckage, without a scratch on her. No blood, no bruises, and no fear.

Eventually, the men became exhausted from trying to inflict pain on this painless child and retired for the day.

A shrimpy white man appeared from behind a window that she thought was a mirror. He was in a white lab coat, horn-rimmed glasses adorning his weak brow, and a muddy blond mustache curving around his slim upper lip. He smiled and typed something onto a computer.

A series of solid steel walls popped up from the floor before her. Having been through all of this before, she took her cue and lifted her tiny hand to throw a single, solid punch at the wall in front of her, causing them all to topple down like dominoes.

A familiar, haunting voice started to speak inside of her head. "It's time to wake up, Nahid."

Nahid was woken up by the sound of her phone, ferociously buzzing. Her bed was covered in sweat. Lisa was texting her. Checking the clock, she saw the time: 11 p.m. The blinding light of her screen initially gave her a headache. She felt simultaneously nauseous and energized.

Lisa: Sorry I haven't messaged you
since last night!
Lisa: Uncle Leo has been a bit of a
mess today.
Lisa: You okay? You want to come
over? I hope it's not too late...

She was about to respond when she heard a thud coming from outside the house. She wanted to believe it was just the wind so she could go back to sleep but then she heard the front door open. Suspicious, and knowing nobody else would be up and about in the middle of the night, she got out of bed and peeked into the hallway to see what was going on.

Standing in her living room were three men, all wearing black, with ski masks concealing their faces. They were carrying assault rifles and quietly searching through the house.

Nahid was so scared she had to cover her mouth to keep herself from screaming. She closed the door as gently as possible, hoping they wouldn't hear her. She opened her phone to try and call 911 only to find it dead, with a dead battery. Her panic increased. Her breathing hastened and her heart started pounding so hard, she was afraid the invaders would hear it and find her.

A soft knock came at the door. She tried not to make a sound.

With a great smash, the door was forced open, knocking Nahid to the floor. She tried to get up but one of the men punched her in the face, flipped her onto her front and, before Nahid could do anything, had bound, gagged her, and flipped her up onto his shoulder, carrying her to the kitchen, where she saw her family, lined up against the wall with guns pointed at their faces. Like her, they were bound and helpless.

5

2 JUN 18.

13:00.

LISA'S APARTMENT, El Paso, TX.

Nahid joined Lisa at her apartment for lunch and was having the most wonderful time. It was a Saturday, and both of her parents were working, Lisa had already finished all her homework and her uncle was visiting family. They had the entire place to themselves. They had the entire weekend to themselves.

Lisa had made bacon jalapeno macaroni and cheese, the same kind her mother made for her when she was younger. To Nahid, it was a sweet effort, until she asked Lisa if it was "Kosher bacon."

"No, it's not. Why do you ask?"

She was almost too shy to tell her. "Muslims can't eat pork."

"Oh my god, I'm so sorry!"

"No, it's totally fine. It's so not a big thing."

"But you can't eat this! I feel so stupid. I could've just googled 'what can't Muslim people eat?' but I didn't cuz I'm stupid! Stupid-stupid-stupid!"

Nahid reached across the table and squeezed Lisa's hand to calm her down. "Lisa. It's *seriously* fine."

Lisa's puppy dog eyes looked up at her. "Are you sure?"

Nahid nodded, holding in a fawning sigh as she thought, *'She's so adorable.'*

Despite only having been dating for a week, Nahid could feel this powerful connection to Lisa. It was as if their minds were connected, in perfect sync with one another. She had never felt that way about anybody else in her entire life.

Lisa jumped up and ran to the refrigerator. "I can make you something else. I can make you a salad. Do you want a salad?"

"Sure! I love salad."

Nahid hated salad, but she could tell that Lisa was trying very hard, so she swallowed her hatred of all things green. She also swallowed the salad without allowing it to touch her tongue, a skill she had acquired from years of having to eat her mother's emerald monstrosities.

"So... I know this will be a stupid question..."

"Hm?"

"What is it like being a Muslim? Do you have to go to church or something?"

'Oh great, *this is it*,' Nahid thought as she braced herself. This was going to be another moment in her life when a non-Muslim asked her a bunch of questions about being Muslim. It wasn't the first time that she'd had to deal with this. However, Nahid assumed that Lisa, being a queer woman of color, would be more aware of how uncomfortable this situation might make her. But she didn't want to make Lisa feel bad, so she pressed on.

"It's called a Mosque."

"Do you have to go or is it a choice?"

"I don't have to go if I don't want to, but I still go anyway."

"Why?"

"My mom."

"Oh. Is she strict?"

"I mean… *Kinda* but also not really."

Lisa looked at her quizzically. "I don't understand."

Nahid gathered her thoughts and took a deep breath. "Okay, so my mom's from Iran where women can't get married or leave the country without a dude's approval and they only just very recently got the right to drive a car on their own."

Lisa's mouth dropped. "Wow."

"Yeah, but honestly it's not as bad as some places."

"Are those places Muslim too?"

"Ha, no. Some of the worst places are run by Christians."

"What about those, um… head mask things?"

"We're Shia Muslim, so we wear Hijabs. It's just, like, a headscarf. It's not a full mask or body shroud or anything. Those are niqabs and burqas."

"Yeah… but you don't wear one."

"We're not forced to, except in places where we are forced to, but this isn't one of those places. It's more of a cultural thing these days.

"But is your mom okay with that?"

Nahid took another deep breath. This wasn't something she planned on talking about until at least the sixth or seventh date, but Lisa's cuteness convinced her to continue.

"She wasn't at first. It was a *very long* conversation, but she came around eventually."

"What about your dad? Is he super strict?"

"My dad was born in New Jersey, so he has a lot more liberal viewpoint of these kinds of things. He's always been super supportive of all the stuff I do."

"Is it illegal to not wear Hijabs in Iran?"

"Yeah. Women's rights are… bad there. I'd rather not talk about it, to be honest."

"Oh. Sorry."

Nahid pushed through her serious discomfort once more. "I think that's why my mom has always been so difficult about it. She's from Iran, so she still has that culture shock of coming to America and dealing with American values. My sister wears a hijab, though, so I guess she helps balance it all out."

"Why did your mom move to America?"

"My dad."

"Really?"

"Yeah."

"How long did they know each other before they got married?"

"A few months or so."

"Wait, they didn't have some kinda arranged marriage, did they?"

"Um, kinda? It's hard to explain."

"Please, feel free."

"Okay, so, my dad was born in America which means he's not technically an Iranian citizen. So, when he went to visit Iran to see his grandparents that was, like, the first time he'd ever even been there. He met my mom at a mosque during a service. Her parents weren't very well-off so their daughter marrying an American '*medical professional*' seemed like a gift from God. He's just a nurse, but nobody was complaining. They tried marrying them off immediately, but my dad insisted on getting to know my mom first, so he stayed in Iran for as long as possible before inviting her back to America with him."

"Wow, was it hard for her to learn the language?"

"No, my mom learned English when she was a kid. The language barrier was never a problem. People treating her like a cockroach cuz she was very obviously not born white or in America is the problem."

"Like how do you mean?"

"My mom thought coming to America would bring more freedom and give her more opportunities to pursue her dreams. She tried going to school to become a teacher but couldn't afford it, so she got stuck in this terrible customer service call-center job and then that turned into an equally terrible job at Halmart. The closest she ever gets to her dream job is when she teaches Sunday school."

"That sucks…"

"Yeah…" Nahid wanted to stop complaining about how her mother was treated, but the floodwaters had already been unleashed. "And *on top* of all that, it's pretty much guaranteed that she'll never become a manager."

"Why's that?"

"Why do you think? My mom is nice, sweet, intelligent, hard-working. A little traditional, sure, but that doesn't stop her from putting a hundred percent into everything she does. And she's been working at that stupid store for, like, a decade. They give *white high school sophomores* supervisor positions, but not my thirty-six-year-old, super experienced mom. Please..."

"Shit... but at least it's better than Iran, right?"

"The same way expired food is better than the food you find on the ground, but that doesn't mean it's going to be *good*. For us - for people of color, Muslims, queer people - it's this constant, never-ending uphill climb."

"What about being queer?"

"What do you mean?"

"What's it like being queer in Iran?"

"Oh! Across the board terrible."

"Like, how terrible?"

"Like, death penalty terrible."

"Jesus... Do you think you'll ever go to Iran?"

"I have been to Iran, it's where my family lives. But I've only been there a few times."

"Aren't you afraid that if you go someone will find out and... you know? Kill you?"

Lisa was exhausted. "I don't think so. My family doesn't even know yet, and I've only known for, like, a year or so."

"Wow."

"Yeah."

"What made you - you know, uh..."

"What made me realize I was bi?"

"Yeah."

"Okay, so I was dating this guy - Raymond, right you met him? At the queer dance thing."

"Yeah, sure. He didn't seem to like me very much."

Nahid didn't want to openly agree with her, but when she told Raymond she was leaving the dance with Lisa, he looked at her like she was out of her mind and tried to get her to let him take her home instead.

"Yeah, well... Anyway, I was playing volleyball at an away game and I met this girl who was playing for the other team-"

"Ha!"

"What?"

"*The other team.* It's funny."

"Oh... yeah!" Nahid forced out a rough chuckle. "I didn't even realize- anyway, the girl's name was Sharon. She was sweet and nice and friendly, so we got ice cream after the game."

"You were hanging out with the enemy? That's a little unorthodox."

"Yeah, I'm not a big believer in intramural rivalry. The other girls on my team treat me like crap so why treat the girls on the other team like crap? Anyway, we went out, and I felt super comfortable talking to her. Like, suuuper comfortable. Comfortable like how Raymond made me feel. There was something about her that just-"

"Clicked?"

"Like a key in a lock. And then she just kissed me, right out of the blue. I think she felt bad after or something. She probably picked up my weird vibes, so she sorta just ran back off to her room. I mean, I was surprised and very confused, but it wasn't like I was upset, or felt violated. I felt... light. I mean, all my life - or, at least, *so far* in my life - I'd only explored my attraction to boys because that's all I thought was available to me. But to be honest, I think the attraction to girls was always buried deep underneath the belief that girls aren't *supposed* to date other girls. So, when I realized that girls were an option, I jumped."

"So, you slept with Sharon?"

"What?! No!"

"Really?"

"Of course not! I was still with Ray. I couldn't go behind his back and start hooking up with girls. C'mon! No, I waited until I got home, then I told him everything that happened, and we had a super long, and super awkward conversation about what it meant and what we both wanted. For a while, we even toyed with the notion of an open relationship, but it became clear that Ray wasn't the kind of guy who could handle sharing his partner with other people, and honestly, neither am I. So, we made the very adult decision to just split up and stay friends. But I guess that flew out the window the minute you and I started dating..."

"You don't see him anymore?"

"I don't know why but, for some reason, whenever we see each other in the hall he just... walks the other way."

Lisa shook her head. "Boys suck. He's probably just jealous."

"Yeah…"

She didn't like to think about it, but she missed Raymond. He was her first real relationship, and she didn't like how they left things. Whenever anything happened between her and Lisa, she wanted to talk to him about it, but now she felt like he'd moved to the other side of the world.

"Have you talked to your family about it all yet?"

Nahid, once again, had the displeasure of answering an awkward question she wasn't prepared for.

Lisa read Nahid's body language and got her answer. "I get it."

"Listen-"

"No, I get it. It's super hard talking about this stuff with people you *don't know*. I can't even imagine what it's like talking to *your* family about it. You're still trying to figure it all out."

"I just don't want you thinking that I don't think you're important."

Lisa looked deep into Nahid's eyes. They connected, piercing into each other's very minds. Lisa quietly got up and crossed the table to sit at Nahid's side. She put her arm around her.

"I would never think that, Nahid."

Lisa kissed her. It started sweetly, a slight peck, but it became deeper and deeper. Goosebumps started to cover Nahid's skin as she leaned in. She felt so warm and exposed but in the greatest way possible.

Nahid didn't know when it happened but the two had somehow magically transported to Lisa's bedroom. She was laid down gently on the bed, her head on the pillow with her girlfriend lying on top of her.

"I've never felt like this with anyone before," Lisa whispered, sensually. "You are the most amazing person I have ever met."

Nahid gasped, and then she smiled. "Lisa?"

"Yeah?"

"I think I'm in love with you."

Lisa slowly moved her hand up Nahid's arm. She could feel her goosebumps.

"Are you nervous?"

"No!" She responded in rushed embarrassment. "Excited! Beyond words, excited."

Lisa smiled. "I'm glad."

Lisa moved down to Nahid's jeans, pulling them down gently. She didn't resist. Even though she had never been this intimate with another person before, she felt at ease with Lisa. She felt at peace. She allowed herself to explore every bit of the strange and the new that came with this moment. She allowed Lisa to take over. She felt her inside her heart, soul, and mind. Lisa's name was all she could say, over and over as if she had forgotten the existence of any other words.

To Nahid, it seemed Lisa knew every method and avenue of pleasing her. So much so that as soon as it started it felt like it was over. The sensation of pure ecstasy swept over her like an inferno. Her body was covered in sweat. Her breath was hard to catch, running away from her like a rabbit.

"Wow."

The front door opened and slammed shut, and the sound of clumsy feet coming down the hallway shook the apartment.

A man's groggy voice called out, "Lisa?!"

"Fuck," Lisa said in a frustrated groan. "Look, we-"

"No, I get it. I'll head out."

Even though that was the last thing she wanted to do, Nahid quickly collected her things and ran out the door. On her way, she passed Uncle Leo, who creepily smiled at her from the open kitchen. A shiver went up her spine as she ran out the door, sprinting to the bus stop as fast as her weak knees could take her.

It was 3 p.m. when she arrived home. There she was immediately greeted with her mother's gigantic, Cheshire cat smile.

"Hello, my darling! How was Raymond? How was your date? Did it go nicely? Did he take you to a nice restaurant or was it another lovely study date at the library?"

"Raymond's fine. Our date was fine."

Nahid felt like she was running around with a massive red "A" branded on her clothes. She was worried that as soon as her mother found out that she had decided to become *'sexually active'*, she would march her around the town square, ringing a gong and squawking "Shame!" at anybody passing by. It was either that or fall into a coma of disappointment. To avoid this potential fate, she ran past her mother like her ass was on fire.

"Wait, wait, where are you going?"

"Just to my room. No biggie."

"'*No biggie?*' Nahid…"

"What?" She asked, nervously.

"I feel like it's been forever since you and I had time alone. Your father is at work, your sister is at the mall with her friends, and here we are, same place, same time. Let's talk!"

Nahid so desperately did not want to be alone with her mother and would fight to the death to avoid talking to her.

"Oh, come on, mom. We talk. We talk - all the time - about - everything - all the time!"

"But not like we used to. I know that things change when you go through puberty and start dating and playing the sports but I'm always going to be your mother, no matter what."

"Thank you. Thank you for that! When's dinner?"

Her mother looked at her sideways and sighed. "Five o'clock."

"Sweet. I'm going to go study."

"Okay…" Fairuza said, her voice heavy with disappointment. "Have a nice time."

"You too!" Nahid said without thinking as she slammed the door behind her.

6

20 JUN 18.

00:00.

NASSIRI HOUSEHOLD, El Paso, TX.

The men who had taken her family hostage were talking amongst themselves, discussing their "game plan" and "being prepared for anything". Nahid, however, could only focus on the terrified looks of her family sitting within arms distance of her. She thought of what she would give up to be able to rip herself free and get her family to safety.

One of the men came up from behind, grabbed her by the tail end of her nightshirt, and held her up.

"I hope you're ready, babe," he said with a gross, full-toothed smile.

Nahid tried wriggling her way out of his grip, only to kick him in the shins. With a deep hiss, he pushed the pain away and slapped her across the face.

'Whose dead handless grandma taught him how to slap?' she thought.

"Well... let's find a good spot for the show."

He roughly threw Nahid against the wall opposite her family. She fell onto her side but could still make eye contact with everyone.

"First things first..."

The man punched Nahid square in the temple, slamming her head into the floor with enough force to break open a watermelon. Her family's screams for her safety were muffled by their gags. He started punching her in the face and kicking her in the stomach. The other men joined in, brutalizing her with as much force as they could muster.

Nahid knew that she should be feeling nothing but pain and anguish, but all their hits and slams felt like nothing. They could have been tickling her with feathers and she wouldn't have felt the difference.

She looked down onto the floor, and where she expected to see pools of her blood was nothing but spotless linoleum.

"That should be enough, I think." The leader said between exhausted pants. "Okay, now..." He pulled out a gun and went over to Nahid's family. "Pick one."

The world around Nahid stopped as the vision of a man pointing a gun at her family threw her into shock.

"What are you, deaf? Pick one!"

She started to cry so hard that she almost couldn't breathe.

He pointed the gun at Vida.

All Nahid could do was push out a muffled, "Please don't do this!"

He pointed the gun at her father and then she realized what was happening: they wanted her to choose who would die. She started to feel sick and was afraid she'd choke on her vomit.

"Please, stop," she weakly muffled.

Then, he pointed the gun at her mother.

"NOO!" She screamed as hard as she could until her voice became hoarse. "NO DON'T!"

He pulled Fairuza up and pushed her down onto her knees in front of Nahid.

"Don't scream. Or they all die." He said as he pulled off Fairzua's gag. "Now. Last words."

Fairuza could barely breathe. Her brain hurt from crying so much, her lungs burning from too much screaming.

She looked down at Nahid and saw her daughter as a baby again. She saw their life together flash before her eyes. She saw all the things they'd seen and done together. And then, she saw all the things they'd never do.

From her lips came words so often said but at this moment had never felt truer. "I love you."

A muffled gunshot rang through the halls of the house. Fairuza fell to the floor, lifeless. Vida had curled up into her father's shoulder, refusing to look up and see her mother's dead body. Ebrahim just stared, too scared to move and too shocked to look away.

Nahid's gag was obliterated off her mouth as she unleashed a blood-curdling scream, filled with grief, despair, and the most powerful emotion of all, red-eyed fury. She felt that rage energize her, filling her body with an almost electrical sensation. It lifted her from the ground as she ripped herself free of the ties that bound her.

Everyone could feel the pure force emanating from her body. It shook the room. And it terrified them.

The man who shot her mother struggled to find his words. "As- as- as syringes..."

Ignoring whatever he was trying to say, Nahid flew at him, pulling him up like he weighed nothing and punching her fist straight through his chest.

While she was busy pulling her arm out of his limp body, one of the other men had started shooting at her. She didn't notice until she turned around, the bullets bouncing off of her as if they were made of rubber. Fuel had just been added to the rage burning inside of her. She threw the body of her mother's killer at the marksman, his head hitting against the wall.

The remaining two men tried running away, but she refused to let them leave her house alive, especially since her mother hadn't been given that option. The force that was driving her to commit such preposterous feats of strength propelled her through the air.

She flew at her assailants like a torpedo and grabbed them by their necks. Together, they broke through the living room window and out onto the lawn, where she dropped them. She could barely hear their moans of pain through the din of her family's screams ringing in her ear.

When she saw one of the men attempting to crawl away, she flipped him over onto his back. She pounced onto his chest and threw a hard and heavy punch, feeling his skull crumble to pieces over her hand.

The last man left alive managed to stand up and attempted to say something. "As syringes-". He stopped to spit out some blood.

Nahid, triggered by the very sound of his voice, wanted to make sure he could never talk again. She calmly walked towards him. He tried to run away but tripped and fell. Looking down at him, with mixed rage and pity, she pried his mouth open and ripped out his tongue. His mouth rapidly filled with blood, drowning him.

Nahid's rage turned into numbness as she looked down at her hands, red as the morning sun. Her numbness turned into fear as she looked around, saw the carnage, and remembered her family was still tied up inside the house.

She ran back inside, jumping through the hole she had made where the window used to be, heading straight to the kitchen where her father and sister still laid on the floor in shock.

She ripped off their ropes with ease. She couldn't think of anything better to say so she just said, "Are you two alright?"

They wouldn't acknowledge her. They just stared at Fairuza, lying on the floor. Nahid didn't want to look, she couldn't, so she tried getting her family to leave.

"We have to go," She said. "There could be more coming."

Ebrahim didn't say anything as he crawled towards his wife's body and cradled her in his arms.

Nahid already had cried so much that she was beginning to get a headache. "Vida, please."

Her sister's eyes widened as she was pulled out of her stupor. She stared up at her sister and started screaming until her voice caved in on itself.

"Vida, please, stop, it's going to be okay."

Vida kept screaming until her face was red. Soon her body grew tired of screaming and she fell unconscious.

The sounds of approaching police sirens sent Nahid into high alert. She knew her family wouldn't come with her if she ran, but she didn't want to leave without them.

Suddenly, in a soft, broken voice, she heard her father. "Nahid... just go."

Heartbroken, she did as she was told and ran out the back door. She jumped over hedges and fences, straight through people's lawns. She ran across town until she, by instinct, found herself at Lisa's apartment. She grabbed the hidden key beneath the doormat and let herself in.

"Lisa?" she loudly whispered as she entered the room.

She expected Lisa to be sleeping on the couch with a book on her lap. She also expected there to be a couch, but when she entered the apartment, she found nothing. No furniture, no pictures, and no trace of Lisa. Nothing but a dark, lifeless apartment.

"Lisa?" She called out again, this time louder, desperately needing her girlfriend to be there.

"She's not here, Nahid," A familiar voice, yet still not Lisa's, called out to her from the darkened hallway.

The source of the voice stepped towards the light, her heels clicking on the hardwood floors. Nahid could barely make out a glimmer of long red hair and alabaster skin. When she finally came forward, Nahid couldn't believe her eyes.

"Miss Cooper?"

"It's Special Agent January Cooper." Her calm, counselor's voice had been replaced by that of a cold, heartless assassin. The very air around her seemed to freeze, sending a chill up Nahid's spine. "But please... feel free to call me Jan. All my friends do."

Nahid suddenly became filled with a sinking, heavy feeling. "What the hell are you doing here? And where is my girlfriend? Where is Lisa?!"

She sighed and looked at Nahid with a concerned frown. "Oh. Nahid. This is going to be hard for you to hear but... Lisa doesn't exist."

"That's ridiculous. Where is she?"

"Hold on."

Jan pulled out her phone and typed something into it. Nahid's text alert went off. She saw a message from Lisa.

LISA: 🖤 🖤 🖤!

A soft, slow chuckle came from behind Jan. Lisa's "uncle" appeared in the hallway.

Nahid pointed at the man and yelled, "If Lisa's not real then who's he?!"

"This is Leo."

"Hi," he said with an awkward wave.

"Leo? Nahid is having trouble understanding the circumstances of her situation right now. Could you help her see what I'm talking about?"

He giggled in a strange, disjointed manner before closing his eyes, concentrating very hard on something. Suddenly, Lisa appeared out of thin air, her arms open wide, waiting for Nahid to embrace her.

The world stopped turning as her heart broke for a second time that night. She thought back on all the times they had spent together. All the movie nights in her apartment. All the times that she wanted to call her but couldn't because of a study group, a class, or a family emergency. All of their most intimate moments were restricted exclusively to Lisa's apartment.

The night they met; Raymond looked at her the way anybody would look at somebody who had been seen dancing with somebody that didn't exist. In all the time that they had been together, never once has Lisa ever been seen by anybody else but Nahid.

"She doesn't exist..." Was all she could mutter as Lisa faded away in front of her.

That day had been a cluster of revelations toppling one after the other in her mind. She felt like she was on the verge of a complete nuclear meltdown as she tried to make sense of the senselessness of that night.

"She never existed." Jan corrected her. "She was nothing but an elaborate fabrication."

"Why?"

"We needed to give you someone to run to. A reason to bring you here after your... ordeal. By the way, congratulations. I always knew you'd be a killer."

Nahid thought through what she'd just said. "Wait... those men..." Tears of sorrow and heartbreak were replaced by tears of renewed fury. "*You killed my mother!*"

"She was necessary collateral damage, Nahid. All your life, you've had this amazing power locked away inside of you, and we knew that the only way to open the door was for you to experience severe emotional distress. If we hadn't killed your mother, all of that potential would have been wasted. You're better off. Trust me."

"*You killed my mother.*"

"Yes, life can be cruel. Maybe if you had had more time to make amends with her... you wouldn't be so upset."

With a roar, Nahid launched herself at the frozen-hearted woman in front of her.

Jan calmly whispered, "As syringes and painkillers replaced his strength."

Nahid crash-landed into the ground with a heavy thud, completely unconscious.

"Leo?" She called, signaling her partner in crime to come crawling to her feet. "Grab our new friend. It's time to go."

"Home?"

"Yes. Home."

(Epilogue)

Ebrahim woke up to the sight of blinding fluorescent lights and a splitting headache coursing throughout his entire brain. He quickly realized that he was handcuffed to a hospital bed in the very hospital where he worked.

"What?" He tried escaping but to no use. "Somebody! Help me! Please!"

One of his fellow nurses, Elaine, walked in.

"Elaine! Oh my god, I'm so happy to see you. What's going on? Why am I here?"

She stayed silent and avoided eye contact while checking his vitals.

"Elaine?"

As soon as she was finished, she left the room and spoke with a man in the hallway.

"He's ready for you now."

Then a heavily mustachioed man in a dowdy brown suit appeared in the doorway. He flashed a detective's badge.

"Mr. Nassiri, I'm Detective Sloane with the El Paso Police Department, homicide division."

"Homicide? If this is a prank, it's not funny."

"I assure you, sir, this is no prank."

"Then what's going on?!"

"What's the last thing you remember, Mister Nassiri?"

Ebrahim pushed past the headache to put together his scattered memories. "The last thing I remember is having dinner with my kids. My wife wasn't joining us cuz she was upset with Nahid."

"Why was your wife upset?"

"Our daughter had just come out to us."

"Which daughter?" He pulled out a notepad and glanced at it. "Vida or Nay-hid?"

"It's pronounced Naw-heed, detective."

"Thank you," He said, unphased. "Which daughter, Mister Nassiri?"

"Nahid."

"And your wife was upset at Nahid. How did you feel about the situation?"

"My daughter being-" He stopped himself from saying 'bisexual'. Though, on the whole, he loved and accepted Nahid for who she was, a part of him was significant enough to want to shelter this knowledge. "I didn't care."

"Really?"

"Of course not."

"And how did you feel about your wife's reaction to the situation?"

"Well, I just thought she was being a big drama queen. Slamming doors, not talking to anybody. She gets like-" His mind and eyes went to the restraints around his wrists. "What's going on here?"

"I just have one last question."

"I'm not answering any more questions until I see my lawyer, and my family."

The detective gave a smug smile. "Of course. Sure."

Ebrahim, of course, was not about to let that go. "What was that? What was that face about?"

"You said you don't want to answer any of my questions and I don't have to answer any of yours so, as far as I'm concerned, this conversation is over."

"Where is my family?!"

The detective just looked at him with a face as cold as stone. "Where do you think they are?"

"What?"

"Ebrahim Nassiri, you are under arrest for the murder of your wife, Fairuza Nassiri. You have the right to remain silent. You have the right to an attorney. If you cannot afford an attorney, one will be appointed to you. Do you hear and understand these rights?"

The machine monitoring Ebrahim's heart rate started beeping wildly out of control as panic took over his body. "What? What?!"

The cop suddenly became very smug. "You murdered your daughter because she's queer. You stashed her body, your wife found out and you shot her in the head. Unfortunately, police showed up on the scene before you could hide her or get little Miss Vida, who ran away into the middle of the night."

Ebrahim couldn't believe what he was hearing. He started to hyperventilate. "This is ridiculous! Where's Vida? Where's my daughter?!"

He chortled "Cute bit, buddy. And good luck finding a lawyer. You're gonna need it."

On the other side of town.

Vida thrashed about in her bed as much as she could but the orderlies at the El Paso County Mental Hospital were much larger and much stronger than her. They pinned her down to her bed and strapped her down tight.

"You don't understand! They think my dad killed her! He didn't! It was those men! They came to us at night! They tied us up! They beat up my sister and then they shot my mom!"

"Uh-huh," one of the orderlies said, obviously not believing anything that came out of her mouth.

"Shut up," the other orderly sniped. "You'll just egg her on."

Vida started to cry. "Please... Please, you have to believe me!"

"Oh god, this is so pathetic."

"Dude, seriously, just ignore her."

"If your dad didn't kill her, then where's Nahid."

Vida calmed down as she began to think. If she told them the whole truth of what she'd seen - Nahid flying through the air, ripping men apart with her bare hands before running off into the night - then they would think she was even more out of her mind than they already did. If they believed her, they would try to hunt Nahid down and arrest her for murder. So, Vida tightened her lip.

"That shut her up."

"Try to get some sleep, Miss Nassiri. You're gonna need it."

They turned off the lights and closed the door on her. The windows were covered with heavy curtains protected by bars to keep her from escaping, leaving the room dark and desolate and Vida alone with her tears.

GEMMA LOUISE WALLACE

BIRTH-DATE: 12 AUG 02

SEX: Female

CURRENT HEIGHT: 5'2"

EYE COLOR: Blue.

HAIR COLOR: Blonde.

INSTALLATION: (Currently) Seaview, Isle
of Wight, GB.

(Previously) Washington, D.C., USA.

NATIONALITY: Dual British/American
Citizenship.

ETHNICITY: White.

FAMILY:

Sir Francis Henry Wallace (grandfather,
legal guardian)

Barnaby Wallace (father, deceased)

Adrianna Wallace (mother, deceased)

DeVAUGHN JORDAN HEATH

BIRTH-DATE: 13 SEP 02

SEX: Male

CURRENT HEIGHT: 6'

EYE COLOR: Brown.

HAIR COLOR: Dark Brown.

INSTALLATION: (Currently) Seaview, Isle of Wight, GB.

(Previously) Washington, D.C., USA.

NATIONALITY: Dual British/American Citizenship.

ETHNICITY: Black.

FAMILY:

Vanessa Heath (aunt, legal guardian)

Jordan Heath (father, deceased)

LaShaun Heath (mother, deceased)

1

20 JUN 18.

00:00.

THE WALLACE ESTATE, Seaview, IOW.

She felt as if she were flying, soaring high above the grounds of her family's prestigious Seaview estate. Far above the few, elite schoolmates lucky enough to be invited to her annual summer blowout.

Gemma Wallace: The Star. The Sun. Everybody revolved around her. Everything revolved around her. The World revolved around her.

The alcohol flowed through the house like a river. The drugs - a candy bowl combination of pills, potions, and powders - were being passed around from room to room so everyone had an opportunity to partake.

Her grandfather, Sir Francis Henry Wallace, MBE, was out of town on business per the usual. The maid, Vanessa, was far too terrified of Gemma to ever disclose the knowledge of her excessive bacchanals. Especially when they both knew his lordship wouldn't do anything to correct her behavior.

The house itself was a great, early 20th-century maze. Too many bedrooms and bathrooms to count, a grand library, a kitchen the size of most flats, and a basement full of expensive antiques too large or too valuable to keep around visitors. A fan of the traditional, Sir Wallace filled every common room in the manor with paintings worth more than most people, priceless antiques, and sculptures. Vanessa always saw to it that these irreplaceable works of art were properly hidden before any of Gemma's "friends" arrived for their near-weekly flood of debauchery, leaving Gemma to do as she pleased, and, this evening, what pleased her was LSD.

Gemma looked up and saw the ceiling. She saw past the ceiling and found the night sky. She saw past the sky, the heavens, the moon, the sun, and the stars until she had found herself at the center of the universe.

Communing with the cosmos, she demanded that this night be made to last forever. Let it be her last memory. Let her body and soul be swallowed whole by this one beautiful moment, surrounded by friends, loved by all she saw, so that she may die happy, young, and beautiful.

It was then that Gemma spied a great, magnificent eye, surrounded by fire and halos of space dust. It was the eye of God. It glared at her, wide and open with a curious judgment. She stared right back with an unerring audacity exclusively found in the hyper-confident. However, she found that, despite her courage and strength, the more she stared the smaller she felt, and the smaller she felt the smaller she became.

She shrank and shrank and shrank like Alice through the looking glass until she was an infant again. The eye of God was no longer a great, cosmic watchman but the eye of a strange, wiry, mustachioed scientist hidden behind thick horned rim glasses.

He had placed her in a large maze as if she were a rodent. The prize for passing the test: being allowed to grow up and become the amazing, decadent princess she was always meant to be.

Just as quickly as she had become an infant and then a rodent, she became a ghost. The world around her became irrelevant, and she became irrelevant to the world. Solid walls became like air as she walked right through them. She walked and walked until she had reached the end of the maze. On cue, she decided to stop being a ghost and thus the world became tangible again.

The rodent was ready for its cheese.

"It's time to wake up Gemma."

The following morning.

Gemma's post-party wake-up started better than normal. There was no messy hangover, no feeling of emptiness, sickness, or depression. She felt as she did on her best day: one hundred percent healthy and completely content in her life.

She woke up on the couch in the center of her estate's lounge, surrounded by a teenage wasteland of regret and shame. Barely functioning bodies of barely clothed teenagers were strewn about the room. Some had fallen asleep where they fell - the hardwood floor, the coffee table, underneath the easy chair, and a small collection of partygoers fell unconscious in the coat closet.

A few were already up and processing or regurgitating the night. Thankfully, there were enough bathrooms in the great estate that all could find a safe haven. None of that mattered to Gemma, though, because *she* felt *amazing*.

With the grace of an angel, she lifted herself off the couch and glided towards the kitchen. On the way, she ran into Summer, a red-headed girl one year below her. She greeted her with a warm and chipper voice.

"Good morning, Summer! How are you feeling?"

Summer didn't respond. Her sunken eyes wouldn't even look her way. Her cold hands rubbed her sockets out of exhaustion until they were a heavy reddish-purple. She walked right past Gemma without so much as a "Hello."

Gemma responded to being ignored with a cold, "Whatever… Won't invite you to another bloody party, that's for fucking sure."

She began to take stock of the condition of her home. The damage was typical for a party of this magnitude. There was a mass of broken glasses flung about, but they owned so many that Gemma knew her Papa would never notice, seeing as he never had before. The same was true with the broken dishes and stained furniture. The maid usually took care of covering up the evidence before it ever became a noticeable issue.

She passed by a girl from Grade Nine puking in the kitchen bathroom and thought, '*How the hell did she get in here? Oh well, too late now.*'

She found two of her closest friends, Bella Tooney and Jim Peck, having breakfast in the kitchen.

She greeted them with a vivacious, "Hello, darlings!"

Despite her loud service, she received no response from the exhausted duo.

"Oh, what? Did I say something out of place last night? Did I bring up Jim impregnating Dina Winterbottom again? I swear I don't mean to make fun of that. I just find it so hilarious that it just pops out! You know what I'm like."

Again, no response. They just went about trying to eat without barfing.

She began to get frustrated. "Oh, come on, people. Don't be like that. I couldn't have been *that* bad last night."

Still no response.

"Wow. Wow, this silent treatment is truly Oscar-worthy. Excuse me while I make a call to the BAFTA committee. Ok - ok, I know what I have to do: Bella, why don't you tell Jim about the time you fucked his brother while you two were on a break? Hm?"

Still nothing.

"Ok, what the fuck is going on?! Answer me, you bloody bastards!"

Dean Richards, another *close friend*, appeared from the basement.

"Oh hello, Dean. Guess what? *Your* friends are giving me the silent treatment."

"Hey guys, have you seen Gemma?"

"You can't find her?" Bella responded. "You mean she isn't flouncing around, acting like the queen of the bloody universe?"

After pushing out a goofy guffaw, Jim decided to chime in. "Yeah or passed out somewhere."

Gemma machine gun fired out a fake, unimpressed laugh. "Great lads... just great. But the joke's over. Get out of my house, please. I'm quite tired of th-"

She was interrupted by Dean. "No. I can't find her anywhere."

"No Dean, I'm right-"

"Well, fuck!" Bella said.

At this point, Gemma had been cut off more times in the past few minutes than she had her entire life.

Jim contributed as intelligently to the conversation as he could. "Maybe she just buggered off?"

"Oh please," Bella retorted with a snorting laugh. "When have you ever known *Gemma Wallace* to leave a room without making it *everybody else's* business, much less her own bloody party? Much less her own fucking house?"

"Guys, seriously, stop. I'm getting freaked out."

"Did she leave with anybody?" Dean asked.

Bella tried to remember but couldn't quite form a full picture of last night's events, mostly due to the heavy fog of irresponsibility. "I don't know. Maybe? I was completely passed out by midnight."

"Jesus Christ..."

"Are you sure she's gone?"

"I've checked every room in the house."

"And the grounds?"

He gave her an incredulous look. "Bella... don't you think that if *Princess Gemma* had woken up in the dirt, that bloody banshee would've screamed her head off about it by now."

"Jesus. Why are you doing this to me? You're supposed to be my friends."

Jim took a deep breath and blew it out through his nose. "What are we gonna do? Call the police?"

"Fuck that! I'm not going to the slammer for that lard ass."

"Fuck you, Bella. You got the clap from Jonah Winter and gave it to half the senior class and Jim's brother! I don't need this kind of shit from you assholes."

"So what?" Dean asked. "Do we just split then?"

Bella thought it over.

"We split."

In a flash, she had grabbed the antique vase sitting on the antique credenza - something Gemma's grandfather would surely miss - and ran out through the kitchen door like a bat out of hell.

"Get back here! Bring that back!" Gemma yelled out, loud enough to wake the entire neighborhood.

Dean followed suit. Jim, with the swiftness of a sloth, took several moments to look for something worth stealing before running after Dean and Bella. Gemma noticed this and tried to convince him otherwise.

"Jim, what the fuck do you think you're doing?"

He settled on an expensive cutlery set.

She tried to grab his arm only to watch as it phased right through him as if she were thin air. Jim didn't notice in the slightest and continued on his way out of the house with no regard to Gemma's presence, closing the door behind him.

She couldn't believe what she had just witnessed. She tried grabbing anything she could find - a rolling pin, a pair of scissors, a frying pan - only to phase right through them. She ran to the back door to try and call out for help, but instead of opening it, she ran right through it.

She started to hyperventilate. The hairs all over her body stood on end. Her eyes widened but her pupils shrank to the size of a pin.

She had become immaterial.

She was nothing.

She screamed a loud, glass-shattering scream that nobody could hear.

2

19 JUN 18.

23:59.

HEATH HOUSEHOLD, Seaview, IOW.

Living down the way from the Wallace Estate was the opposite of fun for the stalwartly studious DeVaughn Heath. He didn't mind not being invited to every school social function if it meant not being around stupid people. However, he did mind being kept awake for hours because of the incredibly loud music booming from the Victorian castle that was Gemma's home.

He and his aunt Vanessa, who worked as their maid, had to live in the cottage nearby so that she could rush over at a moment's notice. This was often the case after one of Gemma's ragers. Despite knowing that these parties kept her scholarly nephew awake, Vanessa had no choice but to keep a tight lip about the parties to retain her employment.

She was a strong woman, with beautiful hazel eyes, a medium frame, smooth, dark brown skin, standing a hair below her nephew. She regularly straightened her hair with a hot comb to pull it back into a tight bun, a look she had maintained since her army days. She hated wearing heels but was forced to work in them every day much to her discomfort.

At school, Gemma generally ignored DeVaughn. Her friends would call him names, he'd even gotten into a few fights with some of them, but she completely ignored him. He wasn't entirely sure that she was even aware that he was her maid's nephew. He didn't mind being invisible to her though, as he knew her to be an insensible brat.

DeVaughn was the only black student at his entire school. He didn't want to assume the only reason all the rich white kids actively excluded him from their many, many parties was because of his race. For all he knew, it was because he was poor or that he didn't drink or do drugs. Maybe it was because he didn't play sports, which annoyed the school's basketball coach considerably as he had assumed DeVaughn was athletic. After all, he *was black*.

"I bet you're a natural athlete!" the creepy old white dude said at him without any provocation or context whatsoever.

DeVaughn responded with a casual, "I'm actually quite shit."

For that, he received a week's detention.

DeVaughn needed to study for the upcoming final exams, and he wouldn't be able to do that without sleep. For him losing even a minute of sleep was a step towards poor grades and a step away from getting into a proper university. Despite being in the top ten percent of his entire school, he still worried about any small details that may deter him from his goals.

He pulled out some earplugs from a large container that he had bought specifically for Gemma's party nights. Despite buying them only a few short weeks ago, he was nearly out.

He and his aunt didn't have a lot of money so bothering her about a few pounds for another tub of earplugs seemed futile.

He would have to mow several lawns for that kind of cash. This would involve him suffering through rich, old white people calling him "boy." DeVaughn debated whether or not it would be worth it as the bass dropped a few dozen yards away, shaking one of his books off the shelf.

He plugged up his ears and, while doing his best to muffle out the rest of the world, fell asleep.

He was a baby in a room full of other infants. They began to age rapidly into people he had never seen before but somehow still felt familiar to him.

A slouching, dark-skinned, nervous-looking boy with red hair and violet eyes.

A strange-looking person with pale skin, a flat, almost lizard-like face, and pure black eyes.

A Hispanic girl with wavy brown hair and steel grey eyes.

An incredibly tall, olive-skinned girl with kinky hair jutting out in every direction.

A very young Asian girl with a short bob haircut.

Then a bottle blonde girl with a shapely figure, whom he quickly identified as Gemma Wallace.

'*Gemma?*' He thought. '*What is she doin' here?*'

"It's time to wake up DeVaughn."

The following morning.

DeVaughn woke up feeling sick to his stomach with an immense headache. He stumbled to the bathroom to take a few aspirins before getting himself dressed for the day. It was between his jeans and his belt that he realized that he had slept through his alarm. Despite how gross he was feeling, his anxiety overrode his nausea and overall pain. He quickly finished getting ready before running downstairs for a breakfast that consisted of plain bread and an apple.

His aunt was still too scared to head over to the manor.

Peeking through the blinds, which gave her a clear view of the estate, she said, "I still see those headless chickens runnin' around. I know better."

DeVaughn was born in America. His parents died shortly after he was born, and Vanessa became his legal guardian. They moved to the Isle of Wight when he was five after Vanessa had received a once in a lifetime job opportunity, only for it to fall through as soon as they arrived. She was on a work visa and refused to move back to America, so she took the first job that came her way: working as a maid for Sir Wallace.

Despite the dramatic reduction in pay and general unpleasantness of the job, Vanessa was very intent on not returning to the United States. DeVaughn couldn't count the times he heard her say, "It's not my dream job, but it pays the bills and saves me from having to buy a ticket back to the states. I'd much rather be up in this mess than *that* one."

He kissed his aunt goodbye before running out of the house.

The two were forced to share a very old computer, as Vanessa could not afford to get him his own. As a result, he had to use the PC's at the local library, graciously donated by Sir Wallace himself. To reserve one for the entire day, DeVaughn had to get up very early on Saturday mornings, a routine that brought an incredible amount of stress to the young man's already stressful life.

He walked up the cobblestone path that led him from their shack of a house to the main street, passing by the Wallace Manor as he did every day. Hearing a loud commotion, he stopped and watched as a large group of Gemma's friends ran out of the house, like a horde of ants retreating from a blast of killer bug spray.

He saw Dean Richards come towards him at an incredible pace, and quickly got out of his way. However, that didn't stop the spoiled youth from brushing into him and knocking him to the ground.

"Stay outta the way, tosser."

An annoyed DeVaughn picked himself up off the ground and dusted off the dirt. He looked back up towards the imposing almost-castle and could see Gemma Wallace yelling at someone from the back door. As soon as he blinked, though, she was gone. He took a second glance. Though he couldn't explain it, even though he couldn't see her in his mind he felt as though she was still standing there.

This feeling pulled him into a trance, which itself pulled him towards the house. Before he had even realized it, he was past the gate and standing just a few meters away from where he thought he saw her standing.

Snapping out of whatever state he was in; he quickly ran back to the path and quietly swore at himself.

"What the hell is wrong with me today?"

3

20 JUN 18.

13:00.

THE WALLACE ESTATE, Seaview, IOW.

When Vanessa arrived at the house to commence with the after-party clean-up, she was in greater shock than usual. Nearly everything that wasn't nailed down to the floor was missing. She looked for Gemma throughout the grounds, in all of her usual drop spots, and couldn't find her anywhere. After several hours of searching, she made the command decision to summon her employer, Sir Wallace, away from his professional engagements to help handle the situation.

Despite his age, Francis Henry Wallace still had the presence that caused those around him to stand at attention. His great wealth and privileged upbringing were most likely the cause. His family's influence in the British government went back generations, and the Wallace family name carried a great level of responsibility.

This responsibility caused a great rift between Sir Wallace and his son, Barnaby, who wished to live a more free-spirited, artistic lifestyle. Both men, being too stubborn to attempt a compromise of any kind, eventually parted ways, with Barnaby moving all the way to America to get as far away from his father as possible.

Barnaby met his partner, Adrianna, in Washington, DC, and the two had Gemma, a granddaughter Sir Wallace didn't meet until after his son and daughter-in-law died in a car crash. His entire world was turned upside down as he simultaneously lost his son and was forced to parent his grandchild in his golden years. This would prove to be an impossible task for a man of such importance, so he would often leave Gemma in the care of a multitude of nannies and nurses, who would all eventually quit when her fiendish, self-absorbed attitude became too much for them to handle.

As soon as he arrived, Sir Wallace's face turned a beet red as he examined the state of his home. Trash was strewn about everywhere, furniture had been dislocated, sick covered the floor of the bathroom, and much of his prized possessions had gone missing.

"This is pure insanity! It looks as if a tornado picked up my home and dropped it back where it was found. And where is Gemma?"

"I don't know, sir."

"Typical. Quite typical. Selfish little brat is probably hiding, waiting for the storm to pass so she can sneak back in undetected."

Gemma watched with eyes darkened from crying invisible tears. She wanted to yell out for their attention, but her voice had all but left her after soundlessly screaming for hours.

Without him realizing it, her grandfather walked right through her as he went on about how irresponsible she was.

"Sir, it's quite possible Gemma might be in some sort of danger. This is the first time she's ever disappeared like this."

"Are you daft, girl? I told you: she's just hiding."

"With all due respect, sir, Gemma isn't the 'hiding' kind of girl."

"Oh please. I don't even wish to describe the *kind of girl* my granddaughter could be. Nevertheless, we should call the police, try and see if we can salvage the contents of my ransacked home."

Gemma could barely contain her anger. "Bastard. If I'm a fool it's only because I was raised by one, you wannabe John Major. Of course, *'raised'* would imply that you were present during my childhood."

"She's just as classless and irredeemably witless as her father. I should've sent her to a boarding school in some frigid, foreign land as soon as she was dropped onto my lap. Filled with a cloister of nuns who are still brave enough to slap her on the wrist with a ruler when she behaves like an idiot."

"Or better yet, had me put down like a cancerous dog so I wouldn't have to suffer under your uniquely outdated brand of absentee parenting. Congratulations must be in order. First, you raised my father into an early grave, and now your only granddaughter is a ghost! You are quite possibly the *worst parent* on the planet. Are there trophies for this kind of situation? I mean, what's left for you after paying for a knighthood?"

Vanessa called the police, but her American accent made them think she was a disgruntled tourist and they immediately dismissed her. She called again, this time addressing herself as an employee of Sir Wallace. They fervently apologized and arrived within minutes with a full complement of inspectors and crime scene analysts. They were very dedicated to providing Sir Wallace with whatever help he required. One officer even offered to make him a cup of tea.

After doing an intake of all the stolen and damaged goods, the lead inspector on the case asked Sir Wallace, "Is there anything else we should be looking for?"

"Not that I can think of at the moment."

"Sir," Vanessa interjected, "aren't you forgetting something?"

"What could I possibly be forgetting, Miss Heath?"

"Your granddaughter?"

"Oh yes," he said as if he had just found his reading glasses. "My granddaughter, Gemma. It appears she may be missing."

"Do you think she might be the one responsible?" The inspector inquired.

"Maybe. Or she's just hiding somewhere, drugged out of her mind. One of the two."

The inspector, as well as the other police in attendance, were taken aback by the lord's nonchalance. "Would you care to describe your granddaughter?"

"Oh goodness," He said, struggling to recall Gemma's appearance. "Just a few weeks shy of sixteen. Blonde hair. Blue eyes. Slightly north of five feet. If anything, she's probably in some pawnshop somewhere trying to sell my precious belongings for a quick pound."

"Yes, *so precious*," Gemma said. "Far more precious than your *flesh and blood*."

"You mentioned earlier that your granddaughter has an issue with drugs. Do you think she might be a danger to herself or others, sir?"

Gemma expected a witty and disparaging retort from the old geezer but received silence instead. She turned and saw him with his head in his hands.

"I honestly don't know."

"She's never run off like this before?"

Seeing Sir Wallace's distress, Vanessa responded in his stead. "No inspector."

"But he just said he thought she might be responsible for all this?"

"She's very much responsible for this. If she didn't steal it all herself, those urchin friends of hers did. She's always cavorting around with the lowest rabble."

The detective took a brief pause. "Sir, this is a hard question to ask but… where were you last night?"

The lord's eyes nearly turned red. "What an impertinent question! I was in London for business in service of the crown, if you must know."

"Can you provide proof of all this?"

"Would my private plane's flight manifesto suffice? The flight crew? The footage of me at the airport?"

Vanessa chimed in. "Sir, I think I know something that may help."

"What is it, girl?"

"We have security cameras throughout the house. They may be able to help us figure out where Gemma went."

"Why didn't you bring this up before?" The inspector inquired.

"You're the police. I figured you would've noticed by now."

She pointed to the four cameras in that very room. The inspector did his best to hide his embarrassed face, pink as a pig's bottom.

"And," He cleared his throat, hoping to push out the shame. "Where do those lead to, Miss...?"

"Heath. Vanessa Heath. And they lead to the monitors in the basement."

"Would you mind taking us there?"

"Of course."

She led them all down to the basement. Sir Wallace struggled to descend but rejected an officer's offer of help, too proud to admit that he needed it.

Gemma followed, a glimmer of hope putting a slight bounce into every step. The footage could help them all find out what happened to her. They could use it to solve the mystery and somehow turn her back to normal.

They made their way to the massive monitor that showed the lot every vantage point inside and outside the great manor.

"I'll just set it to the beginning of last night."

With the press of a button, they all watched the entirety of Gemma's drug and booze-fueled orgy unfold. She looked around at everyone's shocked faces and saw on the screen the havoc she helped wrought, as well her own deterioration. She found herself in a position to see how her actions affected other people, and herself.

"May we please not prolong this?" Sir Wallace asked, his voice and face filled with shame and embarrassment.

Gemma knew that look all too well, but this time it had a greater effect on her. This time, she could see how this once proud and upstanding man had been broken by her actions.

"Of course, sir. I'll just speed it up."

Vanessa fast-forwarded through the video, accelerating Gemma's steadfast descent into depravity. Beginning with her guzzling a forty ounce, followed by a heavy dose of LSD, vomiting it all up, and then ending with her falling unconscious on the couch. When they reached the midnight mark, Gemma was still motionless. Suddenly, the video skipped to seven in the morning and she was nowhere to be found.

"What just happened there?" The inspector asked.

"I don't know, sir. It just skipped to this morning. Something must have messed up the footage. I'm sorry."

"What?" Sir Wallace's voice was filled with confusion and worry.

"Someone must have tampered with it," The inspector responded, matter-of-factly.

"But who would want to do that?"

"Sir, forty teenagers were running around this house last night," The inspector reminded him. "One of them probably figured out they were being taped. Do you mind if I take a copy of this to the station? We have people who can examine it."

"Please." Sir Wallace obliged.

As Vanessa compiled the footage onto a hard drive for the police, Sir Wallace left the security room. Curious, and worried, Gemma followed. She watched as he ascended the stairs at an even slower pace than usual and retreated into the entrance hall den. He slumped into the only clean chair left in the room and placed his head in his hands.

In his sudden solitude, Sir Wallace allowed himself to express his frustration and fear without shame.

"Oh Gemma," He sighed in great sadness. However, tears refused to be shed. He was too much of a traditional and unyieldingly stubborn man to produce such an emotional performance, even to an audience of none.

It was then that Gemma realized something. Something that she had done an excellent job of not thinking about until it was all too much to neglect.

"Could I actually be dead? I don't feel dead. I have a pulse and a heartbeat - surefire signs that I'm not dead. I'm also breathing, and that's something a dead person wouldn't be able to do... And if I'm not dead then I can't be a ghost... but then again, I've never actually met a ghost so really this is all just guesswork. Oh god, please help me out here."

There was the sound of a sudden scuffle of feet at the entrance to the den. Gemma and Sir Wallace both looked over and saw a young, black man who looked very familiar to both of them. It took Gemma a moment to place him as one of her classmates. She had seen him around school, but they had never been formally introduced. And then it hit her.

"Oh, he's the maid's nephew! Daniel or Darren or something... I wonder what he's doing here?"

Then Sir Wallace asked, "Who are you? What are you doing here?"

4

20 JUN 18.

13:00.

SEAVIEW PUBLIC LIBRARY, Seaview, IOW.

DeVaughn saw five police cars drive up the street towards Wallace Estate through the window near his computer station. In his experience, he knew that so many cops could only mean one thing: a rich white person was in trouble. He figured that it had to do with all the kids he saw scrambling out of Gemma's house that morning.

DeVaughn wanted to go to university to become a barrister. He wanted to be a representative for all the underrepresented citizens of the United Kingdom. However, he knew that his working-class upbringing would be an incredible impediment. Thus, was the reason behind his need to be at the top of his class, and his incredibly packed research and study schedule.

Several grueling hours and a homemade tuna fish sandwich later, and he was ready to turn in for the day. Knowing that there would be cops lurking about the Wallace Estate, he made a conscious decision to take an extended detour to avoid any possible trouble.

Along the way, he became lost in thought. *'Which university am I going to go to? How would I pay for it? Would they even let me in? Sure, my grades are nearly perfect but then there are dozens of other kids with perfect grades and parents willing to spend millions of dollars to bribe their child's way. Do I have any control over my life or has everything already been planned for me?'*

Coming out of his confusion driven haze, he found himself standing at Gemma's wide-open front door. This great magnetic pull was drawing him inside.

'What am I doing?' He thought to himself. *'This is completely ridiculous. What is going on?'*

Despite his internal protests, he awkwardly walked into the ancestral home of the Wallace family. It didn't feel to him as though his body was out of his control; he just knew that there was something important he had to find inside.

'This is how horror movies start.'

He announced himself. "Hello? Anybody home? It's DeVaughn. Auntie? Gemma? Sir Wallace?"

No reply.

DeVaughn felt the pull again. It drew him further inside as if an invisible rope had lassoed his mind and was dragging him towards some unknown yet mysteriously familiar destination.

He came upon the den, hearing a noise within. He gently pushed the door open. He thought that he could see Gemma through the corner of his eye, only for her to disappear when he turned his head. Instead, he found an irate Sir Wallace.

"Who are you? What are you doing here?" the old lord demanded, perched on his easy chair like a king on his throne.

"Uhh... sorry. I'm DeVaughn..."

Sir Wallace just stared at him as if to say, "is that name supposed to mean something to me?"

"I'm Vanessa's nephew…?"

Another blank stare.

"Miss Heath, your maid?"

"Oh! Pardon me, my boy… my mind has all but left me today."

"What's wrong, sir?"

"Gemma's missing."

"No, she's not," DeVaughn responded instinctively and matter-of-factly.

Sir Wallace's expression went from one of worry to suspicion. "What did you say?"

DeVaughn didn't know how to explain what he had just said. All he knew was that he *knew* that Gemma was in the house.

He attempted to double back. "I meant… I *figured* she'd still be here. I've never been to any of her parties. We're not good friends. I just thought… she'd still be here."

Sir Wallace's right eyebrow had raised itself so high, it was nearly on the back of his neck. "If you're not her friend, then what are you doing here?"

Before DeVaughn could answer, he found himself staring at the empty space behind Sir Wallace. Then, like a church bell ringing through a summer storm, he could hear a voice attempt to break through whatever wall it was trapped behind.

It was weak but he could barely make out the word, "… *see…* "

Sir Wallace didn't like being ignored. "Mister Darren?!"

DeVaughn snapped out of his trance. "Yes sir!"

"What are you doing here?"

"Oh, uh… there was a police cab outside, and my aunt works here… so I was worried." DeVaughn knew that he had to leave before he said anything else. "I'm sorry. I should go."

"Yes… perhaps you should." Sir Wallace said in an accusatory tone.

DeVaughn ran out the door and back home as quickly as he could while trying to look as nonchalant as possible to anybody who may be watching. As soon as he walked through the door, he tried sorting out what had just happened.

'Why did I walk all the way to Gemma's house? What brought me inside? What did I hear? Some disembodied voice? And why does this all feel so familiar to me? Like this has all happened before?'

Without a chance to truly dissect the confounding events of the day, a twirl of squad car lights started blaring through the window. They were soon accompanied by a loud banging on the door. He answered it to find a tall, thin, wiry man dressed in a business suit. He shoved his inspector's badge in DeVaughn's face, close enough to give him a shave.

"DeVaughn Heath? Would you mind coming down to the station with us? We'd like you to answer some questions."

Two more squad cars appeared behind him.

DeVaughn took a deep breath. "Okay."

5

20 JUN 18.

20:30.

THE WALLACE ESTATE, Seaview, IOW.

Gemma was speechless. DeVaughn, a boy she had never spoken to despite their intertwined lives, was making eye contact with her. She didn't know for sure, but she wanted to believe that he was looking at her. The intent in his eyes, and the focus, as if trying to make out a boat in the distance made her feel like he was trying to find her.

Taking a leap of faith, she spoke to him. "Hello?"

He didn't respond but his eyes tightened in on her.

"Can you see me?" She asked.

He looked as though he was about to say yes when their connection was broken by an irrationally angry Sir Wallace.

"Mister Darren?!"

DeVaughn turned his head away from Gemma. "Yes sir!"

"Oh god, please don't go. Just ignore him and focus on me. Focus on my voice."

"What are you doing here?" Sir Wallace demanded.

"Papa now is not the time to be an ass." She couldn't help but chastise her grandfather, even though she knew he couldn't hear her.

"Oh, uh… there was a police cab outside, and my aunt works here… so I was worried. I'm sorry. I should go."

"Yes… perhaps you should."

"No! No, you shouldn't. Please. Please don't leave me."

But her ghostly protests went unheard and, quick as a flash, he ran out the door.

Gemma was heartbroken. "Papa… I wish I could tell you how terrible I think you are being right now. You have no idea what you've just done to me…"

Then, Sir Wallace began shouting, "Inspector! Police!"

The sound of the stampede of footsteps coming up the stairs was deafening. All the cops attending to the surveillance issue in the basement arrived in a split second and lined up like privates waiting for orders from their military commander.

"What's wrong, sir?" The inspector asked.

"A young man was just here. I believe he may know something concerning the whereabouts of my granddaughter."

"Who, sir?"

He pointed at Vanessa, "Her cousin."

Vanessa looked stunned. "You mean my nephew? DeVaughn?"

"Yes, him. They live in the cottage down the road. Sixteen River Nook Lane."

Gemma rolled her eyes. "Oh, but you have their address perfectly memorized… Oh who am I to judge, I didn't even know he existed until twenty minutes ago."

"Wait!" Vanessa protested. "DeVaughn barely knows Gemma. They're not even in the same classes. I doubt they've ever talked to each other."

"You're only saying that because he's your nephew. But you didn't see him. He was acting..."

"What? How was he acting?" She asked, before remembering her place. "Sir..."

"He was behaving *suspiciously*..."

"Oh my god, Papa," Gemma said, rubbing her temples. "You are such an idiot."

"Inspector, I demand that you bring him in for questioning, immediately."

Without wasting a single moment, the inspector nodded, and he and the entirety of his squad marched out of the door.

Gemma's heart began racing, and her mind shortly followed.

'Oh god, what's going to happen? I don't know. I have no clue what's going on. All I do know is that I need to get to DeVaughn. He may be my only hope. He can save me. But he can't save me if... Oh god...'

She started to run, heading straight for the wall. For a moment, she was blind as the brick and wood making up the foundation of her home passed through her eyes. The experience was jarring but still, she pushed through until she reached the outside.

Refusing to lose time ruminating on her phantasmic abilities, she ran as fast as she could down the hill towards DeVaughn and Vanessa's cottage. She arrived just as they were escorting him out of his home.

"FUCK!" She swore to herself. "Well, this is just *bloody perfect*."

Taking a closer look at DeVaughn as they pulled him away, she saw a great bruise circling his now purple and red eye.

She gasped. "Did *they* do that to him? Oh my god! What the *absolute fuck*?!"

He was forcefully shoved into the back of the squad car. From the window, DeVaughn looked in her direction, once making direct eye contact with her.

His beaten face pulled every ounce of guilt out of Gemma. "Oh, DeVaughn... I'm so sorry."

DeVaughn's cuffed hand pressed against the window as they drove away.

Soon after, she watched as her grandfather's car quickly drove down the way. Tail-gating the police, she saw Vanessa in the driver's seat and her grandfather sitting in the back.

Gemma had become exhausted by her grandfather's behavior. "Having her nephew arrested, and *assaulted*, then making her drive you to watch his interrogation? Seriously, Papa?"

Gemma ran after them at full speed. Through her intense focus, she was able to take notice of her sudden stamina. Running the many miles it took to get to the police station felt like nothing to her. She didn't sweat, she didn't pant, and she felt more energized with each step.

"Perhaps I am dead..." she thought to herself.

Shaking those thoughts out of her head, she turned her attention back to reaching DeVaughn. Since physical matter no longer proved an obstruction to her, she was able to take the most effective shortcut to the police station: walking straight through everything between herself and her destination.

Upon arrival, she passed by or went through, any cop in her way as she escorted herself inside. Across the room, she saw a pair of detectives standing watch outside a door that said, "Investigations." Thinking that was the most likely place that DeVaughn was being held, she began to make her way.

She passed by two detectives discussing the latest news report on the television. "Are you kiddin' me? *Another* school shooting in America?"

"This is ridiculous."

"Right?! I mean, Jesus Christ mate… how many of their kids are gonna die before they get their shit together?"

She phased through the door marked "investigations" and found a hallway. The first door on the right said, "Interview in Progress" and she knew that DeVaughn was inside.

Walking in, her intuition was proven right as she saw DeVaughn Heath. However, all of her relief was immediately replaced with grief and guilt as she saw that he was handcuffed to the table and the floor, trapping him in a hard metal chair.

"Do you know where Gemma is, DeVaughn?" The inspector coldly asked.

As soon as she walked into the room, DeVaughn's attention turned away from the inspector as his eyes fixated on her. It was just like when he was talking to her grandfather. As their eyes met, Gemma's heart began to race.

She knew DeVaughn was in serious trouble. Though she was aware that the police had no evidence against him outside of her grandfather's paranoia that didn't stop them from smashing his face in. She needed him to help her, but she also needed to help him.

"I can get you out of here," Gemma said.

"DeVaughn?!" The detective yelled into his face.

"What?! Sorry... What was the question?"

"Where's Gemma, DeVaughn?!"

DeVaughn didn't answer, he just looked at Gemma again. This time more intensely. Following his quiet lead, Gemma moved closer. As if reacting to her nearness, he reached his hand out across the table towards her.

"Can you see me, DeVaughn?"

"I think so..." He softly responded, igniting a bright light of hope in Gemma's heart.

"You think what, boy?!"

"Uh... nothing sorry! Sorry. I- I'm sorry. I-"

"If you're just going to fuck with me then I can't help you."

DeVaughn looked up at Gemma. She smiled down back at him.

"I don't need you to help me," DeVaughn said to the inspector with great confidence. "And I don't need to help you."

"Boy, you do need help. I have a mountain of evidence that points a very damning finger at you. Your aunt's the maid! You've been inside the house before! You probably know where everything is, including the security room! You could've snuck in during the party, had your way with the girl, stashed her, and still have time to delete the footage! I could lock you up right now if I wanted. Now answer the question: Do you know where Gemma Wallace is?!"

DeVaughn stared up at her again.

"Yes. I do."

Gemma grabbed his hand and felt a surge go through her body.

"She's right here," DeVaughn said with a smirk.

Gemma screamed in joy as she could feel DeVaughn's hand in hers. She looked at the two-way mirror and could see herself, plain as day. She looked at the inspector, his jaw dropped at her sudden appearance.

"I'm right here! I'm right here!" She began to cry. Dropping to her knees she embraced the still shackled DeVaughn. "Thank you."

"No problem," He said with a smile.

"What the fuck?!" The inspector screamed in horror.

08 DEC 17.

11:45.

SEAVIEW SECONDARY SCHOOL, Seaview, IOW.

"God, you're so fucking hot," She said through hot breaths as they made out in the darkness. "Where did you get all these muscles?"

"Hard work," DeVaughn said, with a confident grin.

She giggled. He hoped that she was laughing *with* him and not *at* him.

DeVaughn slipped his hand up under the back of her shirt and massaged her soft, warm skin, causing her to let out a precious moan. This excited him beyond words. He had never skipped out on lunch period to make out with a classmate in a supply closet and of all the people he could be with it was Charli Rudner, one of the most beautiful girls at Seaview Secondary.

Her hands roamed around his entire body, gripping his butt, massaging his back, caressing his arms. Then, she reached up to his head and started groping and stroking his afro. Petting it, like he was a dog. For DeVaughn, the mood of the room shifted entirely, and he instantly became uncomfortable.

"Umm, what are you doing?"

"What?" She asked as she continued her hair treatment, now combing through it as if checking for lice.

"That - that thing you're doing with my hair."

"You don't like it?"

"I mean, I might, if I knew why you were doing it."

She immediately stopped kissing him and gave him an annoyed look before sighing. She turned the light back on and grabbed her stuff.

"I'm out."

"What, why?"

She looked at him, disappointingly. "I mean I just can't believe you. This is completely fucked up. I was just trying to have a nice time and then you had to go and spoil it by turning this into a *race thing*."

"I wasn't trying to make this a race thing! Is it a race thing for *you*?"

She just stared at him again. DeVaughn could tell that she was trying to find the words to help her flip the conversation in her favor.

"Unbelievable," was all he said as he walked out of the small closet.

"Oh yeah?! Well... fuck you, you tosser! You just made a big mistake! Huge!"

'*Jesus Christ,*' he thought to himself as he heard the bell ring. '*I* fucking *hate this place.*'

On the other side of town.

Dean had taken his father's blazing red sports car, which was worth more money than Dean's education, for a joyride. Jim and Dina were making out in the back while Gemma was vaping THC in the passenger seat.

Despite all that was going on, Gemma found herself in the deep trenches of boredom. The thrill of truancy and casual illegal activity had lost its edge for her. To try and inject some excitement into her day, she pulled out a bump of coke from a small container in her purse and huffed it up her nose.

Although Gemma was fully aware of how lucky, how privileged, she was, she felt this aching in her stomach. A void of pure emptiness, nagging at her, was telling her that she would never be satisfied and that nothing would ever make her truly happy.

Then, the coke kicked in and the void was filled once more. Life was wonderful. Being bored was fun again.

Dean sped down the roadway, nearly sliding off the edge of the road with every turn. A cop started driving behind them, full lights and sirens, signaling for them to pull over.

"Oh look," Dean said, "I think this little piggy wants to play tag."

"Just pull over, Dean," Gemma said with a sniff. "I'll take care of it."

They parked on the side of the road with the cop coming in just behind them. He slowly got out of his car and walked up to the driver's side window. He wanted to produce an air of intimidation. Unfortunately for him, these teens were rarely intimidated by anything.

"Shouldn't you lot be in school?" He said in a deep, commanding voice.

"Shouldn't you be in a donut shop?" Dina retorted.

Her friends laughed like hyenas, the sole exception being Gemma who couldn't be bothered.

"Do you even know why I pulled you over?"

"The mud in the pigpen dried up?!" Jim confidently yelled out.

The cop huffed and said, "You were going eighty in a forty, you little prick."

"Ooooh," Dean and Jim said in an entertained unison.

"License and registration. Now."

"Gemma?" Dean asked.

"Yeah, I got it," She said as she leaned over Dean, poking her head out of the driver's side window, nearly headbutting the cop in the gut. "Do you know who I am?"

"You're, sure as hell, not the driver, that's for damn sure."

"My name is Gemma Wallace. As in *Sir Wallace*."

"Pardon?"

"Awww, he don't know!" Jim said, giddily.

"He must be new in town," Dean said.

"What the fuck are you lot goin' on about?"

Gemma continued. "Why don't you call up your superior officer and tell them you just pulled over Gemma Wallace?"

Skeptical, the man looked at her sideways before heading back to his car. He was out of earshot, but the spoiled quartet could see his stunned face through their rear window. He looked over at them with gruff annoyance before jumping back into his car and driving off quickly, for his job's sake.

"Fuckin' pigs," Dean said as he started the car back up.

"Yeah, we showed him, didn't we, Gem?" Jim asked.

"Yeah, we did," Gemma said with an electric grin, bouncing around uncontrollably in her seat.

20 JUN 18.

20:45.

SEAVIEW POLICE DEPARTMENT, Seaview, IOW.

"What the fuck?!" Was all the inspector could muster as he fell back onto the floor.

Gemma Wallace, a girl who had mysteriously disappeared, mysteriously re-appeared before DeVaughn's very eyes and was hugging him like the savior she saw him to be. As she did, something just as mysterious overtook his mind. A great level of knowledge revealed itself in his mind.

He pulled her off of him and took her in. "Gemma..." Her face was full of joy and his mind was full of thoughts. "You can create a phase-shift portal that enables you to enter a pocket dimension directly parallel to our own, in the process becoming completely imperceptible to everybody in this dimension - invisible, intangible, soundless and scentless."

Her joyful face was replaced with one of astonishment. "*That's* what happened to me? God... how do you know that?"

"I just do," Was the only way he knew how to explain it. "It's like a sixth sense."

"You see dead people?"

"You're not dead, Gemma."

Confused but happy, she hugged him again. She didn't know what else to do. She was finally able to touch another person after what felt like a century of isolation. She was so grateful to DeVaughn, to whom she felt she owed her life.

"Thank you so much, DeVaughn. But how did you bring me back?"

A new knowledge was delivered to his brain. "I'm a geno-mapper. I can instinctively sense the presence of a special genetic mutation that grants superhuman abilities to very specific people, enabling me to understand how their powers work as well as turn them off should the need arise. Additionally, my mind naturally categorizes these abilities so I can easily explain them."

"Wow..." Gemma said, confused but still hugging DeVaughn as tightly as she could.

Their embrace was brought to an abrupt end when they heard a gun cocking. The inspector was back on his feet, shaking with fear as he pointed his pistol at the two.

"Put your hands up! Both of you! I don't know what the fuck is going on but-"

Suddenly, the door violently flew across the room. An armed Vanessa Heath quickly stormed inside and shot the shuddering inspector through the skull.

"Holy shit!" DeVaughn screamed.

A man wearing a police officer's uniform entered closely behind and pointed a taser at Gemma. She screamed just as he fired on her, shocking her into unconsciousness. Meanwhile, Vanessa holstered her gun and went to work uncuffing DeVaughn.

"Oh my god! What are you doing?!"

"Shhh, DeVaughn, shhh..."

He started to fall into a state of pure shock. Vanessa pulled him up by his shoulders and started to rub them, hoping to get him to come down from his high anxiety.

"What did you do?!"

"Calm down. I'm not going to hurt you."

"Not hurt me?! You killed a man! Gemma's been tased! Why are you doing this?!"

"I won't sugarcoat this, baby… It's not gonna be great… But time's up. I thought it wouldn't happen this soon, I thought we had more time but… well…"

His shouts became whispers as his anxiety consumed his voice. *"Please.* I'm so scared."

She sighed and pulled him into a tight hug. *"But he couldn't run, couldn't hide, he could only wait."*

DeVaughn fell into her arms. She picked him up as her cohort grabbed Gemma.

"Make sure to grab the old man too before you torch the place."

"Yes ma'am."

She looked down at her unconscious nephew. "Life's not fair."

(Epilogue)

21 AUG 18.

09:45.

THE WALLACE ESTATE, Seaview, IOW.

A gas leak and a wayward cigarette left Sir Wallace the sole survivor of a terrible explosion. The police station was completely destroyed, taking everyone else inside, including DeVaughn and Vanessa, along with it. He only managed to escape with a few burns because he had been waiting in the entrance lounge, a safe distance from the center of the blast.

The out-patient psychiatrist wanted to give him an evaluation to determine whether he was mentally fit enough to return home. Not wanting to spend any more time in the hospital, however, Sir Wallace threw as much money at them until they let him leave when he felt like it.

It had been months since Gemma had disappeared. He knew that the longer she was missing, the more likely it was that she would never come home. However, he also knew that his family's greatest gift was their stubbornness, and so he held out stubborn hope that his granddaughter was somewhere out in the world stubbornly trying to get home.

He was sitting in his den, alone, during his nurse's afternoon teatime. He heard footsteps in the hallway.

"Nurse Adley, I'm afraid my tea has run cold. Could you-"

He was interrupted by someone he was told died in the fire. "Nurse Adley had to go home for the day, so I'll be filling in."

"Vanessa?!"

He looked over and saw her ghost standing in the doorway. "Hello, sir. I'm sorry we couldn't meet under better circumstances, but I have to inform you that some urgent business has called me back to the States. So, I'm going to have to put in my two weeks… two weeks ago."

"I must be going out of my mind. This can't be happening. You can't be real. You're dead."

"No, I'm not."

"And how do you expect me to believe that? I'm on so many drugs, painkillers, sleep aids, coffee, you could-"

She lifted the nearby wardrobe and threw it clear across the room with such precision that it barely grazed the top of Sir Wallace's bald head. He could feel the massive gust of wind blow past him. He flinched in his chair so quickly that he nearly ripped whatever the hospital stitched back together.

Scared and shaking, he asked, "What are you?"

"There's no real point in explaining that to you. I don't think your brain's big enough to handle that kind of information."

"How dare you!"

"Bite me, Francis. Just know that at any point in time I could *demolish* you. So, from now on, you live only because of my incredible pity for you."

He sat up in his chair, attempting to appear as if he had regained his long-dead composure. "Alright. I'm sorry. I believe you. Please, just - why are you here?"

Vanessa groaned as she felt a pain rise in her chest. "I can't - tell you that."

A thought sprang into Sir Wallace's mind. "It's something about Gemma, isn't it? If you're alive then Gemma - You know where she is? Please, you have to tell me."

She pulled out a pill and popped it into her mouth, dry swallowing it. "That's not going to happen."

"Please... Miss Heath - Vanessa... if you know where she is, I beg you. Please bring her back to me. I don't think I have much time left."

"Francis, I'm not here to tell you where Gemma is, or to take you to her."

"Then, what-"

Vanessa quickly closed in on the elderly gentleman and slapped him straight across the face with enough force to knock him out. Her earpiece communicator began to beep, informing her of an incoming call.

"Yes?" She answered.

A cold voice responded. "Sir Wallace?"

"Moving him now."

"The jet will be prepped and ready for takeoff when you arrive."

"Roger that."

She wrapped Sir Wallace in a blanket before placing him in an adult-sized suitcase which she was able to lift without so much as a grunt of strain. Grabbing the last remaining set of keys for the manor, the Wallace Estate was darkened and closed for the first time in years.

20 AUG 18.

07:57.

VISTA VIEW LOFTS - #12A, Boston, MA

Beating the clock had always been a game for her, as every day she would make sure to get up several minutes before it went off. Instead of getting out of bed, though, she decided to lie there and listen to her alarm's high-pitched ringing for a few moments. She enjoyed the shrill sound. It took her back to her army days where being shaken awake by the blaring sound of sirens was the norm.

She missed the symmetry and uniformity of her army days, a nostalgia reflected in how she lived her life. She holistically kept her body as sharp and geometrically succinct as possible. She could be split down the middle and each side would be perfectly identical, from the pedicure on her toes to her golden blonde hair, cut into a perfect, sheer style that fell gracefully to her shoulders without a single strand out of place.

Turning her alarm off, she pulled herself out of bed and began her morning routine. She brushed her teeth and took a shower, timing it perfectly with the coffee maker in the kitchen.

While shampooing, she realized that it had been two weeks since her last hair appointment. She would need to visit the stylist soon or else her hair would grow a centimeter or so too long, which would drive her up the wall.

Leaving the bathroom in her robe, she turned on the television in her living room and began working on breakfast as the news played in the background.

"Good morning, Boston, I'm Katie Walters for your BNN News Update at Eight. This just in from Seattle: in the classic story of tragic teen love, gay teen lovers William Howard, age seventeen, and Caio Medeiros, age sixteen, have been reported missing after not returning home from a date out on the town. We now go to Jenny in Seattle for more details. Jenny?"

"Thank you, Katie. I'm standing outside the West Seattle home of Cassandra and Daniel Howard who, just two days ago, reported their son William missing after he didn't return home from a day out with his boyfriend, Caio Medeiros, who has also been reported missing by his parents, Alfonso and Nia Medeiros. The police later discovered William's car parked in the SeaTac International Airport Parking lot. Police believe this to be just another case of teen runaways but William's mother believes otherwise."

The mother's voice was full of grief, confusion, and fear. "My son has never done anything like this before. He's a good boy. He doesn't do drugs. He gets good grades. I know he wouldn't run away."

"Caio's parents, Nia and Alfonso, were not available for questioning, but we did manage to get an interview with their neighbor, Rita Fu."

An elderly woman began speaking. "Cai is a lovely boy. Always helps me up the stairs when he can. But he's always getting into fights at school about one thing or another. So sad. I hope his family finds him soon."

The reporter's voice returned. "The search for William is made all the more urgent as he had just been released from the hospital a few weeks prior, having been admitted after falling into a month-long coma after suffering a devastating seizure."

Her interest had suddenly been piqued by the peculiar turn in the story.

William's mother returned, sounding more depressed and desperate than before. "Please, if you have any information about where my son could be, please call us. And Billy, Cai, if you're seeing this, we love you and we want you to come home."

Jenny returned. "Local authorities encourage anyone who thinks they may have seen Billy Howard and-or Caio Medeiros to please call Detective Anna Holiday at Seattle Missing Persons Unit at the number listed below. Back to you Katie."

"Thanks, Jenny, let's hope they get home safe and sound. We'll return with more news in just a minute. After the break, is your dog reading your mind? More on this after these important messages."

A thought came to her mind as she called her computer's virtual assistant. "Aviva?"

"Yes ma'am?"

She scraped butter onto her toast. "Pull up a search for me, please."

"Yes ma'am. What shall I search for?"

She sat down at her dining room table. "Search *'missing American teenagers,'* sub-search: believed dead - murdered."

"Searching... done. Over one million search results."

"Narrow the search down to within the past three months."

"Searching within specified parameters... done. Twenty-two results."

"Give me a list of the most recent five."

"William Howard, Seattle, Washington. Caio Medeiros, Seattle, Washington. Nahid Nassiri, El Paso, Texas. John Hoffman, New York, New York. Harry Zane, Mill Creek, Montana."

"Aviva, can you expand the search to worldwide? All missing and, or dead children between the ages of thirteen and eighteen from the past three months. And cross-reference the results with mentions of the following keywords: Sokol Manufacturing, MajorTECH, Armitedge, and ERIS Music."

"Narrowing... done. Seven results remaining. Shall I list them out for you?

"Please."

"William Howard. Seattle, Washington. Mother, Cassandra Howard, and father, Daniel Howard, both employed through MajorTECH. Caio Medeiros. Seattle, Washington. Boyfriend to William Howard.

Nahid Nassiri. El Paso, Texas. Mother, Fairuza, now deceased, and father, Ebrahim, both formerly employed through MajorTECH.

Gemma Wallace. Seaview, England. Mother, Adrianna, now deceased, formerly employed through Eris Music. Missing, presumed dead, or kidnapped.

Ming Sanchez-Luckin. New York, New York. Father, Tyler Luckin, co-founder of social media app TimeLock, now owned by MajorTECH.

John Hoffman. New York, New York. Mother, Alyssa Hoffman, employee of Eris Music Company.

Mikhail Markov. Moscow, Russia. Father, Piotr Markov, now deceased. Former CEO of Sokol Industries."

She laughed to herself. "Aviva, I need you to look up the soonest available flights to Seattle."

"Searching..."

As she waited, she thought, *'Oh Frost... You finally caught them all, didn't you? What wonderful news... I've been waiting years for a proper family reunion.'*

She heard a ding as coffee poured out of the machine and into her mug. Reaching out with her mind, she grabbed hold of the mug, lifting and floating it gently towards her without spilling a drop.

Aviva's voice returned. "There are three seats available on a flight from Logan International Airport to SeaTac International Airport on the twenty-fourth of August at twelve-hundred hours. Shall I book one for you?"

"Are any of them first class?"

"No, ma'am."

"Then no thank you."

She sipped her coffee and smiled.

MING SANCHEZ-LUCKIN

BIRTH-DATE: 22 OCT 03.

SEX: Female.

CURRENT HEIGHT: 4'11".

EYE COLOR: Green.   HAIR COLOR: Black.

INSTALLATION: New York City, New York, USA.

NATIONALITY: American (Chinese-Born).

ETHNICITY: Asian - Chinese.

FAMILY:

Oscar Sanchez (adopted father)

Tyler Luckin (adopted father)

1

19 JUN 18.

12:00.

NEW YORK ACADEMY OF ARTS AND SCIENCE, Brooklyn, NY.

To her, the world had lost all of its colors. It was lunchtime. She looked down at her plate, and closely examined her food. Where she was supposed to see a rainbow - the orange of the carrots, the green of the peas, the golden-brown of the turkey, and the white of the mashed potatoes - instead she saw a grey and dull pile on a bland orange tray.

Not only had the food lost its color, but it turned into tasteless mush in her mouth. Her fathers had spent thousands of dollars for her to go to such an expensive school with "specially prepared, high-quality school meals," but it all looked like it was worth less than the dirt it grew in.

She threw the contents of her tray into the compost bin and started walking to her next class.

She felt as if all the power to feel any kind of pleasurable sensation had been drained from her body. The music she used to enjoy turned into a senseless drone. Books had become unending ventures into tedium that she would give up on after the first few pages. The school was a ceaseless parade of monotony, decorated with bright fluorescent lights that did nothing but keep her from falling asleep, and filled to the brim with clowns.

"Hey Ming!" John, a clown she shared chemistry class with, called out to her as they crossed paths - an event that happened too many times in a day for Ming's comfort. "How's your day going?"

"Fine," she answered in her typical deadpan.

"That's great, you know I was wondering if maybe…"

Ming learned early in life the exquisite art of tuning people out when they started to bore her, and John was constantly boring her. Outside of his name and the fact that he was always trying to ask her out, Ming couldn't remember anything else about him whenever he left her sight. To her, he was just another boring white boy.

"That sounds great, John," She said, unaware that she had interrupted him. "No."

Before he had a chance to respond, she entered the nearby elevator, pressed the door close button, and went up to her next class.

Art history with Miss Sidwell.

The teacher talked at length about Michelangelo and Van Gogh, droning on and on about the two like they found the cure for cancer. She showed the students a copy of Van Gogh's The Starry Night, marveling and singing its praises, raving about its "Decadent use of color" and "Vivid imagination".

However, when Ming looked at the piece she didn't see "decadent color" or "vivid imagination." All she saw was an assortment of colors arranged on a canvas by a mentally ill artist.

Ming was scholastically advanced for her age. She had tested out of so many grades that she only had one school year left before graduating. She and her fathers were already touring universities, but this was difficult for her as she still had no idea what she wanted to major in. She toured at least a dozen colleges during spring break, met so many professors, and looked up so many possible careers she could succeed in, but all of them rang hollow in the void that had become her mind.

She had become numb to everything, be it portrait or person. She had been feeling this way for what felt like an eternity. She wanted to tell somebody, possibly her fathers or the school counselor, but she would always stop herself with the same thought:

'What's the point? What could anybody do that could make me feel better? I'm going to one of the best magnet schools in New York. My parents make enough money for me to be comfortable but not spoiled... at least I don't think I'm spoiled. I don't get sick. I don't get bad grades. I skate by relatively unbothered by everyone except John... ew. I'd bet a hundred dollars that if I told anybody how I was feeling, they'd give me a pat on the back and tell me I was just dealing with "typical teenage stuff." '

She felt as if she were living in another world, completely disconnected from everybody else, a ghost walking amongst the living. She could hear, she could touch, she could see, but she couldn't feel. This dissociation even extended to her loving fathers, her dad, Oscar, and her pop, Tyler.

The end of the school day had come, and Ming was walking out to meet Oscar, who walked her home from school every day. He worked from home, editing and contributing for an online newspaper, as well as writing the occasional book, so he was the most present in her life compared to Tyler.

Tyler was the co-founder of a social media app called "TimeLock". TimeLock allowed people to post short videos that they could share with every user and had algorithms designed to direct users to videos that they might like. Tyler wasn't as much of a tech genius as he was a very talented networker and socializer. A king of the "social" aspect of social media, his major contribution to TimeLock was organizing the customer service department and sucking money out of investor's wallets.

After years of butt-kissing and working hard to please others, Tyler felt confident enough to vie for a soon-to-be-vacant Senate seat. At first, it seemed shaky, since most of his opponents were centrist straight, white democrats all operating on the platform of "why change? Everything's fine!" which directly contrasted with Tyler's leftist platform - fighting for socialized healthcare, redirecting resources to delay climate change, and working to improve the lives of the working class.

While he had already gained a lot of attention as an upstart, everything changed after he won the Democratic primary.

Everyone knew he was on his way to a surefire victory in November since his only competition was a right-wing nutjob named Alfred Bullet - having legally changed his last name in college - running on a platform of outright white supremacy.

Ming often wondered if Tyler truly believed in what he preached or if he was just simply grandstanding. She tried to believe in the best of her fathers, but that faith had begun to waiver due to recent events.

She would find herself wandering into a dark headspace, where she questioned if she truly loved her fathers. She questioned whether the feeling of emptiness she felt whenever she entered her home was a symptom of the indifference she felt towards everything else in the world, or because of a greater problem that nobody in the Luckin-Sanchez family was willing to discuss?

Despite being forced to pretend to be the perfect daughter for the cameras in support of Tyler's ambitions, she still went on with the show. She smiled in every picture, answered every reporter's questions politely and succinctly, and worked hard to be a face value model daughter. She wanted to believe that this was a sign that she loved her parents at least on some level.

'Surely,' She thought, *'nobody would ever do this kind of crap for people they don't love... right?'*

As she walked towards her dad, she found her shadowy train of thought interrupted, once again, by the unwanted arrival of John.

"Hey Ming, how was school?" He said as if he had never asked her that same question a hundred times before.

"The same as it's always been."

"Oh... that's nice."

"Sure, it is…"

"Hey, I just wanted to ask if maybe-"

"I'm not interested, John."

"But-"

"I've told you no a thousand times. I don't understand why you can't just get that. I'm very tired of you constantly bothering me, and I'd like to think I've been very patient, but today I am just completely done. I am exhausted, and I'm one hundred percent not interested. And I never will be. So please go away!"

"But Ming-"

"Did I stutter?"

"I just don't understand. Why won't you just go out with me?"

"Get it through your thick head, John: I'm. Not. Interested."

In a split second, John's face had contorted into a mask of rage. His sudden, very visible anger sent a chill up Ming's spine and pulled her out of whatever trance she had been traveling in, forcing her to finally give him the attention he always wanted.

"BUT WHY?!" He screamed in her face.

She was so terrified; she didn't realize his hand was gripping her wrist so tight it felt like she was going to lose circulation. People were staring, but not intervening, which terrified her even more.

A voice that eased Ming's terror shouted from a short distance away. "HEY!" Oscar, with the timeliness of a knight in shining armor, had arrived to rescue his daughter. He got in between them and ripped John's hand from her wrist. "Get your hands off of her, you little punk."

John's devil stare never stopped glaring at Ming. Oscar stepped into his line of sight, his figure expanding like a pufferfish to intimidate the aggressive young man. Forty-year-old Oscar was a Hispanic man of fair height, standing at a solid six foot two. His stomach had become slightly paunchy from years of being too preoccupied with everything else in his life to care about working out. He kept a trim beard, because he liked how masculine it made him look but if it ever grew longer than a couple centimeters his greys would appear. Meanwhile, his thick, black hair was perfectly free of the signs of aging.

"Walk away, or I'm calling the police."

John's face quickly turned back to normal, his rage contracting like the hood and fangs of a cobra.

"I apologize."

"Don't apologize. Leave."

John quickly walked away as Oscar led Ming towards the subway.

"Are you okay, sweetie?"

"I'm fine, Dad."

"Has that guy been bothering you?"

"I don't want to talk about it. Let's just go home."

But Oscar wouldn't relent. "What's his name, Ming?"

"Dad, no."

"What?"

"I don't want to give you his name because I don't want this to be a thing."

"It became a thing the minute he put his hands on you."

"I don't care."

"That cannot be true. And even if it were, it doesn't matter because I care. I don't like the idea of my daughter going to school with an imbalanced-"

"Just drop it, okay! I have barely a year left of school before I go to college. I do not want to make any waves."

"Honey, please."

"I said no, and I need you to respect that."

He gave her a look of incredible concern and confusion. "Fine."

They spent the rest of the ride home in silence.

That evening.

"Hello, my beautiful family!" Tyler announced as he arrived late for dinner, as usual, from a full day of political peacocking.

Unlike Oscar, the thirty-six-year-old Tyler maintained a trim, fit physique. He consistently dyed his muddy brown hair a sweet, strawberry blonde, and his fair skin tone gave off an almost glowing effect. He was barely an inch taller than his husband but would sometimes jokingly call Oscar "Shorty."

"Heidi ho! Anybody home?!" Darcy Winchester, Tyler's personal assistant, yelled out as he closely followed his boss inside.

Ming hated Darcy. Talking to him always felt like listening to a serial killer trying to sell you medicine. He was smooth, arrogant, always dressed in a slim fit suit with a matching tie, constantly invited himself over for dinner at the last minute, and he always looked like he was scanning her as if he were trying to peer into her soul. He managed to get her to hate him within the minute they first met.

Tyler and Darcy made their way to the dining room, where Ming and Oscar were waiting to start dinner.

"Mmm, what's that delicious smell?" Darcy said as he sat himself down next to Ming, who inched her chair away from him, not caring if he noticed.

Oscar looked at Darcy incredulously. "Are we really doing this again?" He whispered to his husband.

"Yes, so please just be nice," Tyler pleaded, too tired to deal with his family's hatred for his assistant.

Oscar relented, putting on a show for Tyler's sake. "I'm glad you asked, Darcy," He said with the fakest smile in the history of fake smiles. "Tonight, it's seafood risotto with steamed vegetables and garlic bread."

"Mmm, yummy!" Darcy turned his attention to Ming, his eyes once again trying to drill themselves into her brain. "So, did anything fun happen at school today, kiddo?"

"Kiddo?" She responded dully.

"What? You don't like that?"

"No. I don't."

"Well, what would you like me to call you then?"

"Ming would suffice."

"But that's just your name."

"Exactly."

"I'm just trying to make you smile, girl. You need to smile more."

Ming's eyes widened as she imagined Darcy's head exploding. Seeing this, Oscar shot Tyler a look, cueing him to change the subject towards anything else.

"So! You guys will not believe the people I shook hands with today. First, the mayor because, duh why wouldn't he be-"

Ming phased out of the conversation and began forking down her food as quickly as possible in order to escape Darcy's less than welcome presence.

"Ming, slow down," A worried Oscar said. "It's not going any-"

Before he had a chance to finish his sentence, she'd licked her plate dishwasher-clean. "I'm done."

"Already?"

"May I be excused?"

Oscar sighed. He didn't want to be left alone at the table with his husband, Darcy, and their boring conversation, but he also didn't want to torture his daughter by keeping her at the table.

"Go on, get outta here."

She got up and sprinted to her room as fast as she could. Once there she finished what little homework she had and started flipping through the thousands of television channels she had at her disposal. However, once again, she found herself drowning in a pit of boredom and listlessness.

Downstairs, she heard the front door slam signaling Darcy's departure. Barely a split second after he left, she could hear the muffled sounds of her fathers' arguing. This had become a nightly routine at this point in their lives.

She wondered about which subject they were loudly discussing. Maybe it was about John. Maybe it was about Darcy. Maybe Oscar repeated his "I don't like what this campaign is doing to you!" speech. Maybe Tyler repeated his "You always told me you'd support me in everything I did!" retort. Or maybe it was about her.

She remembered the one time that she listened in on the two of them.

"You don't even try to be a part of her life!"

"I try! I honestly do!"

"Oh please."

"I do!"

"I don't see you at the parent-teacher conferences. You're barely here most days! We're lucky if you even spend dinner with us, and when you do you bring that bejeweled jerkwad along with you!"

"I try to make a connection with her, okay? But she never-
"

"What, Tyler? What does she never do?"

"She just doesn't seem to be there. When I talk to her it's like talking to a robot."

"That's our daughter, Tyler!"

"I know that. And I love her but sometimes- I mean, haven't you noticed it? She's so… disengaged."

"She's fine."

"If you say so. It's like you said, you spend more time with her than I do."

Afterward, she actively avoided listening in.

The shouting started to get louder. For a moment she found herself preferring to be around John or Darcy, people that she hated, over being lost on her fathers' endless battleground, which made her feel trapped and numb.

She knew it was unhealthy to chase negative emotions. She knew she should be trying to fix whatever was keeping her from feeling anything but hate and despondency, but she just didn't want to. She was too emotionally exhausted to address her obvious emotional problems, a dark paradox to be trapped in.

Her phone started buzzing on the nearby bedside table like it was on fire. She had received several texts from the same blocked number.

'That's weird,' She thought to herself as she opened her phone, wondering why the app that kept blocked numbers from contacting her had decided to stop working.

BLOCKED: Sorry for the way I acted today.

'Oh, for the love of god...' She thought.

BLOCKED: I didn't mean to blow up like that.

BLOCKED: I shouldn't have touched you like that either.

BLOCKED: That was wrong...

BLOCKED: Are you okay?

BLOCKED: I'm sorry.

BLOCKED: You just drive me crazy sometimes.

BLOCKED: But that's no excuse.

BLOCKED: I'm so sorry.

Ming couldn't figure out how John had gotten a hold of her phone number. She had worked very hard to keep it out of anybody's hands, save for her fathers' and her grandparents'.

Ming: How did you get this number?

BLOCKED: Are you okay?

Ming: Seriously John. How did you get my phone number? Only four people have this number, and none of them are supposed to be you.

BLOCKED: If you meet me tonight, I'll tell you.

BLOCKED: Trust me.

Ming couldn't lie to herself; she was intrigued. She knew that she was chasing danger and fear as a remedy for her emotional vacancy. She also knew that, despite the temptation, it was a very bad idea.

She reactivated her blocked number blocking app before pushing herself to try and go to sleep early. She had to take melatonin and some allergy medication to calm down enough to close her eyes. The last thing she wanted was nightmares of John bouncing around her head.

Ming could always count on her dreams to be twice as vibrant and colorful as her day-to-day life. She would get lost in green meadows, mountains coated in purple majesty, and beautiful blue-green oceans untainted by the pollution of humanity's excesses.

She often wished that she could stay dreaming forever.

That night, however, a terrifying change occurred.

The flowers surrounding her began to turn a blood red as they melted away. The rainbow hues of her mindscape were made grey by the decay of all that she saw. In the blink of an eye, her world became a black hole that swallowed her mind, body, and soul.

She found herself trapped in a gray room with a two-way mirror. A man was laid before her on a slab. He was on the cusp of death, having been stabbed repeatedly. The wounds were clean and small, as though they had been made to make the march towards the grave as slow and painful as possible.

The image of his writhing body began to burn itself into her brain. She couldn't remove the painful nightmare from her vision. She closed her eyes, and it was still all she could see.

"Put your hands on the wounds," a cold man's voice echoed into the room.

She did as she was told, putting her hands on the open cuts, closing her eyes, and wishing that they would disappear. In that instant, she felt a physical connection with the dying man. Energy flowed between the two of them with her hands acting as a bridge. She could feel his slow heartbeat speed up to match hers. She opened her eyes, and his wounds were gone. She had wished them away, and away they went.

"It's time to wake up, Ming."

She woke up at three in the morning in a cold sweat.

"It was just a dream," she reassured herself as she tried to shake the gory images from her mindscape.

She jumped as she heard a knock at the door.

"Ming?" Oscar's voice rang through from the other side. "Are you okay, honey? I heard some weird noises."

"Yeah, sorry, I was just having a bad dream. I didn't mean to wake you."

"It's okay, sweetie. Do you need anything? I can get you a glass of water if you want."

"No, it's fine. I'll be okay."

"Okay, good night."

Just as she was about to go back to sleep, her phone chimed. It was yet another text from yet another blocked number:

BLOCKED: You need me as much as I need you.
BLOCKED: Don't ignore me.

2

20 JUN 18.

07:15.

SANCHEZ-LUCKIN HOUSEHOLD, Brooklyn, NY.

Ming didn't sleep at all for the rest of the night. She was afraid her nightmare would revisit her, or that she would receive more texts of terror from John. However, despite her lack of sleep, she felt more energized than ever, like she could light up all of Broadway.

Walking down into the kitchen, she saw Oscar sitting at the table. Not wanting to add more stress to his life, she decided to try and mask her exhaustion and dread.

"Good morning dad."

"Morning. How was the rest of your night?"

"Fine."

"Slept well?"

"Yup."

"Ming?"

"Yeah?"

"Do you know what time it is?"

"Yeah, it's-" Ming pulled out her phone only to realize she'd turned it off to block out John's messages. This meant that she had also turned off her alarm. "Oh my gosh, dad, we're going to miss the train! Why didn't you wake me up?"

"Honestly? Because I don't feel safe about you going to school today."

Like Ming, Oscar also had trouble sleeping. He was too busy worrying about his daughter and, even more so, her lack of interest in her own well-being.

Ming could sense this. "Is this about what happened yesterday?"

"Of course, it's about what happened yesterday! Why are you ignoring this?"

"Dad, it's fine. He's a blip, and I can handle myself."

Oscar shook his head. "I have all the faith in you. But I think we should speak to a-."

Ming changed the subject. "Dad, I'm going to be late."

"Fine, but I'm driving you."

Ming gave her father a stare filled with disbelief. "Dad…"

"What?"

"Nobody drives in New York except people who get paid to drive in New York."

"Well then the meter starts now, cuz I'm driving you to school. And I am definitely going to be talking to the principal when I get there. I don't care what you're about to say. I am reporting that little turd and grab something to eat on the way."

Ming swiped a banana from the fruit tray on the way to the garage.

As they drove, she noticed Oscar anxiously looking at his phone, perched on the dashboard's holster. She knew he was hoping for a text from Tyler after the previous night's fight. After a long time of ignoring it with all her might, Ming decided to transform her electrified brain into an electrified spine. She knew it was time to talk to Oscar about something that the entire family had been avoiding for months.

"Dad?"

"If you're going to try and convince me not to talk to your principal, the answer is 'girl, bye.'"

"No, it's not that... You and pop... you're not doing okay."

Oscar paused at his daughter's blunt statement. "Ming... I don't want to talk about this with you right now."

"I know but I think we have to."

"Ming, this subject is - it's all very complicated."

"I know it's complicated. But I also know that we need to talk about this."

"Ming, stop. What's that boy's name?" He tried to distract her.

She wasn't easily distracted. "Why don't you think that I can handle this?"

"Because *I* can barely handle it. Ok? Because it's all very confusing for me."

"Why is it so confusing?"

"Because - Because I love your father. And he loves me. But... Marriage is... it's..."

"Dad, please. Just talk to me."

"It's hard, okay?! It's hard. It's ridiculous. It's incredibly difficult. It's two completely different but also similar people trying to be themselves **and** the people they *need to be* to make the person they're married to happy because that's what you agreed to do when you exchanged the vows that bound your souls together forever. You start off in love and then life happens and suddenly you're not spending as much time together and then when you are spending time together, you're fighting. And when you're fighting you completely forget why you married this person. This person that you used to find so fascinating and kind and full of life and hope. And then you look at yourself in the mirror and realize that you don't know why he married *you* anymore. You see an old, angry, exhausted person who tries so hard to... I don't know..."

"What don't you know, dad?" Ming said, suddenly feeling like the parent.

"It doesn't matter."

"It does though."

He drove into the school's driveway. "We're here. I'll see you after school."

"Dad..."

"Just go, Ming. It's ok."

Ming gave him a look of sad longing but knew that she couldn't force this conversation any further than it had already gone. She grabbed her backpack and ran into the school, extra fast in case John was anywhere on campus waiting for her.

Oscar was disappointed in himself. He didn't want to admit his failures, as a husband and as a father, especially not to his daughter. He felt like he didn't have anything left to do but fight against the realization that he and his husband were no longer working. Tyler had become more self-absorbed, to the point that the two hadn't had a conversation that wasn't about him or his career in what felt like years. Meanwhile, Oscar had become more bitter and self-sacrificing, unwilling to voice his sadness, disappointment, and fear until it exploded in Ming's face.

He started the car and drove back home, completely forgetting that he was planning on talking to his daughter's principal.

Ming spent the first half of the morning dreading second-period chemistry, a class she shared with John. The anxiety that she had repressed suddenly burst out inside her as all the articles she had read about girls who were harassed at school flashed through her mind like gunfire. They would tell the school and, of course, the school wouldn't do anything. This would be quickly followed by everyone acting so surprised when the girl suddenly turned up dead, even though they could've seen it coming if they had just paid attention.

She took a deep breath and prepared for the worst as she walked into the chemistry lab but found an empty seat where she expected an emotional and violent John. His absence only served to make her even more nervous.

"Miss Neills, do you know where John is?"

"Oh gosh, I don't know. He didn't call in sick or anything. It's so strange. He's never missed a day of school, you know."

The hair on the back of Ming's neck stood on end as her paranoia increased. John had spent every day for the past two years badgering her at every possible opportunity. He spent all of the previous night sending her terrifying text messages from a blocked number.

'What is going on?!'

Lunchtime.

Ming had gone through her entire day on pins and needles, worried that John would suddenly appear whenever she turned a corner. She thought of him stewing at home, or wandering the streets looking for ways to make her life miserable.

After a lot of internal debate, she made a vow to herself: she was going to talk to the principal. Despite her worries based on how society treats victims of harassment, in particular women of color, she clung to the hope that as the daughter of two very high-profile homosexuals the principal wouldn't be able to ignore her even if he wanted to.

After finishing her meal, she got up to toss the remains in the garbage. Along the way to the exit, she saw Miss Sidwell reading a book - *"Torture in Yellow: A Study on the Life and Talent of Vincent Van Gogh"* - unable to lift herself from it as she mindlessly tossed a half-eaten apple into the recycling.

Ming decided to greet her teacher, hoping to pull her out of her stupor. "Hi, Miss Sidwell."

Just as she turned her head to smile at her student, her body went flying up against the wall. Her colorful sundress was suddenly painted with her blood. Her body twitched and twisted as she slowly died right in front of Ming's eyes.

She had been shot.

Ming screamed. The entire room erupted in screams and the sounds of tables being turned over to act as shields and windows and doors being slammed closed. She turned to find the source of the assault. Her eyes widened as she saw John Hoffman, clad in camouflage colored body armor with a red scarf across his face, sporting an arsenal of assault rifles, pistols, and shotguns.

Years of active shooter drills helped Ming maintain a laser tight focus on the three core principles of surviving an entitled white boy's need for attention through violence: Hide. Fight. Run.

Ming ran backwards to escape but the door to the hallway wouldn't open. She saw the other students and teachers body slamming the emergency doors. They were trapped.

John aimed at the mob and began firing. Ming watched with terrified, tear-filled eyes as they were all cut down.

She glared at John, only to see him smiling like a boy opening Christmas presents. He was enjoying this.

He turned his gun towards the swarms of people trying to break open the sealed windows so they could jump out. He laughed as he mowed down dozens of his teachers and classmates, their screams drowned out by the gunfire.

He yelled at Ming from across the way. "HEY MING! HOW WAS LUNCH?!"

Ming kept her eyes on him as she tried to bust the hallway door open.

He walked towards her, slowly and menacingly. "Oh, that's right! You can't escape! LOL! Here! Let me help you out!"

He pulled out his phone and pressed a button. The door suddenly flew open, dropping Ming onto the hallway floor. She was so shocked that she didn't realize John was a mere few feet away, with a high-powered rifle pointed at her chest.

Bravely, she asked, "Why?"

He responded with a monstrous smile and a point-blank shot, tossing her several feet into the hallway behind her, leaving a bloody trail on the floor as she went. Her momentum was halted by the presence of the custodian's abandoned workstation.

Shocked and bloodied but still awake and alive, Ming reached her hand to her chest to inspect the massive gash. To her surprise, it quickly sealed itself beneath her fingers, healing almost instantaneously.

Confused but alert, she quickly stood up, full of adrenaline from surviving a spray of bullets to the chest. She saw John continuing his easy stride towards her.

"Surprised?" John asked. "I'm not... if only you'd just listened to me. I know you better than you know yourself, Ming. And I'm gonna help you figure out exactly who you are."

Unable to find a logical explanation for what had just occurred, she ran as far and as fast as she could away from the crazed gunman who, once upon a time, seemed like just another innocent irritant.

"Typical. Always making me chase her..."

And with that, he began his hunt.

3

20 JUN 18.

12:55.

SANCHEZ-LUCKIN HOUSEHOLD, Brooklyn, NY.

Oscar was sitting alone in the kitchen. His hands were shaking around his teacup, full of tea left cold from neglect. His head was filled with doubts and fears, all circling the drain of his heavily burdened heart.

He had a plan set up in his head. Once Tyler returned home, they were going to have "the talk." He knew that if it didn't happen that day, it never would.

He started talking to himself, practicing what he might say once he saw his husband walk through the door.

"Tyler... I know that things have been tough the past few months. Your campaign has-" He stopped and started again. "Tyler... I know that things have been tough the past few months. We've fought. I've said some things and so have you. But... I don't want to fight anymore. I'm tired of fighting. And I'm sure you are too. I know that the campaign is important to you, so I don't want to ask you to do anything that might threaten your position with the public-" He stopped again, recognizing how much he had sacrificed so Tyler could play the role of the perfect father and husband for the reporters and voters. He started again. "Tyler... I love you. But I think we love each other too much to continue lying to ourselves. This isn't working. We're not making each other happy anymore. And I want to be happy. And I want you to be happy. I think we need some time apart. I think… I *know* I need time." Hearing his innermost thoughts said out loud brought Oscar to tears. "And I know you think that I should care about what the press will say and how it'll all look, but I don't. I don't care what anybody thinks. I care about what I think. I care about what our child thinks, having to listen to us fight every night. I don't want to fight anymore. I'm so sick of fighting, Tyler, and I-"

Oscar jumped as he heard Tyler's car pulling into the garage out back. He took a deep breath and prepared for the worst conversation a person can have with their partner.

Tyler burst into the kitchen and immediately embraced a still teary-eyed Oscar. "Hello, my beautiful husband! I'm so happy to be home!"

He kissed him on the cheek, briefly making Oscar forget about their marital woes. At that moment, he thought to himself, *'Maybe I'm just being melodramatic. Maybe things aren't as bad as I think they are. Maybe everything's going to be ok.'*

Tyler was gripping him from behind, confusing Oscar. He craned his neck to see Tyler attempting to take a picture of the two of them.

"Smile baby!" Tyler said.

Oscar's face refused to create anything other than a frown. Tyler didn't seem to notice or care as he took the picture. After posting it online, so all of his followers could see how *"in love"* he and Oscar were, he quickly turned the kitchen TV on at full volume and headed over to the fridge.

"I wonder what I should have for lunch today. Sandwich? Leftovers from last night? Are there any leftovers?"

"Not since Darcy started working for you, no." Oscar had to project to be heard over the TV. "Tyler, do you think we can talk?"

"Yeah sure," he said without taking his head out of the fridge. "Do we have any prosciutto?"

Oscar rubbed his temples. "Tyler... please..."

"I said yeah, jeez, calm down, you grinch." He emerged from the fridge carrying a platter of cheese and deli meats. "What's up? What's so important?"

"If only you knew, Tyler..."

"Ugh, what Oscar? What? What could I have possibly done in the twenty seconds that I've been home that could have made you so upset?"

"Tyler, please, just calm down."

"I'm perfectly calm, Oscar. I'm not the one messing up my selfies with my stank face or staring daggers at me while I try to have a snack."

"No, you're just the one who spends fourteen hours a day at the office with the pig who cleans our dishes with his tongue."

"You know, I didn't have to come home. God knows, I didn't come home to deal with..." He stopped himself and redirected. "For the record, Darcy was the one who told me I was working too hard and should take a day off to spend more time with *you*. Honestly, I don't even know why I thought that was a good idea."

"Oh, I'm soooo sorry that I've spoiled your plans for an easy-breezy day at home. But I am just-" Oscar noticed Tyler staring at the TV behind him. "Are you even listening to me?"

"Oscar, shut up."

"I will not shut up, Tyler! You never take my feelings seriously, and I just-"

"No, Oscar, shut up!" He grabbed his husband and pointed him towards the TV just in time to see the headline:

"Shots fired at New York Academy of Arts and Sciences."

The two men, in a level of synchronization that they hadn't shared in years, quickly grabbed their things and ran to Tyler's car, driving off towards Ming's school without saying a single word to each other.

Meanwhile.

Ming kept running through the halls with John close on her tail. Every exit she came to was locked tight. Eventually, she found herself at the library and locked herself inside.

Entering the complicated labyrinth of books, she hoped the many stacks might add protection long enough for her to call for help. She went straight to the center of the literary maze, between fiction Na through Ob and Non-Fiction - Autobiographies.

Sinking to the floor, she used her brief moment of rest to catch her breath and get a grip on her rapidly fraying mental state.

She pulled her phone out. No signal.

'What the hell is going on?' She thought to herself as she began to spiral. *'Am I losing my mind? I should be dead. I could feel the blood drain from my body. How can I still be alive? It's impossible!'*

She became so wrapped up in trying to figure out the mechanics of her sudden and unexplainable resurrection that she couldn't hear the library door open.

"I bet you're confused, right?" John called out.

She had to cover her mouth to keep from screaming. She peered through the books to try and get a good look at him. He was walking slowly through the piles of literature, searching for her. His senses were on high alert. His footsteps were as silent as snowfall. He had become a predator.

He continued shouting out for Ming. "I mean, I'd be shocked, too, if I got up and ran away seconds after someone shot me in the chest. I'd be scared, confused, desperate for answers, and probably in need of a diaper change."

John pushed a nearby bookshelf over, causing Ming to jump and swallow her terrified cries. She started crawling away from where she thought he was. She frantically tried to remember where she could find the emergency exit through a feverish storm of mixed emotions.

"Ming Sanchez-Luckin. Officially adopted by Oscar Sanchez and Tyler Luckin in two-thousand-seven. You turn fifteen this October. You live at four-four-one-seven thirty-fourth avenue in Brooklyn, in a lovely three-bedroom townhouse. You spent the first three years of your life in a state-run orphanage. Tell me, do you remember anything from back then?"

Ming crawled around clumsily on the floor, trying to maintain a distance. She managed to keep his voice out of her head as she ventured towards the exit.

"Tell me," He shoved another bookshelf onto the floor. "Does the name Doctor Frank Gehrig ring a bell to you?"

That name struck more than a chord in Ming's mind. It activated a hellish symphony that left goosebumps all over her body. She became paralyzed as images of her trapped in a grey room, surrounded by other children flooded her mind. She remembered getting poked and prodded by a man in a white lab coat, forced to endure hours and hours of monstrous, scientific experiments.

John's voice pulled her out of her stupor. "Found you!"

He pointed an assault rifle at her face and opened fire. She fell to the floor as pieces of her face, skull, and brain splattered onto the shelves of books behind her.

Time seemed to slow down. She expected pain but instead felt nothing. This nothing was soon replaced by strength enough to push herself up onto her hands and knees. He laughed at her as she started crawling away.

She could feel her entire skull reconstruct itself as she moved. The sensation was jarring but felt strangely natural like she was a snake shedding its skin. Her eye regrew in its socket, allowing her to look back and see John smiling at her.

"Are you starting to get the picture here?".

Ming shot up from the floor and darted to the library door, forcing it open, and running back out into the hall.

'What is happening to me?!' She thought as she fought back tears.

Meanwhile.

Tyler drove to Ming's school like there was no tomorrow, getting as close as he could before the traffic surrounding the mad scene forced them out of the car. He was so wrapped up in fearing the worst that he didn't notice he was parked in the middle of the street.

Police were everywhere trying to field reporters, concerned family members, and passers-by. Tyler and Oscar ran right up to the nearest uniformed officer.

"What's happening?!" Oscar asked.

"Sir, I'm sorry but I cannot answer any questions right now," The cop responded in the roughest, thickest, Long Island accent, with no room left in his voice for sympathy.

"But sir, my daughter goes to this school! Please! Just let me know if she got out!"

"We are still in the process of evacuating the school and evaluating the situation. I'm sorry but you're going to have to wait."

Oscar became hysterical. "WAIT?! You can't just tell me to wait! Please, just tell me that my daughter is okay!"

"Sir," the cop assumed a very intimidating posture as he reached for his gun. "Step the fuck back."

Tyler stepped between them. "Come on, Oz. Let's go." Grabbing him, Tyler managed to put a building's distance between the two in a few seconds.

Oscar didn't want to walk away but he knew he had to. His mind was a tornado. Needing a release for the mental storm, he punched a nearby brick wall so hard his knuckles started to bleed. "Fuck!"

Tyler stayed silent. He didn't want to think about whether or not Ming was dead. He didn't want to think about how much time he had wasted the past few months not being there for her. He knew there was something wrong - that she was hiding something - but he chose not to do anything out of fear. He didn't want to think about how terrible he felt he was as a father.

Oscar walked off to the side of the wild crowd, hoping to get away from the din. He pulled the statue that Tyler had become by the hand.

"This is ridiculous! Our daughter's in there, Tyler! What are we supposed to do?!"

Oscar was becoming more hysterical by the second. His breath was getting heavier. His heartbeat was getting louder. His grip on reality was slipping away.

Seeing his husband in so much pain pulled Tyler out of his stupor. He grabbed Oscar by the shoulders and squeezed him tight.

"It's going to be okay! It's going to be okay."

"Do you really believe that?"

Tyler pulled him into a tight hug, crying into his shoulder. Oscar leaned in and cherished the moment. This was the first time they had truly embraced one another in more than a year.

"Yeah... I do... I *know* that Ming is okay because she has to be. She's gonna get through this. *We are* gonna get through this. And we're not going anywhere until we have her back."

The two heard a distinct "Pssst," the sound of a stage whisper. Confused, they looked around for the source before hearing it again. "Pssst." Turning, they saw a police officer standing close by, his face concealed by a large helmet and a pair of sunglasses.

"Tyler Luckin?" He asked, in a hushed tone.

"Um, yeah?" Tyler confoundedly responded.

"I'm a big fan," The cop said in a husky voice, turning his coat out to reveal a rainbow-colored policeman's badge. "Do you need anything?"

Oscar had never met a more helpful police officer in his life. "Actually, yeah-"

"I was talking to *Tyler*," The cop roughly interrupted him.

Tyler responded with a sharp, "This is my *husband*. Our daughter is inside, we need to know if she's okay."

"I can do you one better; I can let you inside!"

Tyler and Oscar looked at each other, confused and skeptical.

"But we were told there was an active shooter. Nobody's allowed in or out."

"That's just something we say so we can collect evidence. We already caught the guy! Come on, through here, before anybody sees!"

He pushed a partition aside to reveal a small, concealed alley big enough for someone to walk through.

The two looked at each other as if to say, '*Are we really doing this?*' They decided together, without talking, that even though this was an incredibly stupid idea it was still what they were going to do. They would go in, find Ming, and get out as fast as possible.

"Thank you, officer!" Tyler said, quietly. "You have no idea how much this means to us!"

With that, the two ran off into the building.

As soon as they were out of sight, the officer pulled out his phone. "They're heading your way. You should see them soon."

John Hoffman responded, "Thank you, sir. Survival of the fittest."

"Survival of the fittest." He turned off his phone and followed Tyler and Oscar inside, moving the partition back into place behind him.

4

11 SEP 17.

18:15.

SANCHEZ-LUCKIN HOUSEHOLD, Manhattan, NY.

The family was enjoying a quiet dinner at home. Oscar made Ming's favorite: grilled salmon on a bed of couscous. Oscar had noticed that Ming had become quieter and more morose than usual and tried using food to pull her out of her funk. She could sense what was going and decided to pretend like it was working for her fathers' sakes. Unfortunately for everyone involved, she was a terrible actress.

"How is it, sweetie?" Oscar keenly asked.

Ming responded with a near manic, "It's amazing! I love it! Thank you!"

"Glad to hear it!" Tyler said without looking up from his phone.

"Ming," Oscar said, prepared to address his parental fears, only to be interrupted by the doorbell. "Who could that be?"

"Oh!" Tyler said brightly as if somebody had just flipped his on-switch. "That's my surprise guest! He's a little early. Just wait here!"

"Who - Who is it?" Oscar asked.

"It's a surprise!" He quickly responded as he jumped out of his seat and ran to the front door.

Curious, Ming and Oscar craned their heads to catch a glimpse. Straining themselves, they could almost see Tyler embracing a tall, handsome gentleman in a slim fit, pinstriped, navy blue suit.

'Who the hell is he?' Ming and Oscar thought to themselves.

Tyler returned with the mysterious man, smiling excitedly. Stunned by the man's gorgeousness, Oscar nearly jumped out of his seat.

"Family! This is Darcy Winchester from the New York State Democratic Committee. Darcy, this is my husband, Oscar, and my daughter, Ming."

"Hello! Tyler's told me so much about you both!"

'What the fuck is going on?' Oscar thought to himself as a mass of worries flooded his mind. *'Oh god. Is Tyler leaving me for this smiley douche? I tried not to see this coming. But... Am I going to be a single father? Oh god, what's going to happen to Ming?!'*

Oscar stood up and aggressively shook Darcy's hand. "How do you do?"

Ming stared at Darcy, taking him in. Dark, wavy hair. Blue eyes that were as piercing and as bright as a Siberian Husky. A bright, white smile that could burn a forest down. Like Oscar, she found herself drowning in a series of dark thoughts.

'Is Tyler going to leave us for this guy? Of course, not... I mean, he's a little handsome, I guess... but there's just something about him... And why would he do it at dinner time? That would be a serious dick move. This is all very stupid.'

"What's this all about, Tyler?" Oscar asked, using a large smile to mask his paranoia.

"I have some very exciting news." He said, once again preferring dramatic tension over answering any questions upfront.

"And what is that?" Oscar's smile was so large, it started to hurt.

"Okay!" Tyler and Darcy said in unison, inadvertently making Oscar even more paranoid.

"You go first!" Tyler said.

"No, you!" Darcy said.

"Somebody say something! "A frustrated Oscar blurted out.

"Please, it's your family. It cannot come from me. I insist."

"If you insist. Family!" Tyler took an incredibly long pause, trying to build tension, completely unaware of just how much his husband was spiraling. ``I've been nominated to run for the open Senate seat, and I accepted!''

Ming and Oscar looked at him, their eyelids heavy with disbelief.

"What?" Was all Oscar could push out.

This was, obviously, not the answer Tyler wanted. "What 'what'? This is a very big deal!"

"Precisely, a *very* big deal…" Oscar was not prepared to have this conversation in front of his daughter and a total stranger. "I'm sorry, Darcy, is it?"

"Yup!"

"Would you mind waiting here while I speak with my husband? Feel free to help yourself to whatever looks good."

"It all looks good!"

"Well then help yourself to all of it." Oscar pulled Tyler out of the dining room and took him upstairs.

"What's wrong? I thought you'd be happy for me."

"I'm not saying I'm not happy for you. I'm happy for you. I'm proud of you. But that's not what I wanna talk about."

"Then what do you want to talk about?"

"Tyler, I really wish you had talked to me about this before agreeing to anything. I mean, how much time and energy did you put into planning all of this without realizing that it might have a negative impact on your family?"

"What negative impact? It's just a nomination, there's no guarantee that I'll win."

"Tyler, you're a rich, white man. You have all the resources of wealth and youth, and you're a very attractive homosexual. That pretty much guarantees you the *'thirsty liberal'* vote, which is basically half the constituency."

"I appreciate your confidence in me, but I don't understand-"

Oscar hated interrupting his husband, but he wasn't finished. "And I know you Tyler. You fight so hard for the things you want. You're very assertive, which, combined with all you have going for you including that winning smile - that beautiful, beautiful, winning smile - it all works together to make you an unstoppable force."

Tyler paused to take in all that he had just heard. "Were those compliments? You called me pretty and said you think I'm going to win. I'm just not seeing the problem you have with all of this. Yes, I want to win, but there's no guarantee that I will. Elections are unpredictable and difficult to get through-"

"Precisely. Elections are difficult and messy. You have no experience working in politics, government, or with being exposed to the public in a very intimate manner. The press, and your opposition, will look so far deep into your life for any reason people might not want to vote for you. On top of that, being a married, gay couple with a teenage daughter is difficult and messy on its own, made even worse by the political hell we're living through right now. And I don't know if you noticed, but our daughter is going through a very tough time."

"I think you worry too much."

"And I think you worry too little.

"Ming is one of the most chill teenagers in the world," Tyler said, going for reassuring but coming off as condescending. "Whatever you think she's going through is obviously not as big a deal as you think it is. If it were, she would tell us. And even if it were a big thing, she's remarkably intelligent and mature, and she has two dads that love her and will work day and night to get her through anything."

"Does she?" Oscar said, going for brave and coming off as desperate and lonely.

Tyler was taken aback. "What's *that* supposed to mean?"

Oscar took a deep breath, prepared to monitor his words to ensure he wouldn't say anything he might regret. "Tyler, I love you, but sometimes your tunnel vision can make it hard for you to see what's going on around you. I'll support you, no matter what, whether you run for city council, senator, president, or a triathlon. But I just hope that you remember that everything you do until election day will affect everybody in your life. And I don't want Ming getting hurt by the spotlight."

Meanwhile.

Ming waited patiently as her fathers fought upstairs. Their voices were mostly drowned out by the sound of Darcy scarfing down every scrap of food on the table as if he hadn't eaten in years.

Ming gave him a heavy look and thought, *'At the rate he's going, he could inhale the tablecloth.'*

"This is delicious!" He said with a mouth full of food.

She tried to hold back a sneer. *'Ugh, I hate this guy.'*

(5)

20 JUN 18.

14:00.

NEW YORK ACADEMY OF ARTS AND SCIENCE,
Brooklyn, NY.

As she ran through the hallways of her once boring school, she
saw the clock on the wall. It was 2 p.m. That was when school let
out. Oscar would always be there for Ming at the end of the day,
ready to pick her up and take her home with a smile on his face.

'Dad... I wish you were here."

Ming sprinted into the west wing of the school. She tried
opening any of the doors to any of the classrooms, but they were
all locked tight.

"Oh God, please, let me in!" She pleaded, hoping
somebody would hear her and take pity. "Please, please, please!"

Just then, a familiar voice rang through the halls,
"Ming?!"

No sight or sound could have been any sweeter as she
turned and saw her dads.

"Dad? Pop?" She said, in complete disbelief. She ran to
them, as if on air, and embraced them as tight as she could, just in
case they were nothing but a terror induced figment of her
imagination. But they were wonderfully real. "Oh my god! What
are you guys doing here?!"

"We came to get you! Come on, we have to go!"

Before they could move an inch towards the exit, a cold voice stopped them dead in their tracks. "But the party just started, daddies!" John mocked them with a whiny voice. "And you didn't even try the punch."

Ming stood in front of them, prepared to take the brunt of whatever was about to be fired in their direction. "Leave them alone, John."

"Ming." An unaware Oscar pulled back her behind him. The sight of the same boy who harassed his daughter not but a day ago, now armed to the teeth with thousands of dollar's worth of firearms, nearly pushed him into a fainting spell. However, he refused to falter and instead stood strong and stalwart. He puffed his chest and stretched his arms out like a hero of Herculean proportions.

"What's going on?" A terrified Tyler asked in a dog-like yelp. "The cop outside said they already had the shooter in custody."

"He lied," John said. "Millionaire politicians aren't the brightest, are they?"

Oscar didn't have a gun or a bulletproof vest, but he refused to let this young man destroy his family. His only defense would be trying to reach out to him and find the child inside the raging gunman.

"Your name is John, right? It's okay. We're not here to hurt you. We just want to get Ming, and you, out of here, safely, so we can get you some help."

"Oh please. Don't talk to me like you think you know me. I've been going to school with your daughter for the past two years and she doesn't even know me. But, then again, she has no idea who she really is so I guess I can't blame her."

"John, please, just talk to me."

"I don't want to talk to you."

"Why not, John?"

"Because I have a gun and I think that means I'm in charge."

"You can't possibly think you're going to get out of this alive, John."

"Uh, I'm sorry but I think you should be more worried about yourself, *Oscar*. After all, it's not like *you're* immortal. And neither is your husband."

"This isn't about me, John, and it isn't about Tyler or Ming. This is about you. What do you want, John?"

He chuckled, arrogantly. "I want to be remembered."

"Remembered? Do you want to be remembered as someone who hurt dozens of people? Is that what you really want, John?"

"YES! And why shouldn't I want it? After today, after everything I've done, I'll become immortal. I am going to live forever through the tears of every person who lost someone thanks to me. My name will be in all of the history books. I'll have websites dedicated to my life, start to finish, and everybody I've killed today will just be another name on a list. Anything that will be done in their name - any charities or gun laws or foundations -

they will all be because of me! I'll be an omnipresent monument!" He glared at Ming. "And nobody will **ever** be able to ignore me **again**."

Oscar pushed his family further behind him. "John, stop it! Just talk to me. Keep talking to me."

"Talk is cheap." John pointed his gun at Oscar and took a shot.

Without thinking, Tyler pushed Oscar out of the way. The bullet pierced his left lung as it flew through his body, piercing his spine and grazing Ming's side as it exited. Her wounds healed themselves before any blood could be drawn.

Oscar screamed as his husband fell into his arms. He put his hands on the entry wound to try and keep blood from pouring out, unaware that blood was pouring out of the exit wound until he felt its warm stream on his leg.

"Dammit," was all John could say as he reversed back into the main building in what looked like a retreat.

Oscar's screams and cries were muffled as they hit Ming's ears. The world around her melted away as her eyes were painfully stapled to Tyler, bleeding before her on the floor. The only sound she could hear was her heartbeat pounding, fast and fleeting, like a hummingbird in her ears. She fell to her knees and reached out to Tyler, pressing her hand on his heart, hoping to recreate the connection they both felt that they had lost so long ago.

A single tear fell down her cheek as she whispered, "I love you… Please don't leave me."

She felt her body boil over with a mysterious energy, erupting volcanically from her heart outward. She felt strength override her anxiety and her heartbeat continued to speed up.

She remembered the dream where she made that man's wounds disappear. It was at that moment that she realized it wasn't just a dream, but a long-forgotten memory. She took in all that John had said to her and pondered.

'What if I am meant for something greater? What if this day was meant to prove that I could be something greater?'

Let me be greater.

She focused on the bullet hole in her father's chest. She felt his faint heartbeat in her hands. The energy surging throughout her body rivered out through her hand, using the physical connection between the two as a bridge. His heart slowly, but steadily, began to speed up while her's began to slow down until they were in complete synchronization.

She wanted the wound to close. She wanted to keep Tyler alive.

When she lifted her hands, his chest had been healed. Through some miracle, Ming had sealed his certainly fatal wound. He hurdled up out of Oscar's arms, gasping as if taking his very first breath.

Oscar's eyes were so wide that he was afraid they might pop out of his skull. He couldn't believe what he had seen and wanted to pinch himself, but instead, he pulled Tyler into his arms and said, "I love you."

"What happened?" He said with a cough.

"Shhh, just calm down, just relax."

Without further encouragement, Tyler instantly fell asleep on his husband's lap.

Oscar looked up at his daughter. "Ming... what did you do?"

"I have no idea. I know this may sound unbelievable, but... I have to go find John."

"Ming, no, we have to leave." He watched as she wiped the blood on her hands onto her bullet hole ridden clothes and just then noticed that she was covered in blood. "Jesus Christ, what happened to you."

"I've been shot about a thousand times. Go. Get Pop into an ambulance. Get him to a hospital.

He grabbed her arm to keep her from running off. "I'm not going anywhere without you."

"Dad, please, you have to let me do this. I'm going to be okay..." She knew she needed to convince him and could only think of one way to do so. She saw his knuckles, still shredded from hitting a brick wall earlier, and took a chance. "Look."

She held his hand in hers and focused. Within seconds, the wounds had healed themselves and all pain in his hand had ceased. He could even feel his carpal tunnel syndrome evaporate.

"Ming... How did you-?"

"I have no idea. For all I know, I've gone insane, and this is all part of my big delusion trip. Or this could all be a nightmare. I could be at home, sleeping comfortably in my nice, warm bed. Oddly enough, however, I think the more likely story is that I'm some kind of super-healing, immortal mutant girl. All I do know is that John has the answers that I need."

"John?"

"I know it's ridiculous but I'm the reason why he's doing all of this. He's shot me, like, a thousand times and then he just runs away after shooting Pop? He knows things. He's told me things. I need to get to him before he can get away."

Looking into Oscar's eyes, filled with tearful worry, nearly brought Ming to tears herself.

"Just be careful." He said.

"Don't worry. I couldn't die even if he wanted me to."

Scared he'd never see her again, Oscar said, "I love you!"

"I love you! And when he wakes up, tell Pop I love him, too."

"Of course…"

And she ran off, turning the tables as she chased after John.

It only took a little more than a minute before she managed to sneak up on him. He was yelling at someone on his cell phone and never noticed her arrival.

"No, it was Tyler… I know! I know! I'm sorry! I didn't mean to… I know… I don't know. She's probably just finished patching him up. She's a smart girl. She's probably figured it all out by now."

She stepped out into the light and approached her stalker. "Figured out what, John?"

He hung up as soon as he saw her. For the first time since this fiasco began, he looked nervous. He held his gun up at her, aware it wouldn't do anything but slow her down.

"Don't play games."

"I thought you liked games. Isn't this all just one big game to you?"

"Ming…"

She had the power now.

"How about we play a guessing game? Feel free to stop me if I get anything wrong. You have a poorly treated mental illness, a serious issue in today's society, causing you to display obsessive tendencies, impulse control issues, and general paranoia, depression, and anxiety that manifests itself as an outstanding inferiority complex. You found out, through some informant who's connected to whatever secret something or other, that I have the superhuman ability to heal any wound, including my own. This caused you to try and turn me into your 'Bride of Frankenstein,' because you think I'm just as much of a monster as you perceive yourself to be. So, when I rejected you for the billionth time, you decided to take the power and attention you've always thought you deserved by force by shooting up your school and putting my family in mortal danger all while helping me realize that I possess these magical powers. How did I do?"

John was speechless.

"I understand, John. I understand that all the guns, the Kevlar, the fatigues, that stupid red bandana that you think makes you look like a war movie hero, is all part of this stupid game... And now... you're staring down the final boss, and she. Can't. Die." She started walking towards him, mimicking his slow, menacing walk from before. "I can fight through the bullets. I can fight through the bombs. I can walk through any wall of fire you throw at me. And once you're all out of options, I'm going to take the sharpest anything I can find and shove it deep into the most uncomfortable anywhere on your body... and then, I'm going to stitch you back up and start all over again, until you tell me everything you know and who told you. And at the end of it all, you'll realize that the minute you lost this stupid game was when you pointed that gun at my family."

Weapon still in hand, he was about to attempt a response. Only to, in a fit of irony, be interrupted by a bullet flying through the side of his skull. A bullet so expertly aimed that, even under the greatest scrutiny, it would look like a suicide.

"What?!" Ming went down to John. Using her need for answers as motivation, she put her hands on his wound and started healing him as fast as she could.

"I don't know why you're wasting your time on him."

She knew that voice. She turned her head without taking her hands off John's pierced skull. There he stood, in his clean, tailored, navy blue suit with his striped, salmon-colored tie, and a freshly fired pistol in his hand.

Darcy Winchester.

Even without her above-average intellect, Ming would still have been able to see the writing, spelled out in blood, on the wall.

"You're John's informant…"

"Gosh, you're a clever girl. Maybe they gave you super brains on top of that thick skin of yours."

Her work was done. John was barely conscious but still alive without the slightest hint of a scar.

"I'm assuming you organized all of this…"

"Another fifty points to the Asian chick with the bob cut!"

"You pushed John to kill all of these people."

"Now-now, missy, *'pushed'* is a very liberal term for what I did. Truth be told, it didn't take much convincing to bring him to this wonderfully theatrical course of action. You've met him. He's nuts."

"What is wrong with you?"

"I'm having some gastro-intestinal issues I'm thinking of talking to a doctor about, but otherwise I'm fine. How are you?"

"What the fuck does - who are you? Who do you work for?"

"Wow, language."

"I know you know that that gun won't work on me. So, I'll ask again: Who do you work for?"

"My gosh, you got moxie. Don't worry, you'll find out soon enough. But just so you know, in hindsight, you'll see that you were one of the lucky ones. I mean, in my day, the shit you had to go through to get powers was-"

"There are others like me?"

Darcy looked annoyed when she interrupted him. "A few. Not a lot, but enough."

"Enough for what?"

He scoffed. "Wouldn't you like to know?"

Ming was tired of being distracted. "Once again: who do you work for?"

"I'll tell you, but only 'cuz I know that in about..." He checked his incredibly expensive wristwatch. "Two minutes, none of it will matter anyway."

"We'll have to see about that, won't we?"

He gave her a smarmy smile and a dull stare. "I used to think your blind bravery was cute, but now... Anyway... About a billion years ago, when you were just a little babe, you were adopted into a super-secret military program that recognized your potential for superhuman greatness. They experimented on you, trained you to use your powers, and then brainwashed you so you'd forget you ever had them before adopting you out to the home-making homos. Fun fact: There's a little device in your head that locks the control of your powers away, deep into your subconscious, and it can only be unlocked through the combination of two things: the remote trigger, which was activated late last night, and an incredible amount of emotional trauma to provide the need for you to use your powers. In this instance, we managed to kill two birds with one stone: we bring our biokinetic war machine back into our control *and* strike fear in the hearts of citizens through light domestic terrorism. It's quite fun when you think about it."

"Fun? You think all of this is fun? You manipulated me, my family, everyone. You're responsible for the murders of dozens of people."

He rolled his eyes. "Sweetie, trust me if you think a pile of bodies is going to make me see the *'error of my ways'* you'll be wonderfully disappointed. My kill count is a lot higher than all the death you've seen today cubed. I mean, not to be all nostalgic, but you should have seen me in Kuwait."

"How dare you?"

"Hey, has anyone ever told you that you should smile more?"

A lightbulb went off inside her head. He told her that she was a bioweapon, so if she was capable of healing people then she must be equally capable of hurting them. She put her hands out and closed her eyes, trying to imagine the worst possible thing that she could do to him. A brain tumor. An aneurysm. Maybe even a slow, painful heart attack. With all of that in mind, she blindly ran at him.

Unshaken, he spoke a strange phrase out loud. "But no Angels, no Mercy, no help ever came."

Ming fell to the floor, her face a complete blank, her body limp, and her mind shut off.

Darcy pulled out his phone. "Sagittarius checking in."

"Do you have Mercy?" A cold voice responded.

He lifted her over his shoulder, like a sack of potatoes, as he spoke. "She'll be on the next bus home as soon as I can get her out. But…"

"But?"

"There may have been a few complications…"

"Elaborate."

He made his way to the school's basement and started looking for the sewer access grate, knowing there would be one from having memorized the layout months ago.

"The boy is still alive. Mercy healed him. And he shot the *wrong* dad."

Silence came through on the other end until it was broken with a stern but contained command. "Come home immediately. We'll start working on *plan B* as soon as we can get a handle on this situation."

"But sir… don't you think I should stay in the city and keep an eye on the two?"

There was a deep sigh. "No. Make up an excuse. We need you back here. You're too close to this situation. We'll take care of it as soon as all the pieces are in place."

He sighed. "Yes sir."

He opened the access panel and dropped the unconscious Ming down before climbing in and closing the grate behind him.

(Epilogue)

23 JUN 18.

11:00

HUDSON'S HOPE HOSPITAL, Manhattan, NY.

Tyler and Oscar watched the live press conference given by one of Tyler's assistants, reading an official statement to a football field's worth of reporters, absolutely famished for any juicy detail they could swallow.

"To the respected members of the press, thank you all for gathering here today. Out of respect for my family, and for the sake of my own physical and mental health, I have decided to withdraw from the election. I wish my opponent and my party all the best and hope we all can use this tragic moment in history to unite, to mourn, and to remind ourselves to treasure the time we have with our loved ones. This will be my final message on the matter as I kindly ask for privacy as my family and I mourn our tragic loss. Thank you, and good night."

Tyler turned off the TV from his bed, where his husband sat at his side. "Great..."

"How are you feeling, Ty?"

"I don't know... I don't know what to feel... Ming...?"

"She's not dead, Tyler."

"Oz..."

"She can't be. She's the reason you're still alive. She literally cannot die. At least, that's what she told me."

"But that's insane."

"I know how it sounds, but, I mean, do you have a better excuse for how you survived a bullet to the chest?"

"No... I do not. So... Our daughter might be a *superhero*."

"Not 'might be'. *Is*."

"Okay, *is* a superhero. She was trapped in one of the bloodiest school shootings in US history. The building was surrounded by cops and ambulances and press and even some of the national guard. And she somehow managed to completely disappear. So..."

"So, she was taken by the government."

Tyler looked at his husband with dead eyes. "That sounds like a conspiracy theory, Oz."

"Yeah well, do you have a better excuse for why our immortal daughter was reported as *'dead'* in the official report? Or why the police asked us to come down and identify a body. Because there couldn't be a body."

"I mean... if there wasn't a body, then what are they going to show us?"

"We won't know until we go, I guess... But there are ways to fake that kind of thing."

"So, what are we supposed to do then? If the government has Ming-"

"There's nothing we can do."

"But..."

"But what?"

"I mean... Ming might not be the only super out there."

Oscar's ears perked at this idea. "It's more than possible."

"And if the government has Ming, then that means they're probably trying to hide her."

"Because they're probably responsible for her... If - if you think about it, none of this can be a coincidence."

"What, you mean how our daughter has magical powers and even more magically disappeared?"

"She has magical powers, she disappeared, her stalker committed a very public mass murder, you're one of the founders of one of the biggest social media apps of the last decade, and... There's just something about this entire thing that's making my brain go haywire."

Tyler had a lightbulb moment. "We adopted Ming when she was four. We were originally going to have a baby through in vitro then we decided to adopt. I don't remember why, but we changed our minds overnight. Why did we do that?"

Oscar thought about it more thoroughly and he started to feel like a cloud was lifting. "We rushed into it so quickly. We didn't even think to do a check into Ming's background. We didn't know anything about her birth parents or her life before we adopted her... Garden Adoption. I remember. You came home one day and said someone recommended them to you. I don't even remember asking who."

"It was a friend from work."

"What was their name?"

"Well... I don't remember... I guess he wasn't really a friend... Just some guy I saw around the office a little bit. Now that I think about it, he kinda reminded me of-"

"Hey, guys, how ya doing?" Darcy said, interrupting the husbands' private moment.

Darcy's sudden presence startled them, causing Oscar to jump up from his seat. Meanwhile, Tyler saw his PA with brand new eyes, as if he had just been unmasked. There was no doubt in his mind that he had met Darcy many years ago. That Darcy had been the one convinced Tyler to adopt through a very specific agency where they found Ming and immediately took her home. Then, almost ten years later, he had reintroduced himself into their lives only for Tyler to get shot and their daughter to go missing. Using only his eyes, Tyler communicated all of this to his husband, who moved closer to his side.

"Hey, Darcy..." Tyler said feebly, feigning weakness.

"So... It's been a rough couple of days. How are you two holding up?"

Compared to how he usually appeared, Darcy was incredibly disheveled. His hair was a mess, his suit was wrinkled, his tie was askew, and he looked like he hadn't slept in days.

"As best as we can, Darcy. Thank you," Oscar said, actively trying not to expose the incredible rage he felt towards the man he once thought of as just his husband's terribly rude assistant.

"Yeah," Darcy continued, sensing the tension in the room. "If it's okay with you guys, I think I need to head back home. To my family, in Connecticut."

"Really?" Tyler asked, not believing a word he was saying.

"Yeah, you know I'd hate to leave you in the lurch but… I just feel like I need to be around my family right now. You know?"

"Indeed," Tyler said. "Well, you'll be missed."

Darcy walked over to Tyler and gave him a stiff and uncomfortable hug. "Take care, Tyler." And gave Oscar a cold, clammy handshake. "You too, Oscar."

He responded with a fake smile. "Same to you, Darcy."

His eyes flashed. He had sensed something stirring in Oscar's voice. Perhaps even in his very thoughts. Oscar couldn't tell but he somehow knew that, in that instant, Darcy was peering into his very soul, searching for a weakness in the very foundation of his being.

In a fraction of a second, he had transformed from a savvy gentleman into someone they now knew was capable of anything. Both were stricken with great fear but did their best to stay calm.

"Just remember. Ming is in a better place right now. And I'm sure she would want you guys to move on…I mean, if I were you, I'd *definitely… move on*."

Tyler decided to end the aggressive conversation. "I think it's best you be on your way, Darcy. You don't want to keep your family waiting, after all."

"Of course not," He said sharply. "Well... farewell..."

As he made his leave, Oscar exhaled out all the nerves that had been building up inside him.

"What the fuck was that?"

"I have no idea... But Oscar, I swear to god, Darcy is the same exact person as the guy from ten years ago. His hair was different, and he was wearing glasses then, maybe even a little chubbier, but it was definitely him."

"You don't have to convince me, I believe you. And even if I didn't, there is still something very wrong with that man. Did you see that look in his eyes? He looked like he wanted to murder us."

"He looked like he was trying to figure out *how* to murder us."

"I think when we get out of here, we should avoid going home for a while."

Tyler was scared but determined to figure out what was going on. Even more determined in his search for his daughter.

"Oz?"

"Yeah?"

"I think we're going to have to call the adoption agency... I'm not ready for this to be over."

"I couldn't agree with you more."

"And..."

"Yeah?"

Tyler held his husband's hand, caressing it. "I love you."

A little shocked, Oscar had to hold back tears as he looked into his husband's deep blue eyes. For the first time in what felt like forever, he saw the eyes of the man he fell in love with.

"I love you too, Tyler. So very much."

"And I love Ming. And I'm going to stop at nothing to find her."

Oscar caressed Tyler's hair. "Nothing."

And then they shared a sweet, tender kiss, two years in the making.

PROJECT: PARADIGM

BIRTH-DATE: 9 DEC 01.

SEX: Female.

CURRENT HEIGHT (As of 2008): 4'2".

EYE COLOR: Silver-Blue.

HAIR COLOR: Brown.

NATIONALITY: American.

ETHNICITY: Hispanic (Mixed descent).

FAMILY:

Ariana Castellano (birth mother)

Edgar Castellano (birth father)

(1)

9 DEC 01.

00:01.

OASIS MEDICAL CENTER, Albuquerque, NM.

He entered the room quickly and quietly, dropping his medical bag on the ground very gently. The ears of newborns were so sensitive and strong, waking one would cause an unwanted chain reaction that could threaten everything he intended to accomplish. He knew he had the proper doctor's credentials, but he also knew there was no valid explanation for him to be in the nursery in the middle of the night.

He moved to the middle of the room and pulled out his greatest invention: "the Geno-tracer." After years of research, he had devised a way to identify the genetic markers that signified Haartvig's syndrome in someone, simply by holding the device over them.

Turning the geno-tracer on, and plugging in his earphones, he began waving it over every baby in the nursery, until finally: PING PING PING!

The tracer went off over a tiny, cooing angel, tightly swaddled into a pink blanket. He smiled.

'Jackpot.'

He took a quick glance at the name tag: "Baby Castellano."

The next day.

The young couple was embracing one another in the new mother's hospital bed. Her husband had brought her favorite chocolates and the blanket they received as a gift at their baby shower. With great excitement and anticipation, they waited for the doctors to return their little girl to them, eager to go home and start their new lives as a family together.

She turned to see her doctor in the doorway. "Oh, hello Doctor! How's our little angel? Edgar and I think we've finally decided on a name but-"

He put on a very pronounced frown that alerted the tired couple to the terrible news that they were about to hear.

"What's wrong?" Father Castellano asked, filled with dread.

All Doctor Gehrig had to say was, "I'm so sorry…"

The mother fell into hysterics. "No! Please, no!"

Her husband pulled her tight into a protective embrace, as she mournfully cried for the baby they would never get to know.

2

15 SEP 18.
07:00.
BRIG, EDIN.

Cai Medeiros awoke on an uncomfortable metal slab. Taking in his surroundings was a devastating task. He was trapped in a poorly crafted prison cell with restrictive bars patched together from scrap and rubble. He saw a pathetically small toilet popping out of a visually depressing grey well. He didn't have time to become scared or confused before something at the door caught his eye.

Looking through the bars of the cell was a tall, thin, pale-skinned white man with platinum blond hair and piercing blue eyes. He was wearing an expensive white suit, standing as straight as a pencil.

"Good morning," the man said in a cheerful yet somehow robotic tone. "Sleep well?"

"Who are you?" Cai asked, focusing his fear into a voice filled with stoic strength.

"To the point. Respectable. I am Director Frost and I am here to welcome you to EDIN."

Cai looked around. "It doesn't look like much of an 'Eden' to me, Mister Frost."

Frost laughed as robotically as he spoke. "Quite. I love a good joke early in the morning. Energizes me. Like freshly brewed coffee. Tell me: do you know why you are here Mister Medeiros?"

It only took Cai a moment to remember. "Billy!" He tried jumping off the bed, but his legs were still asleep, causing him to fall onto the cold, stone floor. He struggled towards the door, pulling himself up by the bars. "Where's Billy? Is he okay? Can I see him?"

Frost laughed again. "My-my-my. Such tenacity! If they gave out medals for zeal you would win the gold."

Cai looked at him with stone-cold eyes and said, "Where. Is. Billy?"

Frost just smiled. "He is safe. Billy is where he is *meant* to be."

"EDIN…"

"Yes. EDIN. Experimental Developments and Intelligence. Do you like it? I came up with it myself."

"You run this place?"

"I founded it. I command every person within its walls… except you of course. You are what I would call an 'uncontrolled variable'."

"If I'm not meant to be here then why am I here? Not enough space in your closet for more skeletons?"

"Has anybody ever told you how funny you are Mister Medeiros? But you do pose a good question," Frost started to pace back and forth in front of the cage. As he did, Cai could see the outline of a silver, chrome-like mask on the right side of his face. "My intelligence informs me that your families believe that you two *temperamental young lovers* simply ran away in the middle of the night to be alone together forever. And - given the erratic antisocial behavior Billy displayed - your dramatic breakup - and of course his *'medical incident'* - it seemed the most appropriate reasoning behind your joint disappearance."

Cai thought about his family - his mom, his dad, and all of his sisters - and his heart sank. Then his thoughts curved back to Billy and his courage mounted. He gave Frost a determined glare.

"You still haven't answered my question, Frost. Why am I still here?"

"I did not realize we were at the point in the conversation where we asked impertinent questions using only our last names..." He sighed. "If you need it here is the long and short: if I arranged to have you delivered back to *your* family Billy's parents would have quite a few questions for you. I have many tools at my disposal. A significant amount of which I could use to install false memories inside your feeble little mind. But at this current juncture you have been here far too long for me to completely cover all the loose ends I would have if I sent you away. Bigger things going on here require my attention and frankly Mister Medeiros you are not one of them."

Cai became puzzled at all that he was absorbing. "Wait a minute, how long was I out?"

"A month."

"A month?!"

"A month."

"How? Why?!"

"Billy."

"Billy?"

"Billy. Yet another variable whose outcome I did not accurately predict. On top of arriving later than the others he brought you along. Which was just perfect. And as if that were not enough he filled you with enough tranquilizer to keep you unconscious long enough that I had no choice but to keep you here."

This gave Cai pause for thought, *'I was down a month on a tranquilizer meant to keep Billy asleep till he got to EDIN? That's impossible. I bet Billy did something... like a psychic sleeping spell. If I'd just been sedated for a month, I'd be flopping all over the place. But I'm as fit as a stallion. Billy planned this. But why?'*

"So if you're going to blame anyone for your current position please feel free to blame that brilliant boyfriend of yours. Although I am not entirely sure what your relationship status might be now that he is under my thrall and preparing to be delivered for the final endgame... Maybe... *'it is complicated?'*"

"Endgame? What? Jesus Christ, why are you telling me all this?"

He laughed. "That is why I like you Mister Medeiros! Straight to the point no matter what. Like when you and Billy were going to train outside that thrift store, and he wanted to kiss you. But you told him, *'No, I'm not ready yet.'* That took an amazing amount of strength and fortitude far beyond that of a normal sixteen-year-old homosexual."

"Thank you? Wait, what?"

"Ever since you two started dating you have been on my radar. In fact if it were not for you the journey home for Billy would have reached a much more dramatic climax."

"What do you mean?"

Frost's cold eyes locked in with Cai's. "The original plan was significantly less messy and far more expeditious. Mister and Misses Howard would have been called to some drivable distance for a week-long work engagement like Portland or Vancouver. A swanky hotel room with a hot tub and a pool. Your basic family road trip bait. One loose brake line here. A well-positioned sixteen-wheeler there. And boom! Dead mom and dad."

"What?! Why would you do that?"

"Is it not obvious? Billy's powers were activated by extreme emotional stimulation. What greater stress is there than losing a parent? Much less two? But then... you came along. A little rough and tumble passionate muscle-bound bundle of a teenage dream that gave our little Billy Boy all the confidence and strength he needed to get through his dismal days. As I watched you two bond I was reminded of an old friend who told me *'love'* was a powerful motivator. So I sat by and waited. And waited. And waited. If I could be so blunt I was very close to obliterating Mister and Misses Howard in a gas fire until you dropped the L-bomb and drove Billy straight into the hospital while simultaneously awakening his powers. Good job."

"So... you're saying that-"

"I am saying a lot of things that I have no intention of repeating. Waiting for William to manifest his abilities and then adding on that ridiculously long coma did grind more than a few gears. However I think we can both agree that Billy was worth the wait. Such an extraordinary talent he has. And truth to be told I am truly happy we didn't have to kill the Howards. They seem like such lovely people and I hate unnecessary casualties. Spilled blood can truly stain a soul."

'I can't believe any of this... but my life with Billy has certainly been unbelievable. I just need to figure out how to get Billy and myself out of here.'

"I can tell what you are thinking."

"Can you?"

"Yes. Pardon my French but you probably think that I am full of shit."

"Wow, and I thought Billy was the psychic."

"Like I said Mister Medeiros I like you. I think you are a bright and talented young man. And according to the soldiers Billy did not kill you pack a mean punch. As it is reflected in your track record - all those competitions and tournaments..." He looked around, playing as if he were sharing a secret between playground buddies. "And *street fights*. You leave quite the footprint my little wannabe Anderson Silva. When you arrived it would have been a lot easier just to have you killed."

Cai never lost his cool. He never dropped his glare. He had no idea what to expect, but he knew that if Frost was the only thing standing between him and Billy, and their freedom, then he was prepared to pull out all of his cards, jump through every hoop, and cross every ring of fire to beat him.

Frost continued. "But like I said I do not like unnecessary casualties. I do not like collateral damage. And I am always the first to admit how ridiculous that all sounds by looking at my history. So I had to evaluate your skills and see if you could possibly be of any use to me."

"You think I could be useful?"

"Of course."

"How?"

"Oh do not sell yourself so short Mister Medeiros. Your fighting skills. Your ingenuity. Your *spunk* as it were. You could be quite the talented soldier. And I am sure given enough time you might learn to call this place *'home.'* So... what do you say?"

"What, you want me to decide now?"

"Of course *now*. I am on a very problematic timetable. Growing ever more problematic with each fleeting second I spend talking to you. So if you could kindly give me an answer in the next," he checked his watch before continuing, "forty-seven seconds, I would greatly appreciate it. I need to know if I should plan for a new-hire orientation or a cremation. Please take your pick before I pick for you."

"Wait - wait - wait... you mean if I don't join you, you'll kill me?"

"Of course. If you choose to be of no use to me I shall shoot you right here in this cage."

"I thought you said you hated killing people?"

"And yet it seems you completely tuned out when I said *sometimes bloodshed becomes a necessity.*' I may have morals but I cannot be held responsible for the consequences of your stubbornness Mister Medeiros. I have a very important job to do and not a lot of time to do it. So please may I have your answer? Fifteen seconds."

Cai didn't have any choice. He needed to rescue Billy and he needed to escape. Thus, he needed to stay alive.

He heaved a heavy sigh. "Okay... I'll do it. I'll join you."

Frost put on a fiendish smile, with a rigidness and coldness that reminded Cai of Mister Freeze. "Wonderful. Now if you will please follow me."

The cage opened and Cai stepped out into the prison hallway. As he followed Frost out, he heard a clanging noise coming from behind. Looking back, he saw a pair of silver eyes piercing through the dark. He looked closer and saw a young Latina with a bushel of curly hair wearing grey prison rags and lying on the floor of a nearby cell.

"Who's she?"

"Nobody you need to worry about. Now please come along. We have no time to dawdle."

He was taken to a locker room where he was given an official EDIN uniform: a full body suit, gloves, and combat boots, all made from a strange mesh material he had never encountered before. It was sturdy, thick, but somehow light and flexible, with a color scheme that consisted of charcoal grey, cobalt blue, and copper. Wearing it, he felt like a superhero, pulled straight out of the comic books. He was also given a gun, a non-negotiable accessory that terrified him.

Once finished dressing, he was met by a red-haired woman. "Special Agent January Cooper. But please, feel free to call me Jan. All my friends do. Please, come this way." She led him down the hallway. "I'm Director Frost's first officer. All field missions, day to day activities, training, et cetera, et cetera, are all supervised by me. If you need anything, come to me. If you've broken something, come to me. If you have questions about your health insurance, come to me."

"You're giving me health insurance?"

"Of course. And it gets better as you climb the ladder. There are perks to seniority, of course. Amazing dental plan. Remember that if you ever find yourself thinking about quitting."

"I'm pretty sure I'd also be killed if I quit."

"That is very true. Yet another valuable thing to keep in mind." She led him to what appeared to be a simple computer room. "Here we are. Trust me, it's more impressive - and *expensive* - than it looks. Just pick any seat, press any key and wait. The computer will give you all the instructions you need. I'll be back in a few minutes to check in on you."

She walked away without closing the door.

'She's not worried I'll try to escape? Who am I kidding? Where would I escape to? I'm trapped in the middle of the ocean.'

He sat down at the computer in the corner farthest from the door. A beam scanned him through a projector on top of the monitor. A robotic voice spoke out to him, "Welcome, Caio Medeiros. Birthdate: February 28th, 2002."

"Um… hi?"

An old-fashioned media player pulled up on the screen and a video started to play. Frost's voice played over stock photos of scientists in labs looking at beakers full of colorful liquids, soldiers saluting a flag, and fighter jets flying across the screen with red, white, and blue smoke streaking behind them. It all reminded Cai of an on-boarding film he had to watch when he took a summer job at a fast-food restaurant.

"The pursuit of knowledge. The pursuit of freedom. The pursuit of progress. EDIN represents all these virtues and more. And today, you've been recruited to help the world reach the next step in its evolution and achieve an even greater understanding of man's capabilities."

He groaned and rolled his eyes. "Ugh, this place is evil."

Just as the video was getting started, the computer started to flicker. It turned itself off and quickly rebooted with an entirely different screen. Confused, he started clicking on things and moving the mouse around to see if he could fix it. A series of texts appeared on the screen:

DNT B ALRMD. DNT CLL 4 HLP. DONT TRUST FROST. READ.

A folder named "THE WONDERS PROGRAM" downloaded itself onto the computer. Cai, not sure what to do, decided he might as well fall further down the rabbit hole. He opened the folder to find seven folders: In order, Project: Changeling, Project: Psych, Project: Paradigm, Project: Impact, Project: Ghost, Project: Reach, Project: Mercy.

He clicked on the first folder on the list: Changeling. Inside were several files, each marked with different dates going as far back as 2001. He opened the latest, marked "02 May 06 - Final Report."

> Birthdate: 5 NOV 01.
>
> Date of Acquisition: 15 NOV 01.
>
> Sex: Negligible - subject possesses neither male nor female sexual organs or corresponding genitalia.
>
> Nationality: Unknown due to ethnically ambiguous appearance caused by disfigurement, and anonymous parentage.
>
> Capabilities:
>
> - Matter assimilation enables them to ingest all kinds of material to increase their mass, which they can easily discard without too much injury or pain.
> - Metamorphic cellular structure constantly rearranging and adapting to suit subject's

present needs / to match physical or molecular attributes of any human being or physical object.

- ○ Capacity for non-human shapes includes wings (though flight capabilities might be limited), tentacles, spikes, etc.
- ○ Metamorphic cellular structure compensates for any damage done to the main body, reconstituting any broken, damaged, or missing tissue by replacing it with the ingested matter.
- ■ Note: Effectiveness of tissue replacement depends on how much matter the subject had recently ingested. At max capacity, the subject can replace entire limbs or grow to the size of a small building.

-CLEARED FOR DISPATCH

-DFG

Cai was shocked. He had been given a detailed dossier of one of the kids, like Billy, who had been experimented on to give them superpowers. Changeling spent their entire childhood in EDIN, the last place he would designate as "child friendly".

His thoughts rushed to Billy as a child, being trapped in EDIN, poked and prodded by scientists all for some strange experiment. He, and all the other children, were kept under Frost's "care" for so long. All of these images clashing in his head nearly brought him to tears until he remembered that he was being watched. He read on.

"The Wonders" was what the person running the program, known only by the acronym DFG, named them. Each was implanted with a special device called an "artificial neural transmitter," lodged somewhere inside their brains, so small that even an x-ray couldn't find it. The ANT locked away all their memories of EDIN, as well as their powers. They remained sleeper agents until they were activated by a remote trigger. Once turned on, the transmitter then required an agent to utter a special and unique "wake-up" phrase within earshot of the subject to place them back under Frost's thrall.

Cai moved onto the files of the other Wonders.

Project name: Impact. Her entire family was arrested shortly after 9/11 when her mother was believed to be related to a member of Al Qaeda. She wasn't, but when their baby daughter, Nahid, was revealed to be a candidate for "extensive genetic modification" they relocated all of them to EDIN.

They kept her parents under the illusion that both of them were working for a customer call center while experimenting on Nahid. When her powers manifested, her body started producing a special kind of force field that absorbs kinetic energy, making her invulnerable to physical harm. She can then use the absorbed energy to increase the power of the field surrounding her, granting her superhuman strength, with no recorded limits, and even providing thrust for flight.

Project: Ghost. Her real name was Gemma Wallace. Frost made a personal note that she was a "convenient asset" due to her direct relationship to British Ambassador, Sir F.H. Wallace. After her "potential" was discovered, they murdered her family and then, years later, falsified documents that claimed they were killed in a car accident before passing her along to her grandfather.

Project: Psych. Billy.

The files didn't provide any information on him that Cai didn't already know himself. However, he kept looking to get a better idea of what they did to him, stumbling upon a very interesting note:

> What Psych lacks in combat capabilities, he makes up for in his capacity for enemy infiltration, subterfuge, and psychological sabotage. Socialization sessions show a tendency towards submission, and slight anxiety in crowds, but this may be due to his extra-sensory nature. Conversely, his ability has enabled him to

advance intellectually far beyond
his years. Great aptitudes for an
espionage agent.
-DFG 24 FEB 05

'Billy as a spy? There's a wild idea...'

The door opened.

Jan had reappeared with a large crocodile grin. "Hi there! Everything going okay?"

Cai slapped on his best poker face. "Yeah. Totally fine. Couldn't be better. Just enjoying my training video on how to be a super-secret soldier for a super-secret government agency."

"Not too bored, I hope."

"No, I'm fine. Sorry. It's just a... a lot to take in all at once, you know?"

"I understand. Do you want me to bring you anything? Cocoa? Tea? Juice?"

"Do you have kombucha?"

"Sure! I'll be right back." She left, closing the door behind her.

Cai waited until he knew that she was as far away as possible before continuing.

Project: Mercy possessed a power called "biokinesis" - the manipulation of organic cells which, when focused inward, accelerated her healing process. Focused outward, she could either heal people or kill them through a variety of methods, including replicating symptoms of a super virus.

EDIN planned to turn her into a weaponized "patient zero." She would be dropped into a heavily populated metropolitan area, spread symptoms throughout a specific community, and cause a quarantine. Cai was about to press on an attached video titled "Mercy: Demonstration" but he was interrupted by whoever, or whatever, had sent him these files in the first place.

2 slw. No tym. Here:

The dossier for Project: Paradigm opened without any provocation while the nearby printer started quickly printing off everything that was sent to him.

Within the first few seconds of reading her file, Cai could easily tell that Paradigm wasn't treated the same as the others. Cascades of notes filled her folder, all of which were incredibly detailed. She was "obtained" at birth and possessed "electromagnetic capabilities" with her body acting as a superconductor for electricity as well.

Additional notes from the elusive "DFG" informed the curious Cai that they believed she showed too much promise to be released into general society, like the other "Wonders". They petitioned Frost that she be allowed to stay on for greater study and training. It was around this time that the notes started to become more confusingly personal.

04 APR 05:

> To assist in developing fine
> motor skills, which have shown to
> have a direct link to their power

capabilities, we have arranged for Paradigm and the other subjects to recreate paintings by such classic artists as da Vinci, Michelangelo, and Picasso. While the others performed fairly, Paradigm managed to not only replicate the paintings but also the soul and the life force behind them. It was as if she took these masterpieces and made them her own. I'm beginning to believe that it will be very difficult for her to be placed anywhere outside of EDIN. She's so much more powerful than the rest of them and harder to contain. This more so than the others because of the nature of her powers and how they may interact with the ANT.

As soon as Cai had finished this section of Paradigm's dossier, the printer had finished. He found some hidden storage pockets in his suit and began folding every file up until he could hide all of them somewhere on his person, going as quickly as he could.

Just as he had finished, Jan reappeared with a drink in her hand, smiling. "All done?"

He nodded, with a smile meant to convince her that he wasn't nervous or terrified.

She grinned even harder, "Wonderful. Let's move on."

She led him to a room far on the other side of the building. It was dark, with a large mirror on the wall.

"Now, this is going to be your 'observation' module. As you saw in the video-"

'God, I hope she won't be testing me on that…'

"-everyone here at EDIN has a very important job. Not only are we in charge of creating new weapons for the American military, but we're also in charge of caring for the greatest weapons of them all."

The mirror was revealed as a two-way when a light in the massive room on the other side went on. He could see down into a large, cylindrical room where six people stood in a line, all straight as arrows and stiff as boards. Looking closer, a pair of familiar, violet eyes sparkled up at him.

"Billy!" Cai screamed out as he saw him standing below. He couldn't stop himself as he pressed against the window, banging on the glass and calling out. "Billy!"

"He can't hear you."

"Because he's in a trance?"

"No, it's soundproof glass. But he is also in a trance." She pressed a button on a nearby wall, activating an intercom that sent her voice into the room below. "Sound off."

They all stepped forward to announce their code names.

"Psych." Billy.

Cai was happy to see that he didn't look at all injured or traumatized in any obvious ways. His once beautiful, wavy red hair had been trimmed into a typical military buzz cut, but otherwise, he looked okay.

"Changeling." The shapeshifter called out. They were androgynous, with tall, intimidating stature, a long torso, a bald head, and chalk-white skin.

"Impact." Nahid. She had deep olive skin and her dark, curly hair was pulled back into a tightly braided ponytail.

"Ghost." Gemma. She was short, curvy, fair-skinned, and her hair was squeezed into a tight bun. Dark roots were taking over her once honey blonde hair.

"Reach." DeVaughn. He had a handsome, angular face and a clean-shaven head.

Cai didn't have enough time to do any research on Reach. He assumed that whatever he could do would have been just as terrifying as the rest of the Wonders.

"Mercy." Ming. The youngest, but her robotic, expressionless face made her look older than Billy.

They were all wearing outfits similar to Cai's. The only deviations were that the girls were wearing skirts layered over their pants and Changeling's was a simple pair of black shorts.

Through the loudspeakers, Jan gave the command. "Begin!"

A group of two dozen heavily armed soldiers emerged from various doorways around the room. Cai did his best to count every door and memorize their locations to the best of his mental ability. The soldiers, meanwhile, quickly surrounded the Wonders.

"Attack!" She commanded.

The soldiers opened fire on the entranced teens.

In the blink of an eye, Gemma had disappeared into thin air.

Changeling quickly became a form of liquid metal and wrapped themself around both Billy and DeVaughn, shielding them from the bullets.

Nahid planted her feet and stood her ground, bullets falling to the floor around her as her force field absorbed the energy fueling their momentum.

Ming also stayed stationary, not moving until the spray of bullets pierced through her body from every angle. Her body dropped to the floor, seemingly dead, giving the cue for the soldiers to cease their fire and move onto the next target. However, she quickly rose back to her feet, her wounds healing themselves as she ran at the nearest soldier. He opened fire, but while the bullets did make contact it did nothing to slow her down. She reached her hand out to his face and pressed firmly. He began to scream as hideous boils and blisters began to coat his face. Releasing him from her grasp, he fell to the ground with a lifeless thud.

Changeling's metallic, cylindrical form began to move about while soldiers sprayed them with bullets. A cluster of metal tentacles slithered out of the main body and, reaching out, grabbed at the soldiers and threw each across the room in different directions.

Across the room, the soldiers attacking Nahid had run out of bullets and began lashing out physically. She allowed herself to take the heavy beating, but nothing any of them did made any dent, bruise, or cut on her body. She absorbed all of the force they were unleashing on her, and then:

BAM!

The men surrounding Nahid were thrown backward as she erupted into the air like a rocket. Creating an upward thrust with the energy contained in her force field, she hovered briefly before thrusting herself at any soldier in her line of sight, cutting through them like a scythe through wheat.

After this onslaught, only a few soldiers remained standing. Changeling opened up their cylindrical body to release Billy, who leaped out at the nearest gunman, quickly ripping his rifle out of his hands and touching his face. Creating a bridge between their two minds, he unleashed a powerful psychic spike that caused the man to foam at the mouth and his eyes to roll up into his head before keeling over.

The few leftover were quickly decimated by a single touch from Ming, who left them shriveled, quivering, green-skinned skeletons on the ground.

Sensing safety, Changeling returned to their original form, exposing the long-protected DeVaughn.

One of the fallen soldiers, having survived the incredible assault unleashed on the powerless men, saw a window of opportunity. He grabbed his pistol, pulled himself up off the floor, and prepared to take fire on the unknowing DeVaughn. Without any time to react, Gemma's hand materialized inside his chest, obliterating him from within.

Robbed of the ability to scream, he gasped for air as his lungs and heart displaced themselves. Pulling her arm out of him, she watched as he fell to the floor.

"Wasn't that entertaining, Cai?" Jan said, with a terrifyingly pleasant grin.

"Fuck."

3

9 DEC 05.

08:00.

EDIN.

Doctor Franklin Gehrig, in the small amount of time he had been working as Chief Science Officer for EDIN, had managed to accomplish more than all of his six predecessors combined. He had developed technology to detect the presence of the "Haartvig Gene" in human DNA, innovated EDIN's advances in altering the mutation, inducing superhuman abilities in the subject, and had successfully produced three "super soldiers" - Changeling, Psych, and Ferro.

At every possible opportunity, Director Frost would sing Gehrig's praises. "This man is a genius. He has literally crossed everything off my Christmas Wishlist in the past few months alone. Everybody else: follow his example!"

Gehrig's results gave him the green light to continue with more intensive geno-mapping experiments. EDIN had acquired three new test subjects who had already begun their first round of gene therapy. Another subject, a newborn they had "adopted" from China, was resting in the facility's nursery until she was old enough to be experimented on.

He ruminated on his successes. *There's going to be seven of them. The seven wonders… Yes, that's it! They will be the new Seven Wonders of the World. Project: Wonders.*

It was Ferro's fourth birthday. At EDIN, birthdays were regarded as the same as any other day. The tests and experiments continued as normal and no recognition was made towards the occasion. The only reason Gehrig remembered it was her birthday was that he was the one who "requisitioned" her mere moments after she arrived in this world.

As a person who believed he possessed the human power of empathy, he would occasionally feel sorry for the children he experimented on. However, he always kept those feelings from affecting his dedication to his work by reminding himself that it would all be for the greater good. The results of their suffering would save millions of people.

The day would start at 08:00. The children would be given fifteen minutes to get dressed and head to the mess hall, then thirty minutes to eat the provided breakfast which normally consisted of essential nutrients, vitamins, and minerals blended into a sticky paste. They would then have forty-five minutes to adjourn in the "socialization lounge," a small playroom where they were given various puzzles to work on together. This was meant to test their potential for teamwork and their problem-solving skills. When this "playtime" was over, they were then each sent to their respective labs for two hours of testing.

Each of the older Wonders had begun showing clear advancements in the progression of their abilities. Changeling had learned to camouflage themself as well as taking on such complex shapes as miniatures of the statue of David, the Thinker, and even a Picasso painting. Psych, who had been advancing the furthest and the fastest, had most recently learned how to use his psychometric talents to absorb the intelligence of others, accelerating his speaking, reading, and writing abilities.

All Ferro could do was passively absorbing electricity and pulling magnetic objects towards her. This, to Frost, was baby steps compared to the strides of the others. He issued Gehrig direct orders to further supervise all of Ferro's experiments until she showed greater progress.

"I could do what she does with a refrigerator magnet... we need to toughen her up."

Gehrig would rather have been focusing on the younger subjects and their development. Additionally, he wanted to perform greater tests on Psych, whose talents and skills were far beyond his peers. However, he did as he was told and performed all the necessary tests on Ferro.

She was strapped down to a wooden chair with leather restraints while a five-pound iron bar was placed on the table in front of her.

"Levitate the bar," He coldly instructed.

Ferro's face scrunched as she struggled to use her power over electromagnetism to lift the log of metal. Resisting her influence, it nudged slightly only to stay cemented to the surface. Sweat dripping from her brow, she sighed from exhaustion.

Gehrig sighed from disappointment. "Hook her up."

"Yes sir," his assistant said before attaching electrodes to Ferro's temples before returning to the control panel.

"Are you ready?" He asked Ferro.

She nodded with a worried frown.

Gehrig nodded to his assistant. With the press of a button, he activated the electrodes, sending several volts of electricity coursing into the little girl's brain. Having grown used to this treatment, Ferro barely flinched. He knew her powers over magnetism and her ability to absorb electricity were linked, so he hoped filling her with as many watts as possible would release whatever she may have been holding in.

"Now, lift the bar."

Her face scrunched even tighter as she attempted to levitate the iron bar once again. She managed to lift it just over a few centimeters off the table before she let out a strained whine and it fell back down.

Gehrig made note of the failure before nodding to his assistant again, signaling for them to turn up the wattage, amplifying the electricity surging through Ferro.

"Lift the bar, Ferro."

The bar lifted slightly before swiftly falling back down. With it, came another sigh of disappointment from Gehrig. He decided to take a different approach. Pressing a nearby button, a strange mechanism fell from the ceiling above Ferro, uncoiling itself like a metallic snake until it was positioned at Ferro's exposed forearm.

Knowing what was to come, tears began to form in the girl's eyes. When his test subjects cried, Gehrig had to push down the instinctual desire to ease up on them; to coddle them. Ferro was crying like a normal girl, but he had to remind himself that she wasn't a normal girl.

"Lift the bar, Ferro."

Tears streamed down her face as she visibly struggled to do as she was told. A few seconds of the bar not moving a single centimeter passed until she exhausted herself from the strain and the stress.

Gehrig pressed another button. A needle extended from the mechanical arm.

"One last time, Ferro."

She lowered her head in defeat. She was too tired and too scared to press forward.

"Ferro, please... You have to try."

No response.

Just as exhausted as Ferro, Gehrig pressed yet another button, causing the needle to quickly pierce Ferro's skin. It never drew blood, but it always hurt.

She swallowed her scream.

"Lift the bar, Ferro."

No response. Another pierce. Another swallowed cry.

"Lift the bar, Ferro."

Once again, no response. Another pierce, but instead of screaming, Ferro dropped her head down into her chest.

"Lift the bar."

He heard a mumble. She had said something under her breath.

"What?"

"I can't." She said, loud enough for him to hear.

"What did you say?"

"I said I CAAAAAN'T!" She started to scream at the top of her lungs as tears of pain streamed down her face.

He stood and looked into her piercing silver eyes. She met his stare and he watched as her gaze changed from fearful to furious. He could tell that she wanted to use her powers to rip him to pieces, but even then, her control failed her.

She started sobbing. "I can't do it… I'll never be able to do it."

He had never seen any of his Wonders cry before. Changeling didn't feel pain like a normal human and Psych had progressed so quickly that there was no need to apply such methods to advance his development.

It was at that moment, Ferro's tears, reflections of all the pain he had inflicted on all the children in his care, hit him like a wrecking ball. He couldn't suppress his pangs of guilt any longer.

"Stop the machine."

"Sir?"

"Stop it. Stop everything."

"What do you mean?"

"You heard me. Turn everything off."

He deactivated all the machines in the lab.

"Now leave."

Confused but obedient, he quickly left.

Gehrig pulled up a chair next to his "test subject" and quietly sat down. Then he said something he had never said to any of the Wonders before. "I'm sorry."

She looked at him, piercing him with paranoia and suspicion. She had never heard the words "I'm sorry" outside of socialization classes. She was afraid it would be a trick.

"*Why*?" She asked.

"Because I hurt you."

"You've never said sorry before."

"I know."

"Why now?"

"I don't know."

"I don't understand."

"I felt bad about what I'd done. So, I'm saying I'm sorry. I'm sorry for every time I've ever hurt you."

"Then why do you do it?"

"Because I... I thought it would help you become more powerful."

"It's not working. I'm still struggling. The others can do so much more than I can. I'll never be good enough."

"No."

"No what?"

"I think you can be."

"Why?"

"I don't know. I just do. I know you have an astounding amount of potential hidden away inside you. I'm just waiting for you to unlock it."

"But I told you, I don't know how!"

"I know. I know. You've used your powers before. How did you manage to use your powers before? Way back when you pulled those little metal trinkets towards you."

"I mean... I just wanted to play with them. They were shiny and looked like puzzle pieces, so I took them."

His thoughts began to race as he envisioned a new approach to honing her talents. "I think I understand the best way to pull your powers out of you. Listen, I believe in you... I know I may seem- I know I've done terrible things to you, but I think you can do amazing things if you just try your hardest."

She wanted to believe him, but all her instincts led her to the same conclusion. "And if I don't, you'll hurt me again?"

Gehrig felt that wad of guilt in his stomach as he watched her tear up again. He was terrified that if he didn't continue to keep his composure it would explode within him. Ever since he had taken her away from her family, he had seen her as nothing more than a science experiment. Now, he saw her for what she was: a scared child, desperately wanting love and hope.

"No..." He said, as the bomb of emotion went off in his stomach, causing tears to pour out and his heart to rapidly beat. "No, I won't. I want you to succeed. And I want you to be strong. I thought the way to make you stronger was to hurt you... I was wrong. I'm so sorry."

The room began to shake as nuts, screws, and bolts began to fly out of their sockets. The needle claw came apart, piece by piece. The iron bar floated through the air like a butterfly. A shard of metal ripped Ferro out of her constraints as she stood up on her seat and levitated the multitudes of shrapnel around her, dancing within the weightless parade. The image looked much like a young ballerina inside a snow globe. There was no strain on her face, only a look of pure, angelic joy and pride.

He was stunned. The only part of his body that was moving was the hairs standing on end.

"Wow..."

That night.

Gehrig made a special request of Frost in person.

"Paradigm?" A confused Frost echoed his idea for a new code name for Ferro.

"Yes sir."

"It is catchier than 'Ferro', I will give you that. That always sounded too... simple. Paradigm is fancier but... what does it say about the *other* kids? Hell, what does it say about her? Last I checked, she could barely lift a spoon."

"As far as my opinion is concerned, Ferro - *Paradigm* - is the ultimate in capability. In the span of a few seconds, she showed me an incomprehensible level of power and growth than the others took months to accomplish. She is the example to which the other children should look up to. The *Paradigm*."

He rolled his eyes. "I get it, Frank. Must you always be so dramatic? Speaking of: were you not an English major before you switched over to genetic engineering? That is quite a leap."

"Yes, it is." He quickly responded, not wanting to waste too much time in this meeting. He so desperately wanted to run back to his lab and think of new tests for the superhuman child formerly known as Ferro.

"What inspired that?"

"What?"

"What inspired you to go from studying prose to making astounding advances in the study and manipulation of genetic mutations?"

"Oh. Um... My father... He died of Haartvig's Syndrome..."

"Aaah. I see... the symptoms skip a generation, am I right?"

"Yes, they do."

"By the time it is even noticeable on a health screening, it is too late. And the time between that and death is just a slow, painful, agonizing march. Am I right?"

He nodded, images of his father's final days flashing before his eyes. "My proudest moment was when we successfully found a way to detect Haartvig's Syndrome in children. Once this is over-."

"Of course... once this is over. What are your plans for once this is all done?"

Gehrig could sense a deeper meaning behind this conversation. "Sir, is everything okay?"

"I am sorry it is just... before you came around, I was flying blind, modifying human garbage with makeshift gene-

steroids. Then I brought you in, not expecting much from a fresh out of the dorm grad student. Now, here you stand, my glistening white knight. As soon as you started working here, my worst-case scenarios turned into hidden treasures. You are a *genius*."

"I'm just doing my job, sir."

"You've been flying under the radar for far too long, Frank. It is time to stop pretending like you are *not* the most important person here. You can humble yourself and say you were just jumping off whoever came before you, but we both know EDIN would be *lost* without you. And I just hate to think about all of this ending."

"I understand, sir. I didn't mean to offend."

"You will find, Frank, that I am nearly impossible to offend. I know what you want to do: develop a cure for Haartvig that does not involve giving children superhuman powers, live out the rest of your days saving millions of people from a slow, agonizing death, and die knowing you changed the world."

"That is my long-term goal, yessir."

"And EDIN wants to help the world too. I want to heal it."

"I'm happy to hear that sir. Now, may I be excused? I have much to do and a short amount of time to do it in."

"Of course. Of course. I did not mean to keep you. Go."

"Thank you, sir." He walked to the door but was halted by Frost's last word.

"Frank, before you go... Can you promise me something?"

"Yes sir?"

Frost's ice blue eyes gave him a terrifying stare that challenged him to look away. "No matter what happens, you must never leave me.

"Of-of course not sir. We're doing good work here. I would never think to leave."

"Of course, Frank... but... Also... *Never. Leave.* **Me.**"

"Y-yes, sir."

As soon as he felt it was safe, he marched as quickly as he could out of the room. He so desperately wanted to run. He wanted to climb through the nearest escape hatch, find a boat, and row himself to safety. He wanted to escape, but he knew that he couldn't.

Later.

Part of his job was keeping track of the children's individual energy signatures, movements, and vitals while they were alone in their rooms.

Changeling's way of relaxing was liquidating themself, deactivating all the pieces of their mind and body holding their solid form together.

Psych would always immediately fall asleep once the day was over, a soft side effect of such a tiny mind cursed with such awesome psychic power.

He watched Ferro - or Paradigm, per her impending official name change - as she played with a few scraps of metal, floating them around and contorting them into various shapes.

Thanks to her, he was able to see them all with different eyes. He saw children who needed to be protected, not just from whatever Frost had planned, not just from whatever the government had planned, but also from himself.

'Happy birthday, Paradigm… and many more.'

4

15 SEP 18.

18:25.

AGENT MEDEIROS' QUARTERS, EDIN.

Cai's room was the size of a spacious studio apartment. He had been given a hotel-quality comfort, queen-sized bed, a closet full of uniforms, an L-section couch with a coffee table at the center, a private bathroom, and a work desk with a state-of-the-art personal computer.

The room was exclusively lit by overhead fluorescents. That, mixed with the incredibly white walls, made it impossible for him to relax.

Adding to his discomfort were the security cameras hanging in every corner of the room, as well as one in the shower, which made him think twice about bathing. He was still in prison, the cell was just prettier.

While checking out the PC, he soon discovered that the only activities he could use it for were to look up his schedule, play solitaire, a list of the various activities available during agent downtime, such as the swimming pool and the gym, and re-watch the orientation video. He couldn't look up "unlikely animal friends" videos, he couldn't watch porn, he couldn't look up the news, and he couldn't send out emails.

He was just about to get up from the table when the computer started beeping. Sitting back down, he saw four videos, each pulled from the different cameras positioned around his room. He could see himself, lying on his bed, eyes closed, as if he were sleeping. Then a message popped up on the screen: Loop cut. Read. Now.

He figured that this message was from the same someone as before. It appeared to him that they had managed to hack into his bedroom's camera feed to give him time to catch up on his "homework".

He finally had the chance to read about Reach, or DeVaughn, in greater detail. He didn't see him display any real combat capabilities during the earlier "training exercise" massacre. All he ever saw him do was hide behind the other Wonders. Their primary mission appeared to be maintaining his safety, as whenever a soldier came close to him, one of the others would dispatch them as quickly as possible.

DeVaughn had the power to feel the presence of anyone with the genetic mutation that provided them with superhuman abilities. This also granted him extensive knowledge about their powers and how they worked, as well as giving him a destabilization field that enabled him to deactivate those abilities.

'Duh,' Cai thought to himself. *'He's Frost's way of tracking down any of the Wonders in case they go rogue. He's their leash.'*

Cai then revisited Paradigm's file in order to find a clue as to why she was imprisoned in the brig below. However, as he read through it, he only became more confused.

'In what possible universe would favorite food: chocolate cake *and* favorite color: silver *ever come in handy in battle? Or,*

really, in any situation outside of a preschool writing assignment?'

As he read on, he started to notice a distinct change in how Paradigm's notes were written as time passed. What started as simple scientific reports became more detailed until it began to read like the diary of a proud parent.

'But why? The others aren't even half this detailed. Sure, you can see that the scientist or whoever this DFG dummy is, softened up on them. Their experiments became less gross and more focused on "positive reinforcement" *but it's still super obvious that they cared more about this one girl than they did everybody else and I can't figure out why!'*

Out of frustration, Cai tossed the papers into the air. He screamed into his arm, not wanting to alert anybody who might be listening in. He looked directly at the screen, hoping whoever was sending him those messages was paying attention.

"I could use some help here."

The light near his door started to blink, but he had no idea what it meant.

"That's not helping," Cai said, plainly.

Both lights near his door started blinking. The screen beeped. Another message: Hllwy. Now. Cai rolled his eyes, heaved a heavy, annoyed sigh, and went to the door.

Peeking his head out into the hallway, he looked down both ways before declaring it safe to move out. A light down the way started blinking, giving him the cue to follow. He prayed that whatever mumbo jumbo this person was doing to the security camera in his bedroom, they were also doing to the cameras along his path.

'No guards… how confident… of course, why would you need guards when there are superheroes everywhere?'

Every turn he made was marked by a blinking light, guiding him all the way back down to the brig in the dungeon. He passed by Paradigm, sitting perfectly still in her cell. Trying to get a good look, he managed to make direct eye contact with her. She didn't move. She just sat there, doing nothing.

The lights led away from Paradigm, all the way to a cell more heavily fortified than the others on the block. Inside, was a man with pasty skin, long arms, a long, blond beard speckled with grey, and a completely bald head. The door unlocked, beckoning Cai within.

"Um, hello?" He said to the prisoner.

The man turned, surprised. "Aren't you a little short for a guard?"

"If that was a pop culture reference, I need you to know that I have absolutely no time for that shit. What am I doing here?"

"What?" He said in a faded, Bronx accent as if he had spent years trying to erase it. It sounded familiar to Cai, but he couldn't quite place it.

"What 'what'?"

The man gave Cai a pondering look before saying, "Ohhh, I get it. Clever. What's your name kid?"

"You don't know?"

"Of course, I don't know. How would I know?"

"I don't know! I can't- what the fuck is going on here? I am getting so frustrated. I followed a bunch of stupid lights. They led me to you. Now it is *your* job to tell *me* what's going on. So, for the love of God, please… give. Me. A break."

He looked at him blankly. "Okay, I think it's a good time to chill out. Why don't you sit down?"

Cai let out a frustrated sigh and sat down on the uncomfortable, concrete floor.

"So much more relaxing than standing, right?"

Cai gave him a look as hard as the floor.

"So, what's your name, kid?"

"Cai."

"Oooh, mononymous. Like Cher or Usher."

Cai gave him another look. "Cai Medeiros."

"Hi, Cai Medeiros. What brings you to my lovely home?"

"I followed the flashing lights, duh."

"No, I meant what brings you to EDIN. You look too young to be a military recruit."

Cai gave him an intense look.

"What?"

"You're not the one who brought me here, are you?"

"Nope."

"You don't know what I'm doing here, do you?"

"No, I do."

"Well, I don't, so please enlighten me."

"Paradigm."

The realization hit Cai like a ton of bricks. "Oh."

"Yeah. But the deal is I don't know why she brought you here. I only know that she thinks you'll be helpful. So why don't you tell me why you're not trying to kill me right now."

Cai was hesitant. He didn't know who this man was or why he was being held prisoner, but he figured that any enemy of EDIN's would be the kind of best friend he needed to escape. "My boyfriend's name is Billy Howard."

"Ohhhh, intriguing. Please, go on."

"He got called back here, I rode in the passenger seat and now we're both stuck and I need to figure out how to get us out."

"Hmmm…"

"What?"

"Why are you still alive? What do you bring to the table?"

"Frost thinks I could become an assassin."

"Ha!" The man laughed so hard his eyes nearly bugged out. "You? An assassin. *Please*."

"What's that supposed to mean?"

"No offense kid, but you're not a killer."

"Oh… is that supposed to be an insult?"

"Yeah. It takes a lot of guts to be a killer, kid."

"I have guts. I just also don't want to kill anybody. Does that make me a bad person?"

"Not a bad person. Just a stupid one. You're trapped here, Cai. You're going to have to kill somebody to get out, and then you'll have to deal with the guilt that comes with it."

Cai didn't like where this conversation was going and quickly changed the subject. "I answered your question, so what's your story?"

He sat up on his bed with a heavy groan. "Okay... My story is a very short one: My name is Doctor Frank Gehrig, and I'm responsible for all of us being trapped here."

Cai couldn't believe his ears. "What?!"

"Yup." He said, in an ironically proud tone. "I was hired by Frost to engineer and innovate new ways to map the gene that causes Haartvig's Syndrome and mutate it in order to grant people superpowers, giving EDIN the super-soldier army they wanted. I created the Wonders, gave them their field assignments, distributed them out into the world, and I'm also responsible for the technology in your boyfriend's head that pulled him back to EDIN. So... yeah, that's it."

He looked at him with wide, but tired eyes. "So, what are you doing in here, then?"

The good doctor took a long, deep breath as every memory from the past ten years flashed before his eyes. "Now *that's* the long story."

"Ugh..."

5

While the other Wonders were sent off to their various installations, Doctor Gehrig advocated for Paradigm to be kept at EDIN, claiming that her abilities required further study. Frost could only approve as, at that point, he had come to rely entirely on Gehrig's counsel. And so, she continued her training alongside the younger Wonders, Impact, Ghost, and Reach.

Her skill and power, as well as Gehrig's obvious favoritism towards her, intimidated the other children. As a result, she would often be separated from the group and placed under the direct supervision of the good doctor. Gehrig, meanwhile, had begun keeping two, separate logs: his professional log that was accessible to any of EDIN's executives, including Frost, and the personal diary he kept encrypted in his PDA, which he worked very hard to keep not only a secret but also completely unhackable.

In this diary, he would keep detailed records of every interaction he had with Paradigm. What she would say, how she would say it, what he would say, and how she would respond were all documented with incredible impunity. Most specifically, though, he kept track of all the times she made him feel guilty for being a part of EDIN.

She would say, "I like hanging out with you!"

This would make him feel guilty about not being able to take in the other Wonders and caring for them in the same way.

His only excuse for being so close to Paradigm was because of her advanced age and position.

She would ask, "Why are they piercing Impact with needles?"

This would cause him to emotionally shrink as he attempted to make an excuse for why he couldn't stop all the invasive and cruel experiments they were performing on the other children.

Once, she looked at a picture of him and his family and asked, "What is your mother like?"

He responded with, "She's a good person," all while choking back the dread and sorrow he felt, knowing how he stole Paradigm away from her family. His heart would cripple as he imagined the despair and grief they must still have been feeling so many years after he told them she was dead.

He endured these painful emotions because he wanted to feel punished for all he had done and what he had become. It was the only way for him to regain his humanity after so many years of repressing it.

9 DEC 07.

It was Paradigm's birthday and Doctor Gehrig had baked her a cake for the very first time. He made it using ingredients he had collected through several different requisition orders, claiming them as materials for "important scientific research." Using a trick he had learned during a security tech seminar he had taken in college, he placed the cameras in the mess hall kitchen on a feedback loop and baked it in secret before quietly walking to her cell.

With the cake hidden in his medical bag, he did his best not to wake her too early. He pulled it out, carefully placing it on the floor near her bed, and lit the candles. Then he gently nudged her awake.

Opening her eyes, she saw the spectacle and had to cover her mouth to keep from screaming in glee.

He hushed her before she got too excited. "Shhh... Happy birthday, Paradigm!"

"Thank you!" She said, desperately trying to contain her joy as she bounced up and down. "Thank you so much!"

"I hope you like it," He said with anticipation as he watched her bite into the first slice of cake she'd ever had in her life.

"Oh, my goodness!!!!" She quietly shouted. "This is amazing! How did you do this?! It tastes so wonderful! And I love the color - pink, like intestines."

The largest smile he'd ever made in his life grew on his face. "I'm happy to hear that."

"I'm doing my best to keep from screaming. It's almost impossible! This is too amazing!"

Gehrig had wanted to do something special for her birthday that year. He felt she deserved it. Since her last birthday, her powers had greatly expanded beyond his wildest imagination. She could turn a teaspoon into a gear and back again and could mentally throw a dull bullet fast enough that it could pierce bullet proof glass.

"Thinking about it, I think you need another present."

"I'm happy with just the cake, Doctor. Don't worry!"

He thought about it and realized that there was only one thing he could truly give her that would be irreplaceable and unbreakable. "I'm going to give you a name."

"But Doctor... I already have a name. I'm Paradigm."

"That's not really a *name* though..."

"What do you mean?"

"Paradigm is the name of a science project built around your powers. It's also the name of the group of people whose job it is to try and figure out how to make you stronger. It's what my name badge says," he pulled it out of his coat pocket to show her. "See?"

"Oh..." She said, slightly crestfallen.

"A real name is something people who care about you can call you."

"And you care about me?"

"Yes. I very much do."

"Okay then! What shall my name be?"

"What name do you want?"

"I don't know, Doctor. I'm not familiar with many names. I know Impact, Ghost, and Reach all have names that aren't Impact, Ghost, or Reach. They came here with them. But I don't know them."

"That's true..."

"What name do you think I should have?"

"I think I have an idea, but I'm not sure."

"Doctor, I very much respect your opinion. I promise not to shoot down your first recommendation."

"Theresa?"

"That's a pretty name! What does it mean?"

"It means 'summer' in Greek."

"Is there a special reason why you chose that name for me?"

"It's my mom's name."

"Oh! Wow! I've seen her in your pictures. She's very pretty, I'd love to share her name. What was your father's name?"

"Gregory."

"That's a pretty name, too. Did you call him Gregory or just father?"

"Father."

"During socialization, they told us that father and mother were very formal. Some people call their father 'papa,' 'dad,' or 'daddy.' Did you ever call him dad or daddy?"

"No, he was always 'father.'"

"Why not dad or daddy?"

"He just preferred being called father."

"Did you love him?"

He choked on his words as he remembered his final days with his father. "Yes, I did."

"Your brow is furrowed, and your Adam's apple is bouncing. I've upset you."

"No. It's fine."

"You just blinked three times in a row. You're lying."

"Ok. You caught me. My father died a little while before I came to work at EDIN."

"And thinking about him makes you sad?"

"No, thinking about how he died makes me sad."

"Oh. I understand. If you died, I'd be sad."

He choked up again. "That's good to know... Theresa."

"Theresa?" She paused to ponder. "Yes. I like it. I am Theresa. Not Paradigm. Theresa!"

He chuckled at her incredible cheer. "Yes. You are Theresa. How do you feel about that?"

"New, and strange, but all new things feel strange at first. Perhaps, one day, I'll give you a name."

"Thank you, Theresa - see, I'm already using your new name. Doesn't that feel great?"

"It's better than Paradigm."

"Good to know. Anyway, I already have a name. It's Frank. But don't *ever* call me that. Please. Especially not in front of the other kids or scientists."

She zipped her lip and handed him the imaginary key, which he placed in his pocket before they gave each other a thumbs up. He collected the leftovers of the cobbled-together birthday party and prepared to leave.

Before he opened the door, he turned back. "Good night, Theresa."

"Goodnight... Father."

This stopped him in his tracks and put him in reverse. "Theresa..."

"Father. That is your name. It's not Frank. It's not Doctor. But it is Doctor in front of everybody else. But if you died, I'd be sad. Like you were sad when your father died. You are Father."

"Theresa..."

"Accept it, or don't, I'm still going to call you father."

He smiled. "Ok. If you want. I won't stop you."

"You couldn't even if you tried. Goodnight, father."

"Goodnight, Theresa. And happy birthday."

After this night, a significant change occurred in Paradigm, or Theresa as she was called behind closed doors. She became more clever, more artistic, more courageous, and more powerful with each passing day.

Despite her incredible progress, Gehrig still worked very hard against EDIN deploying her. Helping him in this battle was a convenient impasse: because of her electromagnetic powers, it was impossible to place an artificial neural transmitter in her skull, as they had with every other Wonder. When he brought this to Frost's attention, he reasoned that he would need more time to properly study a way to create an ANT from materials immune to her powers.

"It might take years before I can duplicate the ANT design using plastic or a non-magnetic metal, and that's not even thinking about the cost of developing a way to counterbalance how electricity interacts with her-"

"Stop. You do not need to say anymore. It is fine. Just figure it out."

Money had been tight around EDIN. "Layoffs" had been becoming more widespread throughout the various departments. Research and development had felt the hardest squeeze as Gehrig watched his team get smaller and smaller as the weeks went by. Though officially, they were simply debriefed and discharged, he knew that Frost would never let anybody out of EDIN alive.

"Thank you, sir." He turned to leave, but just before he could reach the door, Frost's voice stopped him.

"Paradigm has become your pet project, has she not?"

"She's important to EDIN."

Frost was also quick with his answer. "She is also important to you, Frank."

"She's important to everything, sir. When the time comes, I know she'll be a loyal soldier."

"Soldiers…" Frost said, sounding unconvinced. "Be honest with me, Frank. Are we keeping Paradigm on ice to save money, to train a soldier, or to cure your dead father? What is she still doing here?"

Gehrig kept himself from pausing to remain inconspicuous. "All of the above, sir. Of course, she couldn't be released even if I felt she were ready because of the current issue we're facing installing an ANT unit."

"Right. Yes. Well. Good luck with that. Just try not to waste any more money. You know how I feel about unnecessary collateral."

"Yes sir." And with that, Gehrig calmly went back to work, trying to figure out ways to escape EDIN with the child he had grown so protective of over the past few years.

A year later.

It was Theresa's birthday. Gehrig had baked another cake, but this time he had prepared a side of pink strawberry ice cream as a special present. He was so excited to see the look on her face when she woke up to see it. He had a suspicion that she had been counting the days. He wouldn't have been surprised if he opened the door to see her awake, waiting for him and doing her best not to jump on the bed.

However, when he opened the door, it wasn't Theresa's smiling face that greeted him.

"Hello Frank," Frost said with a disappointed monotone.

He froze, terrified. His eyes darted quickly around the room, desperately looking for Theresa.

"She is no longer here, Frank. You know... I like to think of myself as a reasonable man. I do. I am slow to anger. I am quick to trust. I believe that if you are right with me, I must be right with you. However, aside from being a reasonable man, I am also an intelligent man... actually, let me rephrase that: I am *more intelligent* than the *ordinary man* because I learned two incredibly important lessons that the common folk has a dastardly and self-sabotaging way of disregarding until it is too late. Would you like to hear what those lessons are?" He didn't wait for a response. "That was, of course, rhetorical so you can continue being speechless. One: never live dangerously when living *frugally* is an option. And two, even trusting your own eyes can be a misplaced judgment. I will admit, I allowed my respect and, dare I admit, affection for you to blind me. But then... I started to see beyond what my eyes were telling me. I started to do the math, and the visions I had were not adding up. For instance, how you would stay locked in your lab for hours, working through the night on the same date every year, without fail. At least that is how it looked on the surveillance videos... Or how Paradigm, a young girl who, by day, was such a firecracker, and on any other night would stay up as late as midnight, transformed into such a bed bug on *the same date every year*... without fail... and that date just happens to be her birthday." Frost closed his eyes, afraid of the answer to the question he was about to ask. "What is going on between you two, Frank? Is it sexual?"

Gehrig nearly vomited at the thought. "Ugh! I would never! I mean, I view her like she was my own-"

" *'Patient?'* Were you going to say *'patient,'* Frank? Or how about 'science experiment?' Or 'pupil?' ... What is she to you, Frank?"

Gehrig thought very clearly. What he said next would probably be his last words, and he wanted them to count. Searching his mind for the truth, he eventually found it. "She's my daughter."

Frost recoiled in disgust. "How is that worse than what I had imagined? I have been a very fair leader to you, Frank. I have tolerated your unbalanced behavior, your furtiveness, and your many, many excuses for keeping Paradigm here, but this… at least the motivation behind you bedding the poor creature would be clear to me… but this?!"

Gehrig, suddenly full of courage, decided to start asking his own questions. "Where is she, Frost? Where is Paradigm?"

Frost ignored him. "What do you call her when you two are alone, Frank? Do you call her *sweetie pie*? Or *cupcake*? Is it some kind of food? Feel free to stop me anytime. I want you to stop me before I vomit."

"Where is she, Frost?"

The two held each other's stares. Frost, with his cold, husky dog eyes, tried to peer deep into Gehrig's soul. However, the good doctor would not bend or break. He was not going to fail this test of nerve.

Frost broke his gaze and sighed in defeat. "She is leaving, Frank."

His heart sank into his stomach. "What? No, she can't!"

"She is *leaving*, Frank. She has become a liability. *You* have become a liability. And I refuse to stand by and allow you to destroy everything I have worked and sacrificed for."

"Sacrifice? What do you know about sacrifice, *Irwin?*"

Frost glared at him as if he were trying to make his brain explode. "Do not challenge the lengths of my kindness, Frank."

"I'm not afraid of you, *Irwin*. I can't be, because I'm smarter than you. And we both know that."

Gehrig stomped his foot hard on a loose floor panel. As it gave way, a flash-bang device was triggered, and a great burst of light and sound erupted from beneath Frost, blinding and deafening him long enough for Gehrig to make his escape.

Running with the spirit of a man possessed by nothing but fierce resolve and love, he made his way to his laboratory. As soon as he arrived, he grabbed the most important thing in the room: the ANT-trigger. The key to unlocking the powers and programming of all the Wonders living amongst the general population.

He froze as he looked at the small, remote control-sized device. He thought of the torture he put those children through. The ANTs had blocked those memories out of their minds, allowing them to develop outside of the abuse they had endured. Some of them had been adopted into loving families, others reunited with long lost relatives. They were all free of EDIN and Frost until the trigger brought them back into the fold, which Gehrig knew would only be a matter of time.

He could run away with it, but that would only prolong the inevitable. If he destroyed it, they would all die, but he couldn't decide if that was a worse fate than what Frost had planned for them.

Before he could decide, Frost, accompanied by a squadron of security officers, appeared at the lab's doorway. Seeing the trigger in Gehrig's hands, they froze.

"Ok Frank, come along," he said, shaking, as his eyes stayed transfixed on the trigger.

"That's a lot of security for a man dealing with budget cuts, Irwin."

"I do not wish to hurt you, Frank."

"Why not? Are you afraid I'll break this? Kill off all your precious *'assets'* before they can be used for your war games?"

"Just tell me what you want, Frank. Let us talk this through."

"I want you to convince me not to release these children from the hell you have waiting for them here."

Frost gave him a look of mixed terror and confusion. "I do not know how to respond to that, Frank."

"Have your lackeys drop their weapons or I'm shattering this thing into a million pieces, Irwin."

"Okay..." He motioned for the officers to drop their weapons, which they followed. "I am staying calm, and I am listening. What do you want, Frank?"

"Where are you sending Theresa?"

"Away." Gehrig threatened to drop the trigger, forcing Frost to relent. "She will be placed in a Venezuelan orphanage."

"Why?"

"Frank-"

Gehrig held up the trigger. "Why?!"

"We have something planned for South America, several coups if you must know, and her placement there will guarantee military advantage for our agents."

"Are you kidding me? She's not like the others. Her brain hasn't been washed clean of everything she's experienced here. You're sending a superweapon with the brain of a genius to a

South American orphanage? How do you expect her to survive, you monster?"

"She will be supervised."

"She'll be exploited. She'll destroy everything before destroying herself."

"I think if she is truly as attached to you as you have led me to believe, then all I need to do to keep her in line is promise to return her to you if she follows orders."

Gehrig was seething. "You bastard. How could you do that to a little girl?"

"I am not the one who stole her from her family and manipulated her since the day she was born," Frost retorted in a tone so chilly it could give a penguin frostbite.

"No, you're just the one who bankrolled the whole scheme. You're a coward, too afraid to get your hands dirty. You can't even move because of how terrified you are that I'll drop this and ruin everything for you."

"You are right. I am a coward. I allow other people to fight my own battles for me... And that ends today."

He pulled a hidden pistol out of his jacket and fired at Gehrig, but the bullet never went anywhere near him. Instead, it flew backward into the guard standing to the right of Frost.

They all turned and saw Theresa standing in the doorway.

"Leave my father alone," she said, as the metal world around her started to quake, afraid of her power.

Frost tried to hide his terror. "Paradigm, I was just-"

"That's not my name," She said, darkly.

"What?"

"I said: That's not. My. **Name!**"

A furious blast of electromagnetic energy burst out of her tiny body. The various metals that made up the lab flew about in a whirlwind of incredulous terror. Frost screamed as a large bit of shrapnel slashed at his upper right quadrant before being knocked unconscious by debris, buried under the fruits of his labor. At the end of it all, nothing was left standing save for Theresa and Gehrig, still holding the trigger.

He stopped himself from marveling at the display and grabbed Theresa's hand. "Let's go. We need to get out of here."

They ran for an exit. As they went, she cut a swath of destruction throughout the facility, obliterating as much of her "home" as she could before they reached the upper dock, where a fishing boat used to discreetly shuttle EDIN agents to the mainland waited for them. Commandeering it, Frank let Theresa sleep as he drove them towards the shore.

"When we hit land, we ran as far and as fast as we could. We spent ten years living on a single breath. And then, Frost finally caught us. And now here we are."

"Ten years? How did they get you after all that time?"

"We got complacent. We wanted to believe we were safe because we didn't want to run anymore and paid for that mistake by being imprisoned here once again. They got me, they got Theresa, they got the trigger, and then they dragged the other

Wonders back here by their necks... but what they haven't realized yet is that we brought something back with us."

Cai saw an opportunity to unleash his frustration and took it. "Let me guess: bed bugs?"

Gehrig put on a devilish grin. "Laugh all you want, buddy, but there's one last piece of this puzzle nobody's figured out yet. Nobody except me and Theresa"

"And what's that?"

"We have a secret weapon."

A few moments later.

Cai approached Theresa's cell with great caution.

"Hello Cai," she said without looking at him. Her voice was hollow, raspy, and cold as if she hadn't spoken in days.

"Hello, Theresa."

"So..." She cracked her neck before turning her head to him. "Shall we get started?"

"Yes."

He pulled out the gun he had been forced to carry and was about to fire it at the cell door's lock when Frost appeared in the hallway, flanked by his guards.

"When will you people ever learn?" He said, victoriously. "I never fall for the same trick twice. I mean seriously Paradigm? How stupid do you all think I am? Though I will admit I am slightly impressed. Lyons?"

"Yes sir?" The guard to his right quickly responded.

"Remind me to ask the good doctor how he pulled it off this time."

"Yes sir."

Frost's eyes turned back to Cai. "Now… what to do with you? And here I had such high hopes for your future."

"What a nice way of saying you thought I'd make a good murderer. But let's be real here: you wanted me to choose death."

"I resent that. Why do people insist that I am some sort of psychopath when I am in fact quite the opposite?"

Cai knew that he had to stroke Frost's ego to keep him talking. "Really? If you're not a psychopath then what are you?"

"Something I know you would never be able to comprehend Cai."

"Are you underestimating me, *Irwin*?"

Frost looked at him with dead eyes. "Seriously? I understand that Frank believes me to be a creature of habit. And he is not entirely wrong. But still… I learn from my mistakes and I grow. I evolve. Like what a proper human is expected to do."

"Yeah, you're such a *proper human*."

"This is no joke Cai. Allow me the opportunity to show you my incentive to grow these past many years." Frost pulled his mask off, revealing extensive and graphic scarring that started from the right hemisphere of his scalp, working its way down through the right half of his face to his shoulder. "I mean you have to respect her thoroughness. Our dear Paradigm is quite the expert sculptor when it comes to war wounds. Every day I wake up I have this lovely piece of artwork to remind me of my failure. So…" He replaced his mask. "In anticipation for her inevitable return I had this entire building reconstructed entirely from non-magnetic materials. Every machine. Every weapon. *Everything*. And more importantly I now regard situations of suspected treason with a shoot-first ask questions later attitude."

Cai remembered what Gehrig told him. He thought of Billy and his family, and he forced himself to cry. "Please… please just let me talk to Billy one last time. And then you can kill me. I promise I won't run. Or scream. I'll go quietly, I promise."

Frost curled his lip into a demented grin. "I have a better idea…"

6

15 SEP 18.

22:00.

TRAINING ROOM, EDIN.

To prevent further attempts at an insurrection, Paradigm was moved to another cell in another part of the building, to keep her as far away from Doctor Gehrig as possible. Meanwhile, Cai was taken to the very coliseum where he had witnessed the Wonders demolish a horde of armed soldiers.

The guards laughed as they handed him a ceramic knife and threw him into the large, empty room. A door on the opposite wall opened and he watched as Billy marched in alongside his fellow entranced superhumans. They assembled in a rigidly straight line across the way, staring him down with the eyes of predators.

This was Frost's plan: to have Billy watch helplessly, unable to control his own body, as he murdered his boyfriend. If Cai wasn't killed, then he would be executed.

Jan's voice blared over the loudspeakers. "Begin."

Gemma instantly disappeared. Billy, Ming, and Changeling lunged at Cai, while Nahid and DeVaughn stood their ground behind them.

He stayed sharp, knowing that Gemma could reappear at any time with her hands inside any body part she wanted. However, he also had a suspicion that Frost, not wanting to deny himself the dark poetry of Billy and Cai killing each other, had given her orders to avoid killing him in favor of keeping him paranoid. But he wasn't about to tempt fate based on assumptions and suspicions.

He started running towards DeVaughn, knowing the others would try to stop him. Ming was the first to lunge at him, but her clunkiness lent itself to Cai's strategy. She tried grabbing at his legs, but he expertly dodged her, grabbed her by the hair, lifted her over his shoulders, and launched her into Billy, sending them both toppling to the ground.

Changeling expanded and slithered through the air at Cai like a great snake. Thinking quickly, he slid underneath them. However, they thought quicker and summoned extra arms directly underneath themselves, grabbing him by the legs and jerking him up into the air before binding him into their body.

As Billy began running towards them, Cai started wriggling within the confines of Changeling's semi-liquid mass. As he rocked, they compensated by covering more of his body with their flesh.

Billy stretched his hand out, prepared to unleash a psychic attack on Cai only for him to curve his partially concealed head ever so slightly, causing Billy to unwittingly attack Changeling instead. The shapeshifter melted down into a puddle on the floor, releasing him in the process. Capitalizing on Billy's shock, Cai quickly swung his foot across his jaw, sending him to the ground.

He turned and saw Nahid, standing between him and DeVaughn. She stood, stationary, waiting for him to make the first move. Knowing he couldn't use brute strength, he decided on a more unconventional tactic. He ran as fast as he could past her, grabbing her left arm and holding it up against her back while pressing his free hand hard into the pressure point behind her neck. She went down long enough for him to start back on DeVaughn, who had run to the other side of the room during their scuffle.

With his senses at high alert, he felt a shift in the air. Gemma had returned to the battlefield, making herself visible long enough to attempt a sneak attack. However, her slow and clumsy attempt at a punch was easy for him to avoid. He could tell that she had exhausted herself trying to chase him around the room. As soon as she realized she had missed her opportunity to strike, she returned to her void.

A heavy stomp on the ground informed him that Nahid was back on her feet. Her face red with fury, she flew at him. Cai, however, could tell from her flight pattern that she was still dazed from their earlier encounter. This made it easy for him to leap over the loose cannon, grabbing her by the hair as he did so. Mounting her like a horse, he guided her up into a loop before forcing her to crash land straight into DeVaughn.

Ming had returned to the fray and resumed her assault on Cai. She tried lunging at him, but her slight figure, short stature, and clear lack of combat training gave him so much of an advantage that he almost felt like giving up if only to keep from embarrassing her. He grabbed her by the sleeve and threw her up against the wall.

Another quake in the ground. Nahid was, once again, up and ready to fight. Repeating the same strategy as before, she threw herself at Cai. Just as she was about to land a killing blow, he harnessed his inner jungle cat and leaped out of the way.

With a great crash, Nahid had made a perfect hole in the wall, leading out into the hallway. Ming and the attending guards were left trapped under the debris while Nahid had managed to land gracelessly on the ground next to them. Seizing the opportunity, Cai ran out into the hallway.

Behind him, he could hear the clacking of twelve boots clambering after him as the Wonders gave chase. Unflinchingly, he outpaced them at every step as he sprinted down towards the dungeons, the blinking lights working to guide him to where he needed to go.

Eventually, he had reached the end of the line. A dead-end at the deepest, darkest part of EDIN. He turned around and saw Billy's face emerge from the darkness, the others close behind him.

Just as Billy's hand was within grasping distance of his face, Cai yelled out. "Now!"

The lights of the dark hallway quickly turned on, flooding the scene and blinding everyone as Theresa, trapped in the cell behind Cai, unleashed her powers onto her fellow, unsuspecting Wonders.

Earlier.

"And what's that?" Cai skeptically asked Gehrig.

"A secret weapon." He responded, with a smug smile.

"And what- Can we stop with the suspense, doc? Just tell me what your plan is so we can get a move on, here."

"Okay, calm down."

"Don't tell me to calm down, just tell me what you want me to do."

"Alright. Jeez. It's rather ingenious. It's so ingenious that I wasn't even aware it was an option until a few days before we were captured. I'm assuming you know about the ANTs in everybody's brains, right?"

"Yeah, those things *you* invented to turn them all into Frost's slaves."

"Yes. All of the Wonders have one except Theresa. And why is that?"

"Oh my god, Q and A, I'm not here for it. Just-" His eyes widened as the realization dawned on him. "*Ohhhhh...*"

"They're made of metal! Every fucking one of them! And now they're all in one confined area, trapped here with a living electromagnet." He let out an obnoxiously confident laugh. "She can deactivate all of them at once with one, big, directed electromagnetic pulse."

"Yeah!" Cai was filled with incredible excitement at the prospect of a quick victory. However, this was soon replaced with more questions. "But... wait... how come she hasn't already done that from down here in her cell?"

"Her power works more efficiently within her line of sight. Releasing a pulse strong enough to knock out all of the

Wonders' ANTs from far away might also completely rearrange them in their skulls... So... You know..."

"She'd kill them. Yeah. I got it."

"I'm assuming you'd like to avoid that as much as I would."

"Very much so."

"Yeah, so we need *you* to get *them* down *here*."

"Why don't you just do that weird 'light blinky, sending messages directly to my computer thing' you like to do? That sounds like a helpful trick."

"That wasn't me, that was Theresa. With all the care and encouragement I could offer, her powers grew until she learned how to manipulate electronics and machines. It's called *'Electropathy.'*"

"Ah. Yeah, that makes more sense."

"Indeed. But this power only works along straight currents. And nobody knows she has this power, so..."

"So, keeping it a secret as long as possible from Frost would be the best thing for everybody."

"Indeed. That's why she hasn't tried to pull a prison break on her own yet. And on top of that, there are no metals she can manipulate in this entire goddamn building. Frost, the smart-ass crackpot that he is, rebuilt the place to be immune to her powers. Even if she did try to escape, she'd be gunned down by ceramic bullets in seconds."

"So, we need a plan..."

"We already have one. I told you. We need you to get the Wonders *down here*, within eyeshot of Theresa. She'll work her magic and then they'll be free of Frost and EDIN forever. Or, at least, hopefully, long enough for all of you to escape."

"And how am I supposed to do that?"

"I have no idea. I was hoping you might bring something to the table."

"Ugh, really?"

"I'm a mad scientist. Not a super martial arts boy."

Cai groaned as a dark and dangerous plan filled his mind. "I have an idea… but I'm *really* not gonna like it…"

Theresa focused with all her might, working with great precision to carefully detach the microscopic bits of metallic wiring inside each of her fellow Wonders' skulls. Within a small moment, she had dismantled all of the control devices. However, the feedback caused them to collapse in crippling, mental pain.

"Billy!" Cai shouted out as he ran to his boyfriend's side. He could hear the guards marching in their direction. "Theresa! They're coming!"

"Don't worry," She said without a hint of panic in her voice. "I think it's about time we all left, anyway."

She placed her hand against the nearby wall, connecting her mind with the cybernetic currents within. Cai heard a surge as her cell door opened itself. She saw the guards coming down the hall and, with a cocky smirk, placed both of her hands on the floor.

Finding the sweet spot within, she caused an entire electrical panel in the floor to explode, blowing them all into different directions.

"Sleep tight," she said, with a devilish grin. "I'm enjoying making smart comments after winning a fight. I so rarely get the opportunity."

Her triumph was interrupted by the lights of the hallway turning a bloody red and the sound of a siren blaring through the air. It was at that moment that the other Wonders began to come to.

"Cai?" Billy said, looking up into his boyfriend's eyes as he was cradled in his arms.

"Oh, my god, Billy? Billy, are you okay?"

He blinked, wanting to make sure he wasn't dreaming. "Cai? Oh my god, Cai!"

The two started kissing until Theresa interrupted them.

"I very much respect everything that's going on here, but I do feel it's wiser that we escape first and then explore each other's bodies later."

"Oh, sorry," Cai said as he helped Billy onto his feet. "Is everyone else okay?"

"For the most part," DeVaughn said as he was lifted off the ground by Nahid. "I have a lot of questions... but... Gemma, you alright?"

She took a deep breath as she washed her mind clear of all the emotions that were stampeding around inside it. Sweat was beading on her forehead. She was shaking. "I'm fine. I can do this."

"Good..." DeVaughn rubbed his temples as his face scrunched.

"Is something wrong?" Cai asked.

"Oh... no... Nothing. They shaved my head... It took me years to grow my 'fro out... the bastards."

Theresa responded with a stern, "We need to leave. Preferably before they capture us again."

"Wait," Nahid looked down at her skirt. She ripped it off and wrapped the fabric around her head to produce a makeshift headscarf. "I'm ready now." The others stared at her in confusion. She responded in a dry monotone, "I don't like skirts."

Theresa had become exhausted by the continued delays. "Yes, well, I'll be very pleased to learn everyone's name and pronouns at a more appropriate time, but right now we *seriously need to leave.*"

She began to run, and the others followed suit. However, Billy knew the way to the exit and also knew that it wasn't in the direction she was leading them.

"Where are we going?"

"To get my father, of course."

This immediately inspired panic and anger within Billy. "Gehrig?! Oh, fuck that! I am not risking my life to save him."

Cai knew he had to intervene. "Billy, please."

"No! Do you know what he's done?"

"Yes... and that's why we need to get him out of here. If we don't, then Frost could force him to do something even worse..."

Billy wanted to fight but knew better. "Fine... but we should split up. Half of us can go with Theresa to get..." A heavy sigh replaced the name of the man he would rather forget. "While I take the others to clear the hangar and prep a jet."

"And who will fly said jet?" Ming asked.

"Me."

"Are you sure you'll be able to?" DeVaughn asked.

"It's how I got here."

"I'm going with Theresa," Changeling said. "You'll need muscle. And I'm literally all muscle."

"I will also go with you," Ming said. "In case one of you gets shot."

"Cai, you should go too."

"Billy?"

Their hands touched briefly. *'Just go, okay? I can't face him right now.'*

"Ok. The rest of you? Good luck."

"I trust you... and I love you."

"I love you too."

Theresa was officially done. "We really need to go!"

With that, the group separated. Nahid, DeVaughn, and Gemma joined Billy in seizing the hangar while the others ran towards Gehrig's cell.

Theresa soon became worried about what the other Wonders might do when they saw her father. As they ran, she attempted an explanation. "I feel there is something I need to tell you all. My father-"

"You don't have to tell us anything," Changeling said.

"I don't?"

Ming finished the thought on their behalf. "We know who he is. We know what he did. But we also know that you consider him family. They separated you. Took him from you. Took you from him... We *completely* understand."

"I know you do. And I'm sorry."

"Don't be," Ming responded.

"You're not the one who stole our lives."

It felt like forever for them to reach Gehrig's cell on the other side of the facility. They were all shocked to find the cell door already opened. Theresa quickly ran inside.

The sound of a gunshot echoed through her eardrums as she watched a bullet fly through her father's skull. January Cooper stood over his body, her face as cold as stone.

"NOOO!"

At that moment.

Billy, Nahid, Gemma, and DeVaughn had managed to fight their way to the hangar. Just as Billy had managed to find a soldier that knew how to man a jet, a blackout swept through all of EDIN.

"What the hell just happened?" Nahid said as she punched a man into unconsciousness.

"I don't know, but it just made our jobs a thousand percent harder."

Gemma reappeared behind a man about to take aim at DeVaughn and hit him upside the head with a rifle. "We need to get those hangar doors open."

The Wonders ran at the nearest jet as more soldiers descended on them.

"Nahid, keep them off us!" Billy called.

"Gladly."

She smiled as she began gleefully throwing her former captors around the room. One very brave man hit her over the head with a rifle, but her force field caused the gun to break in half. He let out a whimper of fear as she grabbed him by the neck, flew into the air, and spun around like a tornado. Releasing him, he flew headfirst into a wall, his skull getting crushed on impact.

"What should we do?" Gemma asked Billy.

"I'm going to try and figure out where the others are. You go join Nahid and keep those soldiers off us. DeVaughn, watch my back."

He put his hands to the floor of the hangar in an attempt to get a better grasp of the situation, but instead he received massive psychic feedback by the sheer force of the sorrow and pain of the people who had been tortured within the building.

"I can't get a good read. DeVaughn, can you sense them?"

DeVaughn began to rub his temples again.

"DeVaughn?"

Before he could answer the question, the others ran into the hangar.

"They're over there."

"Thank you."

The last of the guards, with blind fearlessness, attacked them as they entered. One attempted to grab Ming, but she used her powers to cause him to vomit uncontrollably. Changeling transformed their arms into hammers, flooring the last of the soldiers with two clean sweeps.

Theresa placed her hands on the ground, reactivating the electricity in the hangar and opening the doors before joining the rest of the group in the jet.

"Where's Gehrig?" DeVaughn asked.

Theresa's teary eyes gave him all the answers he needed.

"I'm so sorry," he said.

"Get us out of here, Billy."

Billy looked at her with heavy eyes, unaware of Cai's weighted stare in his direction.

"I'm sorry I slowed us down… it won't happen again. I promise."

DeVaughn simply said, "It's no big deal… you had a tough choice to make."

"You have no idea…"

A Few Moments Ago.

Jan's neck was in Theresa's fist. Her gun was on the ground. Her face, however, was void of fear. It was void of any emotion.

"Are we hesitating, Paradigm? Don't tell me Frank raised you to be a pacifist. One of his many regrets, I'm sure."

Tears streamed down her cheeks. "Stop talking."

"Oh, Paradigm. You're getting so emotional."

Ming was on the floor by Gehrig's body, attempting to resuscitate him. It was no use, though. She couldn't help those who were already dead.

"I'm sorry. I can't help him."

"Oh no. Poor Paradigm. Whatever will you do without your father to lead you by the hand?"

"Shut up!"

"I would if I thought it would accomplish anything. You won't kill me. You can't. Of course, if you did, it would be rather poetic. I kill your father, you kill me. And I'm sure Billy would just be so happy to hear that I'm dead once you tell him…"

"What are you talking about? What does Billy have to do with this?"

"Don't tell him anything" Theresa said through gritted teeth.

"Why shouldn't I? He won't kill me either. I swear, I'm surrounded by the most flaccid children. How about you, Changeling? Would you like to do your best to intimidate me?"

They merely glared before turning away from the scene.

"What do you know about Billy? Tell me. Now!"

"Oh, sweetie. Couldn't you figure it out? He's my son."

Cai, Ming, and Changeling were shocked into silence, one only broken by the sounds of guards descending upon them. Thinking quickly, Changeling grabbed Cai and pulled him into their mass.

"Leave her. Let's go!"

"Wait, I'm not done!" Theresa yelled out.

"I'm so sorry."

Changeling grabbed her as well, running off with the two trapped inside their body before they could get any kind of answer from the heartless assassin.

Cai and Theresa both looked at Billy with heavy eyes as he flew the jet out into the night sky.

Cai gave a silent prayer, "Heaven help us…"

(Epilogue)

15 SEP 18.

05:00.

EDIN.

Frost looked around at the waste of destruction polluting his base of operations, flabbergasted and mentally kicking himself.

"Casualties?" He asked.

"Manageable, sir," Jan Cooper quickly responded.

"And Frank?"

"Taken care of, sir."

"Thank you, Jan."

"Of course, sir."

"How soon can we make repairs and begin phase three?"

"Soon, sir. Thankfully there wasn't much damage to the structure. In the end, it was mostly electrical."

"Theresa is always full of surprises."

"Yes, sir. However, unfortunately, it took us quite a while to find the necessary materials after the *previous incident*. As such, it will more than likely take us-"

"We do not have time for such trivial countermeasures. Disregard Paradigm Protocol and begin the reconstruction, immediately."

"Yes, sir. Right away, sir."

"Phase three must begin as soon as possible. If we are to remain on schedule, regardless of the Wonders' presence, we must act quickly. Dispatch the Zodiac."

Her eyes widened as the weight of what she had been instructed to do sunk in. "The Zodiac? Which ones? Sir."

He looked at her as if she had just asked him how much the moon weighed. "All of them, Jan. Have them hunt the Wonders down, without prejudice."

She lost her breath and had to take a moment to recapture it. "Sir, I don't want to speak out of turn-"

"Then I suggest you do not, Jan. The Zodiac. Now."

"Yes, sir." And with that, she made her exit.

Frost noticed a body bag being carried away nearby. Instinctively, he knew who was inside.

"Gentlemen, bring him here."

The two attendants did as they were told and ran over to their leader.

"Just drop him on the floor. And give us a moment."

"Yes, sir."

The bag was dumped on the ground. Frost knelt and unzipped it, exposing the body of a Doctor Franklin Gehrig. His face was nearly obliterated thanks to the gunshot wound, but Frost could still see the man he once considered his closest friend.

"Well, Frank. Here we are. I assumed it might end this way, but I need you to know that I very much did not want it to. You are a good man. And an even better scientist. And, it appears, an even better or, at the very least, smarter father. I will admit, you and your daughter have, once again, derailed my plans. But, as you know, I am nothing if not adaptive. My only regret is that you did not live to see all that you have helped bring about finally come to fruition. It is at times like these I wished I believed in an afterlife. I know I am only talking to a lifeless corpse, but I do truly wish I could pretend that your consciousness was taken to a place where you could see me change the world. Now, you know I am always one to keep my promises. And, once upon a time, I promised that no harm would come to Theresa. And I intend to hold myself to that. I will show her all that I wanted to show you. I will share with her all that I wanted to share with you. She will live to see it all. Goodnight, my friend. And good morrow."

He zipped the bag back up.

THERESA MAE GEHRIG

BIRTH-DATE: 9 DEC 01.

SEX: Female.

CURRENT HEIGHT (as of 2018): 5'5".

EYE COLOR: Silver-blue. HAIR COLOR:
Brown.

INSTALLATION: N/A.

NATIONALITY: N/A (Legally dead).

ETHNICITY: Hispanic (Mixed descent).

FAMILY:

Doctor Frank Gehrig (surrogate father)

Ariana Castellano (birth mother)

Edgar Castellano (birth father)

9 DEC 08.

03:45.

MCNUTT GULCH, CA, USA.

After their fuel ran out, Theresa was forced to use her powers to push the boat to shore. When they reached the beach, she immediately fell asleep, fatigued from overexerting herself.

Frank had no idea what to do next. He had no ID, no clothing except his uniform, and no money. His bank accounts and assets were liquidated when he joined EDIN. Everyone who knew him in his previous life thought he was dead and would have been made targets if he attempted to reach out to them.

With his life at EDIN over, he had to start a third life entirely from scratch. And this life would be built around Theresa, a seven-year-old girl who had never seen the world outside the walls of the government facility she was raised in. It was now his responsibility to keep them both alive, and the only tools he had at his disposal were a service pistol, the ANT trigger, and a Ph.D. in genetic engineering with a minor in English Literature.

He looked down at Theresa, still sleeping. He looked around in the dark of the night and found a street sign: "GAS - 2 MILES." With the potential promise of food and water waiting for them, he picked his surrogate daughter up off the ground and into his arms, carrying her over to the street to begin his trek.

It took barely a few moments of carrying the little girl before the strain became too much for him. Though she wasn't very big, he wasn't very strong, and he also hadn't slept in at least a day and a half.

A possible savior in the form of a large green SUV slowed down alongside him.

"Hey!" The lone, young lady driver with short, bleached blonde hair, cheerily said in a bright, southern California accent. "Are you guys doin' okay?"

Though he desperately wanted to beg her for a ride to the closest motel, he was also aware that EDIN - and Frost - had spies everywhere. This woman's timely arrival could have been part of a plot to reclaim the two of them.

"We're fine, thank you."

The woman didn't want to give away any suspicions she may have had, but also had to ask, "Why you walkin' out here at night?"

He thought fast. "We were out driving home from her grandparents' in Portland when our car broke down."

He knew that he looked more than a tad conspicuous to the young woman. He was wearing dirty and wet suit pants, a partially shredded button-up shirt, covered in a tattered lab coat, and carrying a little girl dressed in a jumpsuit made from incredibly expensive bulletproof material in the middle of winter in California.

"Okay..." She seemed to hesitantly accept his answer. "Are you sure you don't need a lift to somewhere?"

"No, we're fine. I wouldn't want to impose. I'm certain you have somewhere to be."

Her bright smile reignited itself. "You wouldn't be imposing! Plus, you gotta kid. And the nearest gas station isn't for miles."

"Approximately one and a half miles, but who's counting?"

She giggled. "Seriously. It's way past the middle of the night. My mother would murder me if she found out I let a guy with such an adorable daughter walk all alone in the California wilderness."

He kept himself from rolling his eyes. "We're going to be fine. But thank you anyway."

"Okay dude, be safe." And off she drove.

Theresa groaned as the noise of the car woke her up. "Father?"

"Shh, go back to sleep."

She grumbled before turning her head back into his chest and returning to her slumber. Frank kept onward until finally reaching the gas station, which was still open. He heaved a sigh of relief before realizing he then had to deal with the obstacle of not having any money.

He found a bench near the entrance and laid Theresa down gently. Spying an ATM, he walked over and tried to find a way to get money out of it without the use of a card. He kicked and punched it in the hopes that it would break open, exhausting himself after only a few seconds.

He felt like a broken man.

He pulled out his revolver to see if he could shoot the money machine open only to preemptively realize that the gunshot might lead the gas station attendant to call the police. He wanted to avoid engaging with any kind of authority figure as much as possible, so he needed to find another alternative.

Theresa stirred and looked his way. "Father? Is something wrong?"

Frank smiled as a brilliant idea popped into his head. "Theresa, could you come here please?"

"Sure." She bounced off the bench with a sudden renewed energy and sprinted over.

"Are you feeling well enough to use your powers, Theresa?"

She nodded before playfully levitating the gun out of his hand and making it spin around.

He pulled the pistol down from her mental grasp. "Please don't do that. It's dangerous. I need you to use your powers on this machine."

"What is it?"

"It's called an ATM."

"An Automated Teller Machine?"

"Yes."

"We need money. To buy food and shelter. Let me see what I can do."

"Try to be as quiet and gentle as possible."

"Okay!"

"Shhh! Remember: quiet."

She zipped her lip and gave him a thumbs up. With the grace of a ballerina, the ATM was quietly disassembled, exposing the wads of cash within. Frank looked around to keep watch for any passersby only to find a camera pointed right at them.

"Oh, shit…" He said as he heard someone shouting nearby.

"Step away from the machine!" A man appeared, wielding a large, metal baseball bat. "Whatever you are! I'll kill you!"

Frank had no idea what to do. The gas station attendant had seen what was going on through the video feed and stepped outside to investigate. He had seen Theresa use her powers. There was footage inside the gas station. He had no choice. He pointed the gun at the man and fired.

The sudden bang caused a frightened Theresa to drop the front of the ATM on the ground with a loud thud.

Frank pulled her into him, shielding her eyes from the sight of the man bleeding on the ground. He knew she had seen worse, but he had never killed before and wanted to keep her from seeing his shame.

"Theresa, come with me."

Frank ran straight inside the mini-mart and immediately began searching for the security monitor. Having found it, he detached all the cables and pulled out the videotape, removing all evidence of their crimes.

"Grab a bag."

She did as she was told, holding it open for him as he filled it with water, food, money from the cash register, and other survival tools he found; a multitool, lighters, trash bags, gloves, scarves, and a small tank of gas.

Grabbing more bags, they ran outside to the still exposed ATM and squared away as much money as they could carry. When he was satisfied with the amount, Frank grabbed the man's winter coat, bloodied but usable, and the bags and ran into the woods with Theresa as fast as they could. Eventually, they found a small trail that led to a clearing that looked to have been home to a group of vagrants in the recent past.

Theresa was, once again, fatigued into slumber. Laying down the coat on the ground to create a makeshift bed, he let her fall asleep while he tried to plan their next move. However, all he could do was fill himself with more worry.

'It won't take long before someone finds him if they haven't already. They'll do a sweep of the area. They'd find us in minutes. I can't keep running all night. Theresa can barely go a few seconds without falling back to sleep. What the hell are we going to do?'

A twig snapped behind him. He pulled out his pistol and turned around as fast as a man with no pistol training could.

"I have a gun!"

"Dude," A familiar voice called out to him in the dark. "Trust me. That gun won't protect you from me."

Stepping into the moonlight, he saw the face of the young woman from before.

"You?"

"Me."

"What are you doing here?"

"What do you think I'm doing here?" Her voice had a different tone to it. The sweetness had been washed away, and a dark maturity was formed in its stead.

He steadied his hand and straightened his gun. "Are you from EDIN?"

She smiled with a sort of sweet but sinister intelligence. "Yes and no."

Frank only became more perplexed. "What does that mean?"

"If you think hard enough, doctor, you'll probably figure it out on your own. Unless Frost didn't tell you about the one that got away. The first, at least. I bet the look on his face was priceless when you two blew outta there. God, I wish I could've seen it. Please tell me you took pictures."

"You… You're Libra."

She cackled, then sighed. "I love it when you people make me feel famous. Every time I meet an EDIN lackey they can never figure it out fast enough… But when they do, they always give me this look of pure awe. And then, when the magic's gone, I crush the life out of them."

"But that can't be right, you should be much older."

"It's very rude to bring up a woman's age."

Realizing the pointlessness of holding up a weapon against her, he returned his pistol to his holster. "What do you want?"

"Nothing. I'm here to help."

"Why?"

"The enemy of my enemy is my friend, Doctor Gehrig."

"How do you know my name?"

"Is that important?"

"It is if you want me to trust you."

"I don't care if you trust me. You only have to believe me."

"I need to trust you to believe you're telling the truth."

"Listen, doc, I know you're running from Frost. You know *I'm* running from Frost. And that little mess you two left at the gas station would ring a few bells at EDIN, so... I figured it was in our shared interest that I help you throw off the scent."

"How could you help?"

"God, do you know anything about me? For one thing, I know how to properly dispose of a body. And another, I know how to clean up a crime scene. I've been successfully keeping myself out of Frost's sweaty palms for almost nine years. Trust me, I can help."

She reached for something in her pocket, setting off an alarm in Frank's mind.

"What are you doing?!"

She pulled out her keys. "Here ya go!"

She tossed them in his direction. He watched as they slowly and gracefully floated towards him in slow motion, perfectly landing in the palm of his hands.

"I don't understand."

"Those are the keys to my car, or, if I'm being honest, the car of the person whose car I stole. Take it. I just filled the tank. You know, at the gas station?"

"You're letting me drive off with your car? Wouldn't you rather come with us?"

"Why would I do that? A bigger group is easier to find and I can just steal another car. Trust me, it is *not* difficult. Especially if I don't have a middle-aged nerd and a toddler to slow me down."

He frowned. "I'm thirty-four."

"I don't care. The car's parked down the way. Take it and drive as far and as fast as you can without looking conspicuous. There should also be a change of clothes for both of you and some Arizona license plates. I'd recommend switching them out once you cross the border. You should also consider getting contacts and ditch the creeper stache. Your look just screams *'I murder little girls.'*"

He didn't know what to say. "I-"

"The amount of time you continue to waste talking to me about how impressive I am is time that you could be using to run away. So, run away. Now."

Taking the cue, he woke Theresa up. She rubbed her eyes and gently said, "What's going on, father?"

"Come on. That nice lady is letting us take her car."

"What lady?"

"This la-" But when he turned around, Libra was gone.

With no time to reflect on her sudden exit, after such a sudden entrance, he grabbed their things, took Theresa in his arms, and ran for the car. He buckled her into the backseat, where she resumed sleeping soundly, before starting the car and driving east towards the sunrise.

TBC.

(Acknowledgments)

Finding people to support you and your art is almost impossible. It requires a unique level of friendship and trust to be able to listen to someone's opinions, take in their feedback, and appreciate it for the gift that it is. For these friends, I wish to say thank you.

To my family: To my Mama, for your unwavering support and the theatricality, creativity, and your unique perspective that I inherited from you. To Kirsten for providing the drive to strive and reach for what many would say is impossible. To Brendon for being the consistent reality check and for reminding me that I am not the only person rolling my eyes.

To the AMAZING Ezra Komo, of Lost In Thought Studios in Columbia, MO, for creating the most beautiful artwork a neophyte author could ask for.

To those willing to edit this book with kindness and a desire to provide honest critique: Carrie (who is also the godmother of Columbia, MO's Drag Queen Storytime) and Daniel (who also took the About the Author picture!).

To all the people who let me sleep on their couches while I pursued my art: Chris & Seattle Shane, Lynx and Portland Shane, Caio (whom Cai is named after) and David, Katherine, and Bea Jay Enidae.

To the anxiety-ridden phone calls at 2 a.m. friends: Asher (whose talent and strength will take him to heights never seen before, I love you) and Addison (who deserves all the shout outs).

Acknowledgments

To Anson Allseitz, whose incredible emotional and tech support has pulled me out of terribly dark situations.

To the fairy godmother every drag queen needs, Jennifer Dietrich.

To my CoMo Homos: Anthony, Chris, Bly, Brandon, Ben, Dustin, and Slavic.

So Shean & Jami, for being an amazing example of queer love and beauty.

To the drag queens whose power and majesty helped give me the strength to go on: Muffie Beaverhausen, Veronika Versace, Honey D'Amour, D'Manda Respect, Venus O'Hara, Widow von Du, Selena da Fil, and Aeita Buffet.

(To the Amazing Online Donors!)

The following is the list of the beautiful and wonderful people who are the real heroes of "The Wonders Project". If it weren't for their donations, this book wouldn't exist. If you know them, show them love. If you don't, bow when you meet them. I know I will.

Alysson Thompson!

Christopher Matthias!

Darin Weffenstette!

Daniel Young!

David Churchill!

Demitri Wylde!

Derek M. Sheen!

Glenn Brumbaugh!

Hannah from Kickstarter!

Jeffrey Barth!

Joshua Marcille!

Kayla Knutson!

Kim Casey!

Mary Louise Mack!

Melvin Weatherly!

Oliver Faulks Ewert!

Segale Marie!

Skip Lester!

Trent Rash!

Zachery Drillingas!

(About the Author)

Autumn Equinox

 They/Them.
A twenty-something drag queen and lover of all things superhero-related who hails from Seattle, WA, and currently lives in Columbia, Mo with their cat, Archibald McGuire Equinox Thompson.

This is their first published work and can be found on the following social media pages:

Facebook.com/autumnequinoxious
Instagram: @AutumnEquinoxious
Twitter: @Equinoxious
autumnequinoxdrag.com

www.ingramcontent.com/pod-product-compliance
Lightning Source LLC
Chambersburg PA
CBHW030030030726
47500CB00001B/40